ONLY THE LOST

A Death Gate Grim Reapers Thriller Book Three

AMANDA M. LEE

WinchesterShaw Publications

Prologue

SIXTY YEARS AGO

O liver Samuelson shuffled his feet and struggled to maintain his place in line.

He wasn't the patient sort. Nope. Not even a little. He'd been waiting his entire life to see what was on the other side of the doors they were approaching. He could almost taste it, smell it. Yes, he could almost feel it. He didn't want to continue waiting.

He had no choice. He could hardly toss the other recruits aside and barrel his way into the room. If he did that, they would be suspicious.

He didn't want them to be suspicious. That would ruin his entire plan.

"This is exciting, huh?"

Oliver slid his gaze to the man keeping pace with him. Doug Dunning. He remembered the name from orientation. Their qualifications were listed in the packets that went around. Doug was a college graduate who had lived in Michigan his entire life. That's all Oliver remembered about him ... and he wasn't impressed.

"It's work," Oliver replied after a beat. He was determined to play it cool. If the others found out he was resolved to find placement in the gate room they might try to keep him from what he felt was his destiny. He had no intention of letting that happen. So, he had to be nonchalant. That was his only option.

"It's more than work," Doug countered, refusing to back down. "This is ... well, this is so much more than work." His dark eyes sparkled with interest as the line came to a halt. The man leading the tour was explaining something to those at the front of the line. Oliver had researched what they would find on the other side of the door for so long, so deeply, that he wasn't worried about security protocol. He already knew exactly what to do. More importantly, he was familiar with what not to do.

"I just think of it as work," Oliver lied. His fingers twitched at his sides so he shoved his hands in the pockets of his blue trousers. Some of the others were dressed up for this excursion. Again, he didn't want to appear too excited. He dressed in clean clothes, made sure he looked professional, but did not go all out. It was all part of his plan.

"Then you're stronger than me." Doug was the enthusiastic sort and wasn't afraid to show it. "All I've been able to think about since I heard I was moving past the third round of orientation was that I was finally going to see the gate. I mean ... we're actually going to see it."

Oliver fought to control his temper. "That's the rumor."

Doug ignored Oliver's dry response. "The gate was the entire reason I agreed to go through the training. I mean ... on the other side of that door there's a gate that allows you to travel between worlds. It's not just planes of existence either. We're talking the line between life and death. One side of it is in that room."

Oliver was well aware of what the gate signified. He, more than anybody, grasped its true ramifications. He was a vampire, after all. He'd managed to cheat human death a good ten times over and for a very long time. That was one of the reasons he wanted to visit the gate. He had questions about mortality.

Most vampires hit this wall at some point. They eventually started questioning the meaning of it all. Why live forever if you didn't have a purpose in life? Was it better to live fast and die young than linger without a purpose? Was any of it worth it or would he be better at the sharp end of a pointy stick and leaving this world behind? He was asking himself all those questions. He hoped the gate would provide answers.

"I'm curious about it from a scientific standpoint," Oliver said finally. It was obvious that Doug wasn't going to stop talking, so there was no reason to be rude. "Energy and matter meld to make humans. Only energy passes over. At least that's what they say, and I have no reason not to believe them. It's an interesting phenomenon."

Doug stared at him for a full beat, unblinking, and then smirked. "I'm more interested in the philosophical implications. People always wonder what happens when you die. Aren't you curious about that?"

In truth, Oliver wasn't much of a student of philosophy. He'd always been more interested in the science of an afterlife. "Not really. The gate is basically a conduit. Energy separates from the body on this side and then is passed through the opening. I'm wondering if it's possible for that energy to become solid again on the other side."

Doug turned thoughtful. "You're saying that you believe a second body awaits the soul on the other side. That's interesting ... although it sounds impractical. Why would there be another physical body over there? The energy is what's important. The soul doesn't need a body to carry on."

"I know that, but ... if you can't touch and interact with your environment what's the point of living? Are you just supposed to float around and do nothing for thousands of years? That doesn't make sense."

"Your final resting place depends on your belief system," Doug replied. To Oliver, he sounded as if he was reciting from a textbook. "Technically, what's right on the other side of the gate is a waiting room. Everyone is sorted in the waiting room and then transported again."

Oliver's interest was officially piqued. "How do you know that? About the waiting room, I mean. I don't remember reading that in our orientation materials."

"They don't tell us everything. I happened to run into a reaper at the main office — one of the reapers who is actually collecting souls on the streets — and he said that what's on the other side of this gate isn't the final resting place. There's more."

"How would he know?" Oliver wasn't trying to be difficult. No, really. He simply wanted answers to the questions that had been plaguing him. "As I understand it, reapers can't cross over to the other side, check things out, and then come back again. We have no proof that anything we believe is true. We only have hypotheses. That's what I find fascinating."

"Oh, well, I didn't think about it that way." Doug furrowed his brow. "Still, I would think someone had to voluntarily cross over at some point just as an experiment."

"It would have to be a suicidal individual because no one has crossed over and then come back," Oliver pointed out pragmatically. "I'm sure you're right. I'm sure someone did pass over. They never came back, though. Nobody has ever come back."

"How can you be sure?"

"I ... well ... ." In truth, Oliver couldn't be absolutely positive. He had an opinion that he wanted to believe was fact, but he couldn't prove it any more than the others could prove their wild hunches. "I think we would've heard if someone had crossed over and returned," he said finally. "It would've been big news."

"Unless the reaper council wanted to keep it secret for some reason."

It was an offhand comment, but Oliver took it to heart. "You think they're trying to hide the truth from us?"

Doug immediately started shaking his head, fervent. "I didn't say I believed that. Don't tell them I believe anything of the sort. That will severely limit my prospects with the organization."

Oliver held up his hands in capitulation. He wasn't nearly as worried as Doug about punishments the reaper council might dole out. Reapers had magic, so they were a threat, but it was limited. Oliver's powers far outweighed those of a lone reaper. In truth, he figured he could fight three at once if he had to. He doubted it would become necessary, but he'd thought every aspect out when applying for this job. He wanted to leave nothing to chance.

"I'm not going to say anything," he promised, sincere. "We're having a simple conversation. You don't have to worry about me. I have no interest in limiting your prospects."

Doug bobbed his head, placated. "That's good. Still, I know you were half joking when you asked the question, but I have researched the gate a great deal and I think you're right. Someone had to cross over voluntarily."

"Do you think they were unable to come back?"

"That's one possibility, isn't it?" Doug's eyes sparkled with enthusiasm. "Perhaps those who crossed over were unable to come back. Maybe the sentries that ride herd on the souls wouldn't allow it. Maybe the souls separated from the bodies the second they crossed the threshold and there was physically no way to return."

In truth, Oliver had considered that possibility himself. He didn't know how much stock he held in the notion, but he couldn't rule it out. That's why he was so interested in the science of the matter.

The line started moving again, which meant they were finally going to see the big prize of the tour. The rest of the operation had been ho-hum. The gate was something else entirely.

"There's also one other possibility," Doug added after a beat.

"Oh, yeah?" Oliver was distracted now. He could practically feel his skin humming the closer he got to the gate room. Still, he didn't want to be rude. He fancied himself a polite individual ... by choice. There was no need to be rude unless dealing with a boorish idiot. Doug might not have been the smartest man in the room, but he was neither boorish nor stupid. "What's that?"

"It's always possible that once a soul reaches the other side it simply doesn't want to return to this plane of existence."

Oliver was taken aback and inadvertently slowed his pace. "You think what's over there is so great that the souls choose to stay behind. That's ... interesting."

"But you don't believe it." Doug pursed his lips. "I'm not saying it's fact. It's just a premise."

"It's an interesting one." Oliver opted for the truth. "I don't know what I believe. It's possible we'll never know."

"Not never. We all die at some point. We'll find out the truth then. Sure, it might be a long wait, but we'll eventually know. There's comfort in that ... at least for me."

And there, Oliver realized, was the part he struggled with most.

There wasn't inevitability in his death. He could conceivably amble along forever. Even if he did die, chose to somehow end his life, there was no way of knowing if his soul would pass over.

Some people believed vampires didn't have souls. He knew otherwise. He felt things like normal humans. He loved. He grieved. He was even depressed occasionally. If he didn't have a soul, those things shouldn't be possible.

Still, the humans persisted in spreading the lie that vampires didn't have souls. As much as he considered himself worldly, a man who formed his own opinions, part of him wondered if they were right. That's why he wanted to see the gate so very badly.

"Yes," he said as the door appeared in front of him. "We all die eventually."

The gate was resplendent in shimmery goodness when Oliver passed into the next room. He forgot all about Doug and focused on the portal, his eyes going wide as the surface glowed.

The room was absolutely silent except for the scuffle of feet on the floor. Everyone in their orientation group — all twenty men (women weren't yet allowed into the program despite persistent rumors) — were focused on the gate. No one said a word. They only stared.

Then the tour guide started to speak. "This is what you've all been waiting for," he said. "Does anyone have any questions?"

No one so much as raised a hand. The gate was too magnificent to mar the moment with words. All the assembled individuals did was stare ... and stare some more.

"That is amazing," Doug said finally on a shaky breath. "I mean ... I've seen photos, but ... I didn't realize it would be like this."

Oliver couldn't help but agree. He opened his mouth to say just that, but a bright light at the corner of the gate caught his attention and he lost his train of thought. He focused on that spot, wondering if he'd somehow imagined it or if it was a trick of the room, and found a pinprick of light that was somehow brighter than the rest. After staring for a few moments, he glanced around at the other men to see if they noticed the phenomenon. He appeared to be the only one who could see the difference.

To him, that didn't bode well.

As if on cue, perhaps to match the pulses of anxiety rolling through him, the gate surface began to ripple. First small waves, then bigger ones. Within seconds, the gate was making a strange crackling.

"What is that?" one of the other orientation members asked, confused.

The tour guide looked as concerned as the others felt. "I don't know. Perhaps we should head upstairs and get a technician down here. If the gate is malfunctioning it needs to be repaired."

Even though Oliver wanted to stay where he was, study the gate for hours, he realized he was in a different position than the others. He was unlikely to die if something went wrong. Humans were more vulnerable, softer. They weren't as durable as he. That meant they could easily fall if something actually did go wrong with the gate. "We should definitely go," he agreed, reaching for Doug's arm when the man shifted closer to the gate. "We can come back later."

Doug brushed off his new friend's concern. "Just a second," his eyes never moved from the gate surface. It was as if he was entranced. "I just want to see something."

Doug lifted his fingers and extended them toward the gate. He was still a good ten feet away, but he was moving almost before Oliver could register what he was doing.

"What are you doing?" Oliver called out, alarmed. "You can't go through the gate."

"I just want to see," Doug repeated, his voice hollow. He didn't resemble the person Oliver had been trapped in the hallway with. He was devoid of emotion, his face blank.

"You can't." Oliver took a step in his direction, but the crackling the gate was emitting doubled in volume, causing the humans to clamp their hands over their ears and drop to their knees. Even Doug was down, his eyes going wide as he protectively shielded his hearing.

Oliver was the only one in the room who could tolerate the sound. It wasn't exactly pleasant, but he was stronger than the others. That's why he stood there like an idiot as the gate began to pulse. At first it was one pulse every three seconds. Then one pulse a second. Eventually, it was one nonstop pulse.

Even as the light in the room exploded to a level that made Oliver want to cringe, he kept his eyes open. He was almost positive he saw shadows moving on the other side of the gate threshold. He was convinced if he continued to stare long enough that he would be able to see something magnificent.

He was wrong.

At the exact moment one of the shadowy figures moved to the spot directly on the other side of the threshold, what looked to be a shimmering hand reaching for a different world, the sound increased tenfold. Even Oliver couldn't tolerate it. His senses were overwhelmed as he reached out to catch himself.

The last thing he remembered was a pair of cold blue eyes appearing from the glaring light. He couldn't see a face. If there was one, he somehow forgot it instantly, but those eyes were seared in his brain forever.

He hit the ground hard, the whole of his very long life passing in front of his eyes. Then everything went dark.

He almost welcomed it.

Almost.

One

"Give me a kiss."

Braden Grimlock was insistent as he ducked his head and moved his lips toward mine.

I slid away from him thanks to the rollers on my desk chair and gave him a dirty look. I, Isabella "Izzy" Sage, am nothing if not professional.

"I'm at work."

He looked amused rather than offended. "So am I. There's no rule that says we can't kiss on the job. I know because I pored through the rule book last night after you fell asleep ... at ten o'clock."

He had a charming smile, one that probably brought women from five different counties to their knees over the course of his thirty years, but I had no intention of falling for it today. "I went to sleep at ten o'clock because I was exhausted. Your niece kept me up the night before with all that screaming she does at bedtime."

Braden snickered. "She takes after her mother."

I had no doubt that Lily Taylor indeed took after her mother, Aisling Grimlock-Taylor. That didn't change the fact that a six-week-old infant was ruling the roost at Grimlock Manor, a house that had

9

more in common with a castle than a two-story colonial. That also didn't change the fact that the baby was turning into a terror.

"You guys are spoiling her," I pointed out. "The only reason she cries at bedtime is because you all rush to hold her. I doubt she's even spent more than an hour in that crib your father probably spent more money on than I did on my first car. She's figured out that her uncles and grandfather will rock her all night if she plays it right."

"She is a genius," Braden agreed, smiling. "She's cute, too. She looks like me."

I had to laugh. Sure, we were in the middle of an inspection — the head of the reaper council, Renley Hatfield, was touring the renovation of a private library that had been hidden behind a wall for decades — but the statement was too funny to keep a straight face.

"She looks like her mother," I corrected. "The fact that all five of you guys look exactly alike is just a fluke of genetics."

"No, she looks like me." Braden had made the statement more than once and it was obvious he truly believed it. He was the sort of man who puffed out his chest when it came to sparring with his brothers. He was also the sort of man who turned into a big puddle of goo when his niece batted her eyelashes. I thought it was a little early for Lily to be as manipulative as she plainly was, but the kid had obviously inherited the Grimlock charm and wasn't afraid to use it. She knew exactly which relative was most likely to coddle her, too.

All of them.

I grew up in Detroit. Er, well, I spent the first few years of my life in the city. My parents served as gatekeepers until an accident claimed their lives. I was present for the event. Something came through the gate to kill them. I remembered nothing about that night, though. It was all a blank.

After their deaths, I moved to New Orleans to live with my grandfather. A powerful brujo, the man knew his trade and peddled it to those who needed magical help. I was born into magic and with him as my teacher I thrived. Sure, I missed my parents, but I wanted for nothing. That didn't mean I wasn't anxious to return home and unlock the mystery of my parents' deaths. I needed to know ... mostly because I was convinced I was somehow to blame.

Shortly after graduating from high school, I joined the reaper ranks. I worked my way up quickly, although I was never interested in being one of the people on the front lines of soul collection. Braden did that for a living and seemed to enjoy it. He'd been born into a reaper family and knew no other way of life. I wanted something different. Not more, just different.

When the gate position in Detroit opened up I volunteered right away. I wanted to be in the place my parents took their last breaths. I wanted to capture the memories that remained just out of reach. I wanted revenge on whatever creature took them from me. All my wants and needs shifted once I actually got the job.

Braden was one of the first people I'd met. I was determined to keep my heart closed to him despite the pull I felt toward him. It worked for a grand total of five minutes. Obviously there was no denying him. Oddly enough, I found I didn't want to after I got to know him. He was a good man ... who had a few immature tendencies. I had no doubt he would grow out of those ... just as soon as he stopped living in his father's house.

Speaking of his father, Cormack Grimlock was also present. He was high in the reaper council and he'd shown an inordinate interest in making sure I was safe and tended at the gate. It was located on Belle Isle, which was technically in the city but located in one of the prettier places the sprawling metropolis had to offer. The island was my sanctuary, my new home, and things were starting to slip into place in a manner I never thought possible.

Sure, I was still determined to find out what happened to my family. But I was no longer alone. I had a whole family of reapers volunteering their help to give me what I needed. I'd always wondered what it would feel like to be part of a big family. Now I knew.

"Knock it off, Braden," Cormack warned as he slid around the side of the desk and flicked his son's ear. He was an engaged father. All his children were now adults — he was a grandfather, after all — but he once told me that making his children behave was like herding cats after a big bout of catnip play. The visual stuck and always made me chuckle.

Braden shot his father a dirty look. All the Grimlock children were the spitting image of their father. They boasted his black hair and purple eyes. They were beautiful specimens, each and every one. They also inherited his temper, and there was a lot of strife under Cormack's roof. His children seemed to thrive on it.

"I'm not doing anything," Braden complained. "Izzy and I were just discussing her new co-worker, who is supposed to arrive today for a tour." He was smooth as he delivered the lie. I had to give him credit. If I didn't know him as well as I did, I would've believed him. "I don't know why you always assume that I'm up to something, but it's not fair. I'm your good child."

Cormack rolled his eyes, something he had down pat. All of his children were mouthy — something they got from him — and he wasn't dumb enough to fall for a single thing they said when they were trying to snow him.

"I heard you beg Izzy for a kiss," he countered. "Don't bother denying it. I might be getting older — although I'm still in my prime — but there's nothing wrong with my hearing."

Braden balked. "I didn't beg. It's horrible that you would even insinuate anything of the sort. I'm a Grimlock. I don't beg."

"You do when Izzy is around." Cormack shot me a fond smile. He was a warm man, inviting. Sure, he had a short fuse. Given the way his children acted, however, it was warranted. A few times I wanted to point out that he was the reason they acted the way they did, but it seemed unnecessary. It wasn't as if he didn't know that he spoiled them rotten. Aisling especially, as the only girl, was something of a terror. She was the mother of his only grandchild, so he spoiled her more than the rest. I had a feeling it had been that way since her birth thanks to her position as the only girl in an army of rambunctious boys. Cormack didn't believe that boys were stronger than girls. He did believe that his daughter was to be treasured and protected. His form of protection was gratuitous enough that Aisling was even more of a terror than her brothers, which was something to behold when a family dinner got out of control.

"He begs all the time," I offered, ignoring the dark look Braden shot me. "I think it's kind of cute."

"It's not cute on the job." Cormack was firm as he inclined his head toward Renley. "You might not think it's necessary to be professional, Braden, but this is important to Izzy ... so stop being an idiot."

Braden scowled, but climbed off my desk. He knew it was unprofessional to carry on in front of Renley, a man he considered more of an uncle than a boss. He didn't want to bring shame to me, and I appreciated his effort ... even if it was a little pouty.

"Fine." He let loose a prolonged sigh. "I guess I can behave. As soon as Renley is gone, though, I'm going nuts. You've been warned."

"Thank you for the heads-up," Cormack said dryly, shaking his head. "I'll be fleeing as soon as Renley completes his tour."

Because I was legitimately interested, I craned my neck to see around Cormack. The spot where Renley had been standing only moments before was empty. "Where did he go?"

"He's in the library," Cormack replied. "They're going to use that space as a classroom for future reapers at some point. They've already brought over a bunch of books, which I assume you've noticed. I hope you're prepared for the influx of bodies down here."

"It's fine."

"You might not say that when you have students traipsing in and out of here. It won't be for newbies. That's all I can promise. It will be for those who have advanced through the ranks and are getting ready to hit the streets."

That reminded me of a question I'd been longing to ask. "I thought reapers were born. Reaping families are dynasties of sorts, right? If that's the case, why are they starting these new classes? I didn't think the reaper council was the recruiting sort."

"It's a difficult time," he explained. "It used to be that reaper families could keep up with the demands of the dying. Before the families took over, we recruited quite regularly. We trained reapers in classrooms ... and for multiple jobs. When cadets entered the academy, they had no idea where they would end up.

"It could be on the streets collecting souls, depending on their aptitude," he continued. "Other positions were clerical. Up until about thirty years ago, the gatekeepers were selected from the cadet classes, which were much smaller then."

"Did my parents attend classes?" The question was out of my

mouth before I thought better of it. Talk of my dead parents was often depressing. Cormack never shied from the topic, though. He was always open with me. Perhaps it had something to do with the fact that his children had lost their mother in a terrible accident — and then watched a monster return wearing her face ten years later — but he showed infinite patience whenever I asked questions, even if they were invasive.

"Not really. I mean ... all reapers, even those born into the business, attend classes. Your parents both had specific knowledge that helped prepare them for their jobs at the gate. I believe Oliver attended classes, though."

I looked to my co-worker. He seemed engrossed in whatever he was doing, his gaze fixed on his computer screen. He was a vampire. I knew that. He'd been present when my parents died. Well, he wasn't there when the monster came for them, but he did dig me out of the rubble and save my life. I didn't exactly remember him from my childhood, but he gave me a warm feeling. The same went for his boyfriend, Brett Soloman. They both lived on the island and they'd quickly become members of my extended family.

"He's not even listening to us," Braden snarked. "He's tuning us out. That's what he does whenever I visit Izzy."

"I don't tune you out," Oliver countered, his eyes never moving from the monitor as his fingers flew over the keyboard. "I simply pretend I can't see the filthy thoughts written all over your face when you look at her. It's better if I pretend not to see you. Otherwise, I might have to kill you."

Cormack chuckled, the sound warm and inviting. "See, Braden. I told you that trying to romance Izzy in front of her pseudo-godfather was a bad idea. He could rip you limb from limb if he loses his temper."

"I could," Oliver agreed without hesitation. He seemed intent on what he was doing. "There's nothing pseudo about my godfather status, though. I've always been a part of Izzy's life. She might've been separated from me for most of her childhood, but that doesn't mean I don't take my position as her caretaker seriously."

I had to laugh at the statement. "I'm an adult," I reminded him. "I can take care of myself."

"You're still a child to me. Besides, it doesn't matter how old you get, I'll always be your godfather." His gaze was pointed when he finally looked in my direction, although I didn't miss the way his lips quirked. "As for your friend, if his hands continue to wander I will have to break them. He really should be more professional when you're at work."

Instead of being apologetic — which would've been smart under the circumstances — Braden opted to be offended. "I'm a total professional. Just ask my father. He gives me the important assignments because I'm never distracted on the job."

"I give you the important jobs because Redmond has his head in the clouds these days, Aidan is planning a wedding, Cillian is angling for a spot in the research department and your sister just created human life," Cormack countered. "It's not a commentary on your abilities."

Braden's expression darkened, which I wasn't sure was even possible. "Well, thanks for that."

Cormack grinned. "Don't give me that look. You know your sister is my favorite right now." Most fathers deny having favorites, especially if they had five children close in age vying for attention. Cormack was not most fathers. He openly pitted his children against one another and picked a favorite to spoil daily. Aisling had garnered the top spot more often than most the past few months. The reason was obvious.

"And how long is Aisling going to keep being number one?" Braden queried.

"Until one of you gives me another grandchild." Cormack's expression was light when he glanced at me. "I'm thinking another little girl with Izzy's looks and grace would be a welcome addition."

Even though I knew he was teasing, my cheeks flooded with color. "Oh, I ... um ... ."

"Stop that," Braden ordered, his eyes flashing. "You're freaking her out. I don't want you scaring her away. We've been dating only a month. You don't need to pressure her."

"I agree," Oliver offered. He was back to focusing on his computer. "It's far too soon to talk about anything of the sort. Yes, Brett and I would love to play grandfather to a new life, but they need to be married first."

The simple comment made things worse.

"My sister got pregnant before she was married," Braden argued. "It wasn't the end of the world."

"If I remember correctly, your sister found out she was pregnant as she was getting married. Also, your father is more indulgent than I am. If you knock up Izzy before you marry her, I'll make sure you never procreate again." He delivered the threat with grace and an easy smile, which made Braden swallow hard.

"Nobody is getting pregnant," I interjected quickly. I wanted this conversation to disappear just as quickly as it appeared. "Stop talking about stupid stuff. It's way too early to even be thinking about stuff like that."

"Human life happens in the blink of an eye for me," Oliver countered. "It will happen before I'm ready. I guarantee that." His stare was grave as he glanced away from his computer and focused on Braden. "It will be very difficult for you to have more than one child if I tie it in a knot."

Braden shifted uncomfortably, increasing the distance between us. I would've found his reaction amusing under different circumstances. But I felt under the microscope so I wanted to change the subject as quickly as possible.

"What are you looking at?" I moved from my station to Oliver's so I could look over his shoulder, frowning when I caught sight of the energy spikes that had his attention. "What is that?"

"It's the energy pattern from the gate. It is ... *off*."

That was a gentle word for what I was seeing. The line, usually soft and rolling, was hopping up and down with wild swings. "What would cause that?"

"That's what I'm trying to figure out. I've never seen anything like it before."

Curious, I shifted away from his desk and moved in the direction of the gate. I'd almost gotten used to it now, the way it shimmered. It felt like it was alive.

As if on cue, the whispering began. I'd been hearing whispers from the gate since I was a child. Oliver reminded me of that. I was barely back at the gate when the murmuring began in earnest. It wasn't constant, and I could discern no pattern when the whispering kicked into overdrive. I was beginning to believe it started whenever someone was close to the threshold on the other side. Of course, I had no way to prove my hunch. That didn't stop me from speculating.

"Do you hear that?" The question escaped before I remembered there was no way they could hear it. I was the only one who heard the voices.

"Hear what?" Alarmed, Braden stepped in my direction. "Do you hear something beyond the gate?" He'd been present a previous time when I'd heard the whispers and I was convinced he was still edgy about what happened in the aftermath.

"I hear them." I extended my fingers toward the rippling surface, my eyes going wide when the normally small waves turned choppy. "What's happening?"

Seconds after the question was out of my mouth a buzzing filled the room. It was loud, almost overpowering. Out of the corner of my eye, I saw Oliver hop to his feet. He looked paler than normal, which was saying something, because he hadn't seen the sun for the entirety of his life.

"Izzy, get away from that gate," he ordered.

Braden, perhaps sensing that Oliver meant business, took another step in my direction. "He's right, Izzy. Get away from the gate. I think something is about to happen."

I was positive something was about to happen. That didn't mean I could turn away. "I just want to see." I knew better than to touch the surface, but something inside the gate — more likely on the other side — was calling to me. "It will just take a second."

The noise level ratcheted up until the buzzing became excruciating. It was so painful I had to cover my ears. Even then, I couldn't stay on my feet.

The human brain is equipped to acknowledge noise only to a certain decibel level. The buzzing went beyond that. The next thing I knew, a black curtain was falling over my eyes. I fell backward, away from the gate.

By the time I hit the ground, I was already out.

Two

I was in another time.

Heck, I was in another world.

When I managed to open my eyes, the gray pall was gloomy enough that I had to blink several times to make certain of what I was really seeing. I still wasn't convinced, even when I pressed my hands to the ground and felt jagged rock edges poking into my palms.

"Where is this place?" I meant to say the words out loud. They only found form in my head, though. I tried again. No sound came out. Was I mute? What was happening? I rubbed my forehead as I struggled to a sitting position and frowned when I realized I wasn't alone.

It took me a few moments to absorb what I saw. It was the gate, only it wasn't the gate as I knew it. I couldn't see the room I'd been in only moments before. It was gone. Instead, I sat on a rocky cliff, a steep dropoff only twenty feet away. There was no sun or clouds, only gloom.

This wasn't my world.

I rubbed my forehead to help clear the fog and focused on the individuals huddled together several feet away. They'd picked a spot in the shadow of an even greater rock face. They looked shocked, traumatized to their very bones, and they were pale and sallow.

"We have to go back through," one of the men announced. He looked to be the bravest of the bunch, although that wasn't saying much. "We've been here for two hours. We can't continue to sit here."

Another man, this one with blond hair and pale gray eyes, stirred. "We don't know that we'll survive if we go through the gate. In fact, we've been taught the exact opposite. The gate will kill us."

"Obviously not," the first man argued. "We're on the other side of the gate right now. We survived the trip. Our instructors were clearly wrong. There's no reason to believe we won't survive the trip a second time."

"Or we're already dead," a third man volunteered. He was young, in his early twenties, and yet his hairline was already receding. His eyes were filled with fear, the sort I'd seen only in my nightmares. And, well, a few well-acted horror movies. It was enough to make me shudder and look away.

"We're not dead, Stan," the first man snapped, making a face. "I mean ... check for yourself." He pressed his fingers to his neck to feel for a pulse. "I feel my heart beating. That doesn't happen when you're dead."

"How do you know?" Stan, obviously at his limit, didn't fear a fight. "We're out of our element here. Everything we thought was true isn't. We could be dead ... or we could be unconscious. For all we know, this is a figment of our imagination."

"He's right." Another man found his voice. He had black hair and a slightly darker skin tone, making me believe he was Hispanic. "We could be unconscious. This is probably a dream. We were most likely knocked out by the sound emanating from the gate. Now we're unconscious and dreaming. We'll wake soon."

"And this is what, Manuel, a mass delusion?" The first man fancied himself in charge, but he was clearly facing a mutiny. I wanted to stop the arguments, but I couldn't speak ... and they hadn't as much as looked in my direction. That made me believe they didn't see me, which was frightening for a different reason. I chose not to dwell on it. If I did, the fear might overwhelm me. I would never get out of this predicament if I allowed the fear to get a foothold.

"This could be happening in one person's head." Manuel refused to back down. "We should wait, Doug. We could wake up any second."

"If this is a mass delusion, then there's no reason not to walk back through the gate," the man apparently named Doug pointed out. "In fact, that might be the thing that wakes us up. The gate is only dangerous if this is the real world, right? You seem to believe it's not the real world."

"I didn't say that." Manuel turned morose. "I don't even know that I believe that. This being a product of one person's imagination is better than the alternative."

"And what's the alternative?"

I was actually wondering that myself.

"The alternative is that we're in purgatory," Manuel replied, calm. "The alternative is that we're really dead, and because they weren't expecting us we'll be forced to remain here until they figure out what to do with us."

"Who is this 'they' that you're referring to?" Doug challenged. "There's no 'they' for us to worry about."

"Isn't there?" Manuel inclined his chin toward the trees on the far side of the small clearing. On that side of the expanse, there was what looked to be a dark and dank forest. It gave me chills just looking at it. There was no way I was going in there. "Can't you hear them? They're coming for us. They'll be here soon."

Everyone — including me — jerked their heads in that direction. Now that it had been pointed out, the unmistakable sound of footsteps was hard to ignore. I went cold all over.

What was going on here?

Just at the moment the footsteps reached the edge of the woods, my fingertips started tingling. I glanced down and found my vision had started to blur. Oh, well, this couldn't be good.

As if to prove me right, my head suddenly felt as if it had doubled in size. It was too big to hold up. When I fell to the ground this time I was terrified I would never open my eyes again. This was it, I told myself. This was the end.

· · ·

I WOKE TO BRADEN ABSOLUTELY melting down.

"Somebody call an ambulance right now! Right freaking now!"

I opened my eyes and found myself in the gate room, in the same spot I'd lost consciousness. Oliver and Cormack stared down at my face. Braden cradled me against his chest as he held me on the floor. My head hurt and I felt numb. I was alive, though. That was the important thing.

"What happened?" I rasped, relieved to find I had a voice.

"Oh, thank god." Braden held me so tightly I feared he might smother me. "I thought you were dead."

He wasn't the only one. "I'm fine," I reassured him, awkwardly patting his arm. "I just have a headache. I ... what happened?" I looked to Oliver for answers because he had yelled for me to stay away from the gate right before it happened.

"I'm not sure." Oliver looked grave. "But that's not the first time I've seen the gate act like that. It's been sixty years, but ... I'll never forget."

As if testing him, the gate gurgled, causing every head in the room to turn in its direction. To my utter surprise, five bodies were spread on the platform in front of the shimmering opening.

"What the ... ?" I tried to climb to my feet despite Braden's insistence on keeping me close. "Where did they come from?"

Oliver was so pale I could practically see through him. He worked his jaw but no sound came out. It was only the sound of someone clearing a throat near the door that led to the hallway that broke the spell that had settled over the room.

When I turned, I found a pretty brunette studying the scene with impassioned eyes. She had long dark hair, cheekbones so high they looked carved from granite, and a serious expression on her face. I recognized her from the application form she'd sent in.

Her name was Paris Princeton and she was my new assistant. This was one heckuva way for her to be introduced to her new job.

"Oh, um ... hey." I felt like an idiot as I remained prone on the floor, Braden stroking my hair and his father and our resident vampire staring dumbly at the pile of bodies that had suddenly appeared in front of the gate. "You must be Paris. Um ... welcome."

Cormack finally tore his eyes from the bodies and focused on our new guest. He looked dumbfounded and out of his element, two things I thought I could never say about him. "Did anyone see what happened?"

Paris nodded. "I did." She raised her hand, as if in a classroom. "The gate flashed really brightly and knocked you down." She lobbed a tight smile in my direction, one that was almost apologetic, as if she could've stopped what had happened. "I think I was protected because I was so far back. When it flashed a second time, there were five new people here ... and I think they came from the other side."

"But ... how?" Cormack's bewildered expression hurt my heart. "How could this have happened?"

"I don't know," Oliver replied, determinedly moving in the direction of the bodies. "I just ... I ... oh, my!" He dropped to his knees next to the first body, and when he turned the man over I almost jumped out of my skin. I recognized the face.

"I saw him," I blurted out. "When I was on the other side, I saw him."

Braden's eyebrows practically flew off his forehead. "You were on the other side?"

I swallowed and nodded. "I think so. I saw him ... and a few others. I think there were, like, fifteen of them."

"Fourteen," Oliver corrected absently. "There were fourteen."

"How do you know that?" Cormack asked, moving toward another body. I recognized that one, too. As the lone Hispanic of the group, he was hard to forget.

"I was with them when they disappeared," Oliver replied, forlorn. "There were fifteen of us and the gate malfunctioned. It flashed like it just did ... and when I came to I was the only one left. Well, me and the trainer. He was spared, but he was never the same."

"I don't understand." Braden ran his hands over my arms, as if to warm me. Keeping contact was obviously important to him. I still felt weak, so I didn't complain. There was no bettering this scenario for Paris's benefit after all, so why bother? "What is going on?"

"That's what I would like to know," Renley announced as he

strolled out of the library and took in the scene. "I think we're going to need some help."

That was an understatement if ever I'd heard one.

AN HOUR LATER WE HAD more questions than answers. Paramedics arrived and bundled the five men, strapping them to gurneys, and disappeared before any of them regained consciousness.

I didn't know much. All five were apparently alive. They were breathing, although none had regained consciousness. Given the fact that he was present for the initial disappearance, Oliver was the one person who could identify them and fill in a few blanks. He seemed reticent about the latter, but I chalked that up to shock.

"Their names are Doug Dunning, Pat Hill, Manuel Ramirez, Stan Bodri and Hank Morgan," he started, dragging a hand through his dark hair as he paced the area at the bottom of the gate platform. He seemed lost in thought. Heck, he seemed lost in time. I understood that. I had a feeling I'd witnessed the immediate aftermath of the gate malfunction myself, although I was still struggling to understand how. That's why I kept my mouth shut about what I'd witnessed ... at least for now.

"And they were your classmates?" Cormack queried.

Oliver nodded. "We were training to be gatekeepers. Or, we were training to work on the island. Nobody knew what position they would get."

Cormack explained how the training was different back then.

"And this was sixty years ago?" Braden was flummoxed. He'd finally allowed me to stand, but demanded the paramedics check me over despite my insistence to the contrary. They declared me fit, if a little dazed, and suggested I get a good night's sleep. In Braden's mind that meant he should take me to my apartment in the boathouse without further chitchat. When I balked, he grew frustrated. I ultimately won the argument and he continued fuming. He refused to leave my side.

"It was." Oliver bobbed his head. "The gate burbled ... and screamed ... and flashed. I was knocked out, which was a new experience because it had never happened before. When I woke, the others were gone ... except for the trainer I mentioned. I was the only one left behind."

Instinctively, I reached out and rubbed my hand over his shoulder. He wasn't the demonstrative sort, though he rarely denied me when I graced him with a rare hug. Now he seemed almost grateful for the contact. "That had to be horrible."

Despite the serious nature of the situation, he mustered a smile. "Actually, it was difficult ... although not for the reasons you assume. I didn't feel guilty about being left behind, if that's what you're worried about. I was confused. I'm still confused."

"It's probably because you're a vampire," Braden supplied, thoughtful. "The gate took the others because they were human, alive. It might not have been able to recognize what you were because vampires rarely, if ever, go through the gate. It left you behind because it couldn't identify you."

"That's the same conclusion I came to," Oliver confirmed. "I assumed the rest were taken in a mishap and probably died on the other side. Now, though ... they looked the same."

The conversational shift threw me. "What?"

"They looked the same," he repeated. "They didn't age. That's how they looked when they went through the gate. They're humans. Most of them were in their twenties when they went through. That means they should've been in their eighties coming back. They weren't."

"They were young men," Cormack mused. "You're right. They didn't age. That is ... interesting."

I could think of a few other words to describe it. "What's going to happen to them? I mean ... I know they were unconscious and needed medical attention, but what's going to happen to them after that?"

"I have no idea." Cormack bit his lower lip. "They'll have questions to answer. The reaper council will want to know where they've been, what they've gone through. This could be the biggest thing that's ever happened to our ranks. They've actually been on the other side of the gate. Nobody other than an errant wraith or two could ever say that before this happened."

"That's probably why Renley took off the way he did," Braden volunteered. "He was on his phone the entire time the paramedics worked on them, and then he bolted. Did he even say goodbye?"

"He said I was to remain here until the scene was under control," Cormack replied. "After that, I'm expected at reaper headquarters. If they think I'm going to have answers, they're going to be sadly disappointed."

"No one will have answers until those men wake," Oliver pointed out. "In fact ... perhaps I should be at the hospital with them." He looked uncomfortable with the suggestion, but barreled forward. "They're in a new world. I mean ... this might've been the place they lived sixty years ago, but it's like an alien planet now.

"Their families will have changed," he continued. "Their parents will be gone, wives either dead or moved on. Children who are not only adults, but are now older than them. My face is the same. They might react better to me than a stranger."

Cormack agreed. "That's not a bad idea. Maybe you should come with me to the main office. You'll be of invaluable assistance thanks to your knowledge of the men. You should definitely be part of this."

Annoyance bubbled up. I absolutely hated being left out. "I might be of assistance, too." I made up my mind on the spot. No matter how hard it was to explain, the vision of what the men went through not long after being transported to the other side had been shown to me for a reason. I couldn't simply hide the information. "I saw something when I was knocked out cold."

"You saw something?"

I nodded. "I was confused at the time, but I think I understand now. It was a memory fragment of what those men saw in the hours right after they were transported to the other side. I was there for part of it and tried to interact with them. I couldn't, but that's because the memory was already formed. I was meant only to see, not interact or change anything that had already happened."

"You saw the other side of the gate?" Oliver was intrigued. "I forgot you mentioned that right after you woke up. I figured you were confused or had a dream. You seem adamant that's not the case. What did you see?"

"It was a cliff. I ... it was just a cliff." I wasn't sure what answer he was looking for and I didn't have time to think it over. "There was no pearly gate, if that's what you're asking."

"I never expected there to be a pearly gate ... especially that close to the gate. That is nobody's final resting place. It's a waiting room."

"It's more like a clearing on a top of a mountain," I corrected. "There were woods ... and there was something coming through the trees for them. I'm certain I recognized a few of the faces. I was definitely with them ... and something definitely happened."

"It's our job to find out what," Cormack agreed, rubbing his forehead. "Okay, you're part of the team, too. We'll head to the reaper headquarters and see what we can find out. There's always a chance Izzy can read them if they remain unconscious."

That sounded like a plan. When I turned, though, I found Paris watching the conversation with unveiled interest.

"Oh, well ... ." Crap. I had responsibilities as a boss, too.

"You don't have to worry about me." Paris was oddly unflustered, which made me respect her even more. "I get that this is a big deal. I was just here for a tour anyway. My first day isn't until tomorrow. How about we hold off until then?"

I was beyond grateful. "That doesn't upset you?"

"No, but if you don't mind, I'm going to spend a little time in that library researching the gate. There must be some precedent for what just happened."

"There isn't." Cormack was firm. "If there were, someone would've found it by now."

"I still think it's worth checking out."

"If you want to waste your time, go ahead. I guarantee you won't find anything."

"Never say never."

Yup. I definitely liked her. She was going to turn out to be a good choice. I could feel it.

Three

I had been to reaper council headquarters only a handful of times, including when I interviewed for my job. I wasn't familiar with the layout, so I trailed behind Cormack, my mind busy with a thousand possibilities, and exhaled heavily as we navigated the labyrinthine hallways.

"I didn't even know they had a hospital wing here," I admitted.

To my surprise, Braden quietly reached over and linked his fingers with mine rather than verbally respond. When I spared him a look, I found his handsome face lined with concentration. He seemed distracted.

"We're on the job," I reminded him, pulling my hand away.

He scowled. "You're just trying to punish me," he muttered.

I almost laughed at his morose expression. "Actually, I'm not." I studied him for a long beat. "Do you want to tell me what's wrong? If you blame me for this ... well ... I don't know what to tell you. It's not as if I caused it."

He slowed his pace and gave me an incredulous look. "Do you honestly think I blame you for this?"

I was taken aback. "Well ... ." How was I supposed to answer?

"I don't blame you for this." His temper was on full display as he stepped closer to me. "Let's say I did, though. What is there to blame you for? Fourteen people disappeared through the gate sixty years ago. Five came back today looking as if no time had passed. What blame is there to pass around in that scenario?"

That was a good question. "I don't know. I ... ." I frowned, which made him smile for the first time since I'd come to on the gate room floor. "If you don't blame me for this, what's your problem?"

"What's my problem?" Braden's eyebrows hopped. "Seriously? I thought you were dead."

Realization finally hit me. "Oh."

"Yeah, 'oh.'" His fingers were gentle when they slipped a strand of hair behind my ear. "Do you have any idea the fear I felt when I saw you go down?"

I hadn't even considered it, which seemed rude. There was no way I could admit that. He wouldn't take it well. "I'm sorry." That was true. I never wanted him to feel any pain. "I didn't mean to frighten you."

He merely shook his head. "Izzy, I'm not blaming you. You didn't cause this. No one caused this ... at least as far as we know. Sometimes things just happen. That doesn't mean I wasn't afraid."

The admission made me feel warm all over. "I guess you kind of like me, huh?"

He snorted before gently grabbing the sides of my face and resting his forehead against mine. "I kind of like you a lot. That's something my sister would've said, though, and I don't like being reminded that you have so much in common with Aisling."

"Does it make you feel dirty?"

"Oh, don't be gross." He wrinkled his nose and gave me a quick kiss before I could pull back. "I don't really care if you're against displays of affection on the job, I need one right now."

He was so earnest I couldn't deny him. "Okay, but we're not doing more than this." I squeezed his hand and remained still before pulling away. "That's all you get until we're alone later."

His eyes gleamed in a fashion that made me believe he wanted to test my boundaries. Thankfully for both of us, Cormack had realized we'd fallen behind and chose that moment to clear his throat to get our attention. Embarrassed, I snapped my head up.

"It would be best if you two didn't swap spit in the middle of the reaper headquarters when we're dealing with a crisis," he volunteered.

Braden scowled at him as he took a step back. "You have to ruin all my fun, don't you? You've been like this since I was a kid."

"If you're talking about that time you and Redmond decided you were superheroes and were going to jump off the roof, I still maintain I was saving your lives, not ruining your fun."

Braden made an incredulous face. "We weren't going to jump. We were going to float. We made capes with wing things."

"Yes, and I'm certain the sewing prowess of eight-year-olds would've held up against wind velocity." Cormack rolled his eyes. "Stop arguing. We don't have much time. We certainly can't waste any on the two of you making out in an office hallway. That's unprofessional."

"Ha!" I jabbed a finger in Braden's chest. "I told you."

"Yeah, yeah, yeah." Braden ruefully rubbed the spot where I poked him. "I can't tell you how thrilled I am that my father and girlfriend regularly team up to torture me. It makes me feel warm all over."

I couldn't stop myself from smiling at him. "I'll soothe your fragile ego later if you let this go now. I promise to make it up to you."

He brightened considerably. "I'm going to hold you to that."

"I have no doubt."

CORMACK LEFT US OUTSIDE WITH Oliver while he attended a closed-door meeting in Renley's office. That gave me a chance to study the photos on the wall and pace as Oliver stared into nothing, his thoughts clearly overwhelming him, and Braden played a game on his phone.

"I don't remember reading anything about missing reapers when I was researching for my placement here," I noted after a bit, my gaze falling on a faded black-and-white photo. "Don't you think that would be a big part of the curriculum? Or at least mentioned in the history books?"

"Are you sure there's no mention of it?" Braden asked. "I wasn't the best student — before or after reaper training — so I can't say with any degree of certainty that it wasn't mentioned."

"I can." I was firm on that. "I would've remembered that story. I conducted a lot of research before applying for my position here. I knew I would have only one shot. Trust me when I say that a story about fourteen people going missing through the gate when I was trying to dig up information on what happened to my parents would've caught my attention."

Braden nodded in sympathy. "Yeah. I guess that's true. I don't know how to answer your question."

Oliver stirred. "They covered it up."

I slid my eyes to him, conflicted. "Are you sure?"

He nodded without hesitation. "I'm most definitely sure. They covered it up. They didn't want any information to get out. The trainer and I were the only ones who witnessed what happened and we couldn't actually say what went down because we were both knocked unconscious."

That brought up an interesting thread. "I was knocked out, too. Like you, I wasn't transported through the gate."

Braden lifted his chin. "Don't even suggest anything of the sort."

I didn't have a choice. "I have to. Sixty years ago, the gate acted up and fourteen people were sucked through it. Today, the gate acted up. Five people returned. What happened to the other nine? Why wasn't I sucked through? I mean ... other than the vision, nothing weird happened to me. Why?"

"Those are all compelling questions," Oliver agreed, stretching his long legs in front of him. His expression was hard to read as he held my gaze. "You saw something when you were unconscious. I would like to know what you witnessed."

I shouldn't have been surprised by the request. He knew the missing men, after all. Still, it was an uncomfortable conversation. "I don't know if I really saw what happened to them or if I dreamed it."

Oliver arched an eyebrow. "You seemed sure when you convinced Cormack to bring you here."

"That's only because I didn't want to be left out of the adventure."

"No." He shook his head. "It makes no sense for you to dream of men you didn't know existed. You're powerful. When you went under, you saw a memory. You couldn't make that up in your head because you didn't know the participants."

I hadn't really considered that, but he had a point. "I don't know what I saw. There was a group of men — I didn't count them so I don't know if they were all present — and they were huddled together on the other side of the gate. It was like this weird cliff area. There was nowhere to run but the woods, and they were too frightening to consider escaping in that direction."

Oliver nodded for me to continue. "Did they speak?"

"Yeah." I told him about the discussion I'd overheard, leaving nothing out. When I was finished, he looked more agitated than when the conversation started.

"Something was coming for them from the trees?" He leaned forward. "Did you see what?"

"No. That's when I woke up."

"That's ... unfortunate." He rolled his neck until it cracked. "I can't imagine what happened to them. I don't understand any of it, including why they haven't aged. I just ... it's a mystery."

"I think you're about to get a chance to at least try to solve that mystery," Braden noted as he tilted his head toward the door. Cormack entered, looking grave. "Are we clear to talk to the returnees?"

Cormack nodded. "Yes, but we have only twenty minutes. Make them count."

THE HOSPITAL WARD WAS EXACTLY as I imagined. It was like a scene out of Harry Potter, with one long ward and beds lined up on either side, creating an aisle down the center.

The men were spread out, separated by beds, and partitions had been placed to give them some privacy.

They were all awake ... and complaining loudly.

"I want to know what's going on right now!"

"That's Doug," I automatically volunteered to Oliver. I recognized him from the vision.

Oliver slid me a dubious look. "I know." He looked nervous as he stepped forward, focusing his full attention on the man. Doug stopped grousing at the nurse taking his blood pressure and focused on the man at the end of the bed.

"Why don't you have to be strapped down?" he demanded, frustration practically oozing out of him. "Why aren't you getting the hard treatment like the rest of us? What makes you so special?"

Oliver looked at a loss. "I wasn't with you," he said finally. "Somehow I got left behind."

Doug made a face. "Left behind when? We were all in the gate room together and it started making that noise. I think we passed out or something. Now we're here."

I shifted from one foot to the other, myriad questions bubbling for supremacy. Didn't he remember being on the other side of the gate? It sounded as if no time had passed for him. How was that possible? I kept my mouth shut — for a change — because it seemed the thing to do. This was Oliver's show.

"That's all you remember?" Cormack asked, stepping into Doug's view. "You don't remember anything else?"

"What else am I supposed to remember?" Doug's anger had teeth and he was looking to bite someone. Apparently it didn't matter who. Of course, he had no way of knowing that Cormack was one of the highest-ranking reapers in the Detroit office. Cormack hadn't even been born when the men disappeared.

Cormack slid his eyes to Oliver, uncertain. "What have you been told?" he asked finally. "I mean ... when you were removed from the gate room you must've been told something."

"I was told that I passed out and I was fine. I need to call my brother. Do you have a phone?"

Cormack pretended he didn't hear the question. "What happened to the other members of your group?"

"What other members?" Pure bafflement washed over Doug's pinched features. "I don't know what you're talking about."

Oliver made a sound deep in his throat to draw attention in his direction. "Fifteen of us were going through orientation. Did you notice how many people were in the room when you came to?"

Doug glanced around, as if doing the math. "I don't know what that's supposed to mean," he said finally. "Did something happen? Wait

... was it the Russians? I bet it was the Russians. Or it could've been the Cubans. Did they gas us?"

The questions seemed fantastical, and I had to ask the obvious question. "Why would the Russians attack?"

"Sixty years ago things were different," Braden replied absently. "Russia was a superpower until the eighties. They weren't always as bumbling as they are now. Things are much different these days. They have been for the entirety of our lives."

I understood what he was insinuating, but I was still confused. "Why do you know so much about it?"

"My father is a history buff. He used to make us watch things like *Rocky IV*, where Rocky ended communism with a single fistfight."

Huh. I vaguely remembered that movie. My grandfather had been a fan, too. "At least he looked hot doing it."

Braden snickered. "We can play that game later."

Doug was wide-eyed as he glanced between us. It was obvious we'd stepped into *Twilight Zone* territory here and he was incapable of keeping up. "I don't understand what any of you are saying. I demand to know what's going on ... and I want to know right now. Then I need to call my brother and tell him I'll be home late. He's probably worried."

He probably was worried ... sixty years ago. The man might not even be alive today. In fact, playing the odds, he probably wasn't.

"Well, since no one else has explained the situation to you, I guess it falls to me." Cormack was resigned as he tugged on his suit jacket. "Sixty years ago, you and thirteen others reported for training in the gate room. Something happened — the gate malfunctioned — and you disappeared. Today, the gate malfunctioned again and five of you reappeared. Things are not as you think."

Doug's face was a block of ice as he stared at Cormack for what felt like a ridiculously long time. Then he belted out a laugh. "Oh, that's good. Did Willy put you up to that? Where is he, by the way? I'm guessing he wasn't knocked unconscious by whatever happened. Were we out long enough for you guys to come up with a plan to mess with us or something?"

"This is not a joke." Cormack's expression was a mixture of determination and regret. He obviously felt sorry for the man, but it was important to make him accept reality. "I'm sorry this happened. We don't have answers as to the how or why. We're going to do our best to find them. You have my word on that."

"You're so full of crap." Doug refused to back down. "We were out for only a few minutes. Sixty years? Give me a break. I know I look a little worse for wear after losing consciousness, but I clearly haven't aged sixty years.

"For that matter, neither has he," he continued, gesturing toward Oliver. "He was with us in the gate room. He's obviously in on this. You shouldn't have included him."

Oliver took the opportunity to step forward. "I've been included because I knew you back then. The reason I haven't aged is because I'm a vampire." When it looked as if Doug was going to start laughing again, Oliver did the only thing he could — and bared his fangs. They were hidden unless he was fighting or eating, and the shocked expression on Doug's face said it all. "I don't age. That was true even then. I'm sorry, but ... what he's saying is fact. You've been gone for sixty years."

"And ... what? Are you saying we just disappeared? How is that possible?"

"I think you were on the other side of the gate," I volunteered, speaking for the first time. I could no longer remain quiet. "You were all together, on a cliff of some sort, and there were woods to the east. I don't know what happened to you after that, but I know you were stuck in that spot for a few hours."

"And how do you know that? I don't know that. If I don't know, you can't possibly know."

"I saw you."

"You saw me?" He took a moment to look me up and down. "Am I supposed to believe you're more than sixty years old, too?"

"No. I'm in my twenties. I just have ... certain abilities."

"Izzy can see things," Cormack interjected smoothly. "She's magical, and got a flash of what happened to you after the gate malfunctioned again today. We're reasonably assured that what she saw was real."

"Oh, well, if you're reasonably assured." Doug vehemently shook his head. "I don't believe you. I don't believe any of you. I want access to a phone right now. In fact, I demand it. If you try to keep me from my family, I'll sue you."

Cormack heaved out a sigh and dug in his pocket, returning with his cell phone. He extended it in Doug's direction, but instead of eagerly taking it, the man shrank back.

"I thought you wanted to contact your family," Braden challenged. "That's the only thing that's going to make you believe, so I think you should do it."

"On that?" Doug's voice turned shrill. "I don't know what that is ... or what you're doing ... but I demand to talk to someone in charge right now. I mean ... right now!"

The nurse appeared again and shot Cormack a look. "He's upset. You shouldn't press him now. It's too soon given the shock his body has been through."

Cormack held up his hands in defeat. "I'm sorry. We didn't mean to upset him."

"Well, you did."

"We should probably give them time to acclimate," I suggested, as Doug covered his eyes. "I think we approached him too soon."

"If not now, when?" Oliver challenged. "He'll have to learn the truth eventually."

"We'll give him time to settle," Cormack insisted. "We'll come back tomorrow. I think we're done for tonight."

The nurse emphatically nodded. "You're definitely done."

Four

Oliver and I returned to the gate room to finish our shift. Paris had left a note saying that she'd borrowed three books, making sure to spell out the titles in their entirety and promising to return them the next day. We had hundreds of intakes to finish, something Braden wanted to be there for, but his father put his foot down and sent him on his way.

Braden had his own work to do. As much as he wanted to hover, it was unnecessary. I was fine. That didn't mean I was ready to let Oliver off the hook when it came to his past.

"Why didn't you tell me?"

We were packing up for the day when I finally asked.

He tilted his head to the side and met my gaze head-on. "Tell you what?"

"I thought we agreed that we weren't going to keep things from each other. After what happened before … ." I left it hanging. Trust was something that needed to be earned. I was still in a strange limbo with Oliver and Brett due to the fact that they'd kept important information from me.

"We agreed to share information about your parents," he clarified.

"I told you why I didn't immediately tell you about your past. I wanted to see if you would remember me on your own."

I didn't. Well, not really. I felt something when I was near him. It was like a sense memory. I was much more comfortable than I should be around him given the brevity of our relationship. I trusted my instincts, though. Oliver was trustworthy ... if a bit reticent when it came to volunteering information of a personal nature.

"No, we agreed to always tell each other the truth," I pressed. "You didn't tell me about this."

"Because I didn't know it was important. This happened long before you were born. This happened before your parents were born. How does it affect your life?"

"I'm the gatekeeper. They disappeared through the gate."

He considered the statement and then nodded. "Fair enough. Still, it didn't occur to me to broach this particular subject. As I told you before, the reaper council went out of its way to cover up what happened. I was ordered to keep the story to myself."

"Yes, and you so often follow rules," I drawled.

"I followed this one because I assumed whatever happened was caused by human error," he explained. "I mean ... what else was I supposed to believe? Whatever happened that day was powerful enough to knock me out. When I woke, all the men I'd been with were gone. I believed there was a very real possibility that they'd all died and I was told they'd disappeared so I wouldn't inadvertently cause a panic."

Huh. I hadn't really thought about that, but it made sense. "So ... you thought they were dead all this time," I mused. "That must've been difficult."

He held his hands out and shrugged. "It wasn't the easiest of times. Back then I was searching for answers. I was feeling aimless and looking for direction. Most of the questions plaguing me had to do with life ... and death ... and an eternity spent not accomplishing anything."

"Oh, so trivial subjects." I grinned at him to lighten the mood. It worked. "I never asked, but I guess it makes sense you came to work here. You don't die. That probably makes human death even more of a curiosity for you."

"It was at the time," he conceded. "I feel differently now. The gate is a great responsibility. Important things happen on both sides. I truly did believe that my compatriots were dead. Why would I think otherwise?"

"Why would you continue working for an outfit you assumed covered up fourteen deaths?" I challenged. "It seems to me that would be a good reason for finding work elsewhere."

"Not all of us are insistent on being ethical to a fault. Also, I assumed it was an accident. If I believed the others were purposely killed it would've been a greatly different scenario."

"I guess that makes sense." I pursed my lips. "What do you think now?"

"I have no idea. I'm as intrigued by what you saw as I am by the return of men I thought dead sixty years ago. There are so many questions coursing through me I don't know where to start."

"Will you try to go back and see them?"

"Yes, although maybe not for a few days. They need to come to grips with what's happened and I'm a difficult reminder of what was. Most of them have lost everything they knew. Even if parts of their lives remain, they won't be the same.

"Imagine going to work one day, kissing your wife and children, and then falling into darkness," he continued. "Also imagine waking on what you think is the same day only to realize sixty years have passed.

"You're mortal, Izzy. Sixty years to you is a virtual lifetime. These men will have lost everything. Wives gone, remarried or dead. Those who are still alive will look like grandparents to them. Nothing will ever be the same, and that's a bitter pill to swallow."

"And you're worried that they'll be bitter because you weren't taken," I surmised. "You were there, yet nothing happened to you. You lived for sixty years and still look the same, but your end result is vastly different from theirs."

"I want to help them," he clarified. "I will do so to the best of my ability. That doesn't mean pressuring them from the start. I should've thought better about that."

"You were trying to help."

"Yes, and I will do better next time. That's the best I can do."

I squeezed his shoulder and nodded, reminding myself that whatever he said, this had to be difficult for him, too. "I'm supposed to head to Grimlock Manor for dinner. I can cancel and stay if you need to talk."

He looked more amused than touched by the gesture. "I have Brett to talk to if I need it. While I appreciate the offer, you have a life to live. I want you to live it. You can't help with this anyway. It's simply something that needs to work itself out."

He had a point. "Okay. But I'll be here if you need me."

"Thank you. I greatly appreciate the gesture. You and the Grimlock boy will be entertaining yourselves in other ways this evening, though. That is how it should be."

I opened my mouth to reiterate the offer, but he shook his head. The conversation was clearly over. He needed time to absorb things. It was my duty to give it to him ... no matter how agitated I was at the prospect.

GRIMLOCK MANOR WAS BUSTLING WITH activity when I let myself into the house. From the outside, it looked like a castle — complete with turrets — but inside it was full of warmth and family. What I thought ostentatious the first time I entered had turned into a welcoming environment.

I absolutely loved it.

"Look at me, Lily. Look at Uncle Redmond. That's it. Laugh."

I followed the sound of voices into the front parlor. The entire family looked to be gathered, including Maya and Jerry. The former was living with the bookish Grimlock child, Cillian, and the latter was engaged to the youngest boy, Aidan, and planning a lavish wedding. In addition to being Aidan's fiancé, Jerry was Aisling's best friend since childhood. He was watching the scene in the middle of the floor with disgust.

"She's not going to laugh at you until she's old enough to realize what she's laughing at," Jerry challenged, cocktail in his hand and a wedding magazine open on his lap. "You're not going to win this competition."

For his part, the oldest Grimlock child was full of disdain. "That shows what you know," he shot back. "Lily absolutely loves me the best. She's going to laugh for me first."

"She's not going to laugh for another six weeks to two months," Cormack countered. He sat in his normal chair, a coupe glass perched on the table next to him. He was obviously more interested in what his granddaughter was doing than the drink. "You're wasting your time."

"That's not the competition anyway," Braden argued. He was on the floor next to Redmond, holding up a fuzzy unicorn stuffed animal, jiggling it for his niece's enjoyment. "We're trying to see who can make her smile first. That's what's next up on that little development chart of hers. She's old enough to smile."

I remained in the open archway so I could watch the show, folding my arms across my chest. The Grimlocks were the overbearing sort — and that was putting it mildly — but the way every single one of them melted in the face of a pretty baby with violet eyes tugged on my heartstrings.

"What about me?" Aisling challenged from her spot on the settee. Her eyes were bright, her skin glowing, and she looked much better than she had several weeks earlier, when new motherhood was clearly wearing her down. Her tyrant daughter took it out of her, something Aisling understood she had to halt. It was the rest of her family fighting the notion of letting Lily cry herself to sleep. Aisling was determined to break her daughter of bad habits before things completely got out of hand. "I gave birth to her. I'm going to get the first smile."

"As grateful as we all are for you bringing up the birth thing constantly, she can't smile at you first," Aidan countered. He was Aisling's twin and they had a unique relationship. Right now, though, his attention was barely on her because he was doing a little dance behind Braden's back to get the baby to smile. "Everyone knows that babies don't smile at parents first. They smile at uncles."

Cormack snorted. "You're all wasting your time. She's going to smile at me first. Isn't that true?" He stared adoringly at his only grand-child, causing me to have to stifle a laugh.

The Grimlocks weren't happy unless they were competing with one another. It could be a sports game ... cards ... or even a made-up game featuring stuffed sharks and Xbox fishing. They were up for the oppor-tunity to claim glory whenever it arose. Whoever Lily smiled at first would lord it over the others for the rest of her life.

"Hey, Izzy. Why are you just standing here?"

I recognized the voice. It was Griffin Taylor, Aisling's husband. He'd obviously just arrived, because while he held my gaze for a split-second, he immediately turned his attention to the little girl on the floor.

"There's my baby." He swooped into the room, not waiting for me to reply. Instead of bending down to give his daughter a warm greeting, though, he went immediately to his wife and planted a smacking kiss against her lips. "How was your spa day?"

Ah, that explained the fresh glow. Aisling and Jerry took the day off to be puffed and pampered on her father's dime. They were talking about it over the breakfast table this morning. I'd completely forgotten.

Aisling accepted the kiss and gave Griffin an intimate hug. "Good. I really needed it. I also had a doctor's appointment today."

"I know." Griffin sat next to her, his gaze never leaving her face as he brushed her dark hair from her forehead. "I was going to call and see how it went, but I got caught up in other stuff. What did the doctor say? Are you okay?"

Cormack shifted in his chair. "I didn't know you had a doctor's appointment with the baby this morning."

"Not with Lily," Aisling countered. "It was just me. Jerry sat with Lily while I was in the examination room."

"And I was very entertaining," Jerry offered. "She's this close to smiling at her favorite uncle." He held his index finger and thumb about an inch apart. "I'm definitely going to win this particular competition."

Redmond rolled his eyes. "No way. I'm going to win. We all know it. I'm Aisling's favorite brother. That means Lily picked up on it while in the womb. It's already a done deal."

"I'm Aisling's favorite person," Jerry countered. "I'm going to win."

"*I'm* Aisling's favorite person," Griffin corrected, his eyes never leaving his wife's face. "She's going to smile at me first and I don't want to hear another word about it. We're not talking about Lily, we're talking about my wife. I want to know what the doctor said."

Cormack leaned forward, his gaze keen. "Is something wrong? Have you been keeping something from me?"

"Nothing is wrong," Aisling offered hurriedly. "It was just a standard check-up."

"That's not what Griffin seems to think," Redmond argued, turning from Lily and staring down his sister. "He's obviously desperate for a report. That makes me think you're lying and there is something going on."

"Yeah, Ais," Cillian prompted. "Spill. What's going on? What did the doctor say?"

Aisling's expression reflected annoyance. "Don't worry about it. I'm fine."

"We're glad that you're fine," Cormack insisted. "We want to know what you were worried about. Just because you're a mother now doesn't mean you're not my little girl. What is going on?"

Aisling shot her husband a dark look. "I blame you for this."

Griffin's lips quirked. "I'm sorry, baby. I didn't think about the can of worms I was opening. You can flog me later."

Cormack extended a threatening finger in his son-in-law's direction. "Don't say gross things to my daughter. We've talked about this. You have a filthy mind and wandering hands. Both make me want to hurt you."

"You wouldn't have a granddaughter if it wasn't for my filthy mind and wandering hands."

"Stop." Cormack held up his hand. "Not one more word out of you. I'll ban you from the ice cream bar if you're not careful."

Griffin made a pathetic face. "That's just mean."

"And unnecessary," Aisling added. "You guys are getting worked up about nothing. There really is nothing wrong."

"I'll be the judge of that," Cormack countered, firm. "Tell me what's going on. Why were you at the doctor's office?" He looked genuinely apprehensive of her answer.

Aisling let loose a heavy sigh. She looked put upon, which made me laugh ... especially when I got a glimpse of why she was really at the doctor's office this particular day. She was good at shuttering, especially since she figured out I could pick up on surface thoughts, but there was no hiding what was going through her mind at this exact moment.

"If you must know, I needed a pelvic exam," Aisling announced, causing every single man in the room to cringe. "The doctor wanted to make sure I was fully healed so Griffin and I can start having sex again."

Most daughters wouldn't announce that in front of their siblings ... or father ... or friends. Aisling wasn't a normal woman. She wanted to win as much as the next Grimlock, and she'd clearly just declared herself victorious in this evening's Grimlock Gross-out Fest. She looked proud of herself.

"Oh, man!" Redmond rolled to his back and covered his eyes as Braden buried his face in his arms, which were perched on his knees. "I can't believe you just told us that."

"I can't believe it either." Cormack was stern. "You're grounded for the rest of your life, young lady. I hope you're happy. You're going to give your brothers nightmares. What's worse, you're going to give me nightmares."

"You can't ground me." Aisling was blasé. "I'm an adult."

"Do you want to try me?"

She cocked her head to the side, considering. "You know what? Go ahead and ground me. Griffin and I will lock ourselves away in my old bedroom as punishment and you won't have to see us for the rest of the night. You can continue your competition to see who makes Lily smile first and we'll sit in the corner upstairs and think about what we've done."

Griffin brightened considerably. "I love the way your mind works."

"I can't even." Cormack glowered at his drink, which he'd reclaimed from the table. "Why can't I have normal children?"

"Because then you wouldn't be a true Grimlock," Braden offered, his eyes finally moving to me. The smiles we shared were small and intimate. He clearly had plans for the evening, too. They would have to wait until after dinner, though. I was starving. Watching men come back from the dead apparently made me hungry. "I definitely think you should ban them both from the ice cream bar. That seems only fair."

Cormack followed his son's gaze and shook his head when his eyes landed on me. "I'm going to ban every single one of this family's filthy minds from the ice cream bar if you're not careful."

That sounded like a travesty in the making. "What did I do?" I challenged. "I've been good all day ... and got knocked out. Given Grimlock Family Rules, doesn't that mean I'm your favorite?"

Cormack's lips curved. "You catch on quick."

"I was always a good student."

"The ice cream bar is open for everyone," he announced. "Even all those with filthy minds can eat to their heart's content. I ordered plenty of fixings because I figured we'd be having multiple ice cream bars a week now that the weather is looking up."

Lily made a gurgling sound that almost sounded like a laugh, causing every head in the room to snap in her direction.

Aisling leaned closer and made a face. "That was gas, not a laugh."

"In this family it's the same thing," Redmond argued.

Five

Even though Braden retained a room in his father's house — which would've been a deal breaker for another man — I found his digs beyond comfortable. It was more of a small suite than a standard bedroom. I'd gotten used to waking up in his childhood bedroom and didn't think anything of it these days.

"Good morning." His lips brushed my ear as he shifted. He'd spent the entire night spooned behind me, which would've felt smothering with anyone else but seemed natural with him. "How did you sleep?"

That was an interesting question and I understood what was concerning him. "I'm fine," I reassured him without hesitation. "You don't have to worry about me."

"That goes with the territory." He rubbed his stubbled cheek against my ear. "I was worried you might have a few nightmares."

"I did."

He jolted. "You did? Why didn't you wake me?"

"Because I didn't think you would want to hear about my dream. I mean ... your father was in it ... and it wasn't exactly a violent nightmare. It was disturbing for a different reason."

"Excuse me?" His body went rigid. "You had a sex dream about my father?"

I was taken aback and rolled so he wouldn't miss my harsh glare. "That is disgusting."

"You're the one who had the dream."

"I said I had a dream about your father, not that I was having sex with him in it."

"Oh." Braden had the grace to look abashed. "I guess I just assumed."

"You know what they say about people who assume things."

"Yes, that we're awesome and great." He snaked his arm around my waist and tugged until I was plastered against his chest. "Let's be awesome and great together this morning."

I pressed my hand to his chest so he couldn't invade my territory and cause me to lose my train of thought. "I can't kiss you when I'm grossed out about your assumption that I had a sex dream about your father."

"Aw, man. You're going to make this a thing, aren't you?"

"Probably."

"Ugh." He closed his eyes. "At least tell me what you really dreamed about before we start arguing. I need to clean a couple of things out of my mind and I have a feeling whatever you dreamed about will be dark enough to do just that."

"I dreamed that your father found a bayonet and spent the entire night stalking outside Aisling's room to make sure she and Griffin didn't have the romantic reunion they were clearly jonesing for. He even wore a tan pith helmet, and then he said he was hunting handsy cops."

Braden sputtered out a choked chuckle, clearly amused. "Oh, that was so much better than I thought. You make me laugh." He kissed me before I realized he was swooping in. "Have I mentioned how much I love having you here with me?"

He had mentioned it. More than once. And while I understood that he wasn't keen to leave his father's house, it did remind me that it would ultimately become necessary if we expected to move forward with our lives. Now clearly wasn't the time to bring that up, though. It was too early in the relationship to start fiddling with living arrangements.

"I like being with you, too." I rested my head against his chest, taking a moment to enjoy the morning. Then reality crashed into our fairytale. "I need to get back to the gate early this morning. I want to make sure it doesn't malfunction again."

Braden's expression darkened. "No offense, but I would prefer if you weren't around the gate when it's acting up. Why can't you leave Oliver to handle it?"

"Because he's not the boss."

"He's been there long enough to be the boss. Have you ever asked yourself why he didn't take the position himself?"

"Actually, I did." That was one of the first things I'd asked myself, in fact. "He says he's fine being a worker and not a leader."

"Do you believe that?"

It was a fair question. "I believe that his needs are different. To him, the entirety of a human life is the blink of an eye. He might want to be boss, but he's not at the point that it's important to him."

"Fair enough. Are you going to ruthlessly question him about what happened at the gate sixty years ago?"

"I already have. I don't think he has any answers."

"Why didn't he tell you about the disappearances?"

"He assumed they were dead. He thought he was spared some mass catastrophe because he's a vampire, and the reaper council lied about what happened. He was as surprised as anyone to see them appear on the other side of the gate."

"Huh. You know, that makes sense in a weird way."

"I thought so, too."

We lapsed into silence for a few moments.

"You could still call in sick," he said finally. "No one would blame you after what happened yesterday."

"I would blame me."

"Yes, but you're a taskmaster. Nobody normal would blame you."

"I have to go to work." I was firm. "This is Paris Princeton's first day. After what happened yesterday, I have to be there. She'll run if something goes wrong two days in a row."

"I don't know. She seemed pretty calm and collected despite the circumstances. I think she might make a good fit."

I was thinking the same thing. "That's why I have to be there for her first day. I want to see if she found anything during her research."

"You know odds are against that, right?"

"That doesn't mean she didn't stumble across a miracle."

"I think we've witnessed our allotment of miracles for the week ... well, unless you want a personal miracle to start your day."

I cocked an eyebrow. He wasn't exactly subtle. "You have a dirty mind. Do you want your father to ban us from the omelet bar?"

"What he doesn't know can't hurt him."

"He's smarter than you give him credit for."

"And often willfully blind."

That was true. I'd witnessed Cormack's selective blindness a time or two. "Okay, but don't come crying to me if he takes your mushrooms and tomatoes away."

Braden's lips slid into a sly grin. "I wouldn't dare. Besides, there are better things than mushrooms and tomatoes."

"I think you'd better show me what those are."

"You read my mind."

THE FAMILY WAS GATHERED AROUND the dining room table. Aisling and Griffin sat side by side, their plates heaped with food, and cast each other the occasional flirty glance. They'd obviously ignored the complaints of the male Grimlocks and enjoyed their time together, which explained what they were doing at the manor two mornings in a row. They had their own townhouse in Royal Oak and only spent the night at the family manor once or twice a week now for a break from the baby's incessant screaming. Two nights in a row was luxury that Cormack obviously indulged to keep his daughter happy.

"Stop looking at each other that way," Cormack ordered, Lily's head resting against his shoulder as he lightly patted her back. "I know what you were doing all night ... while I was taking care of your baby."

"I should certainly hope so," Aisling said blandly. "We weren't exactly quiet about our intentions."

"Definitely not." Griffin kissed the corner of her mouth before saluting his father-in-law. "You'll never know how thankful I am for your sacrifice."

Cormack scowled, although I didn't miss the momentary twinkle that invaded his eyes. He enjoyed the game as much as his children, which was telling. Even though Aisling was his only daughter, he would deny her nothing. Plus, truth be told, he enjoyed sitting up with the baby. That would probably change when the rest of his offspring started procreating and he was inundated with grandchildren. For now, though, spoiling one wasn't that much work.

"We need to talk about serious things now," Cormack countered, changing the subject. He shot Redmond an evil glare when his oldest son tried to take Lily from him. "Get your own baby. This one is mine right now."

I smiled at the curmudgeonly response. Life with the Grimlocks was never going to be quiet. It would, however, always be entertaining.

"You're such a grump." Redmond flicked his father's ear, shot Lily a winning smile, and then headed toward the omelet bar. "What dire thing do we need to talk about today?"

"The fact that five men returned from the dead," Cormack replied without hesitation. "Word is going to eventually spread that men thought missing for sixty years are back. I'm not saying that it will hit the mainstream media, but rumors are bound to spread throughout the reaper world."

"I've been wondering about that myself," Griffin said. He was a Detroit police detective and he looked genuinely concerned. "These men are going to have living relatives they'll want to contact at some point. The council will be able to keep them locked down for a bit, but eventually someone on the outside will find out and then everyone will hear rumors ... including random humans on the street."

"I've thought about that, too," Cormack conceded. "I don't know what we can do about it. These men have been separated from their families for years. As long as they're not a threat, they're going to be reuniting with loved ones. When that happens ... ."

"Things are going to get ugly," Braden surmised. "Is there anything we can do about it?"

"Not that I'm aware of," Cormac shrugged as he shifted Lily to his other shoulder. "All we can do is take it one day at a time. Izzy, I'm assuming you're going back to the gate today. I expect you to watch it closely. If it starts acting up again, I want you out of that room. Do you understand?"

I was expecting the warning. "You don't have to worry about me. I'm not an idiot."

"You're dating Braden," Aisling argued. "I mean ... I like you and everything, but that kind of indicates to me that you're an idiot."

"Don't make me thump you," Braden warned with a clutched fist. "Your doctor just gave you a clean bill of health. That means things are back to normal and we don't have to worry about breaking you. You're no longer getting special treatment in sock hockey and shark attack. You've been warned."

Aisling rolled her eyes. "Oh, please. I could take you with one ovary tied behind my back. I wasn't the one who demanded the special treatment. That was Dad."

"And the special treatment continues," Cormack boomed. "She can't afford to be hurt."

"How long is that going to be the rule?" Braden whined.

"Until I say otherwise." Cormack was firm. "We all have jobs to do. Cillian will be hitting the research because we need information. The rest of you — including you, Aisling — will gather souls as if nothing has changed. Don't bother arguing."

Slowly, Cormack's eyes tracked to me. "I want you to be careful. You'll be trapped in that room for hours on end. I know it's apparently rare for the gate to malfunction, but it's happened twice that we know of. We don't want anything happening to you."

"Definitely not," Braden agreed, squeezing my knee under the table. "In fact, maybe I should hang around the gate room today instead of collecting souls."

"No." Cormack made a face. "Your idea of hanging around the gate room is begging Izzy for kisses all day. That's not work."

Braden scowled. "I don't beg."

Aisling's eyes gleamed. "Oh, you're such a beggar. It's pathetic."

"Knock that off," Cormack warned. "Everyone is sticking to their assigned tasks today. Is everyone clear?"

Griffin raised his hand. "Does that include me? I mean ... I might want to spend some quality time with my wife. Are you saying that's not allowed?"

Cormack's expression was so dark I felt as if I was trapped in a horror movie. "How far are you going to push me?"

Griffin smirked. "I haven't decided yet. I'll let you know when I know."

"That would be greatly appreciated. Until then, everyone needs to go about their day as if nothing has happened. We're only tangentially involved in this. I don't foresee that changing."

He was right, but that didn't mean I wasn't going to dig as hard as I could. Tangentially or not, I was shown the vision for a reason. I wouldn't stop until I figured out why.

BRADEN PLAYED "KISS ME" GAMES in the driveway for a full ten minutes before he allowed Redmond to drag him away. As I was preparing to leave, I caught sight of Aisling and Griffin playing the same game.

As far as I knew, this was the first time Aisling was returning to work since giving birth. I'd heard her talking about it with her father the previous week. He thought she should take a few more weeks off. She was tired of being stuck at home. They compromised and agreed to two shifts a week. Apparently she was starting today.

Was it difficult to leave the baby? I couldn't help but wonder. Aisling clearly loved her daughter, but she was also fine taking a break. That was probably necessary. Lily was the tiniest tyrant in the land. She was prepared to run the entire family ragged ... and they were willing to let her. Of course, Aisling was leaving the baby with her father. She would be comfortable, safe and completely spoiled.

Oliver was already at his desk when I entered. His eyes were glued to the computer screen and I knew he was running data before I even glanced over his shoulder. The technology we had now was a hundred times better than what they would've been dealing with back then. We might not be able to figure out exactly what happened, but we were better prepared to extrapolate information.

"Anything?" I asked, shrugging out of my jacket.

Oliver slid me a sidelong look. "Not so far. How was your evening?"

"Well, I watched the Grimlocks melt down because Aisling got a clean bill of health and can resume sexual relations with her husband. There was grilled steak, garlic mashed potatoes and an ice cream bar for dinner. Oh, and they're having a competition to see who the baby smiles at first."

Oliver enjoyed stories about the Grimlocks. He said they were a bit much for him, but it was fine listening from afar. Today, though, he didn't as much as crack a smile. "That's nice."

I frowned. "I know that I usually tell stories with a little more gusto – my grandfather says I come by the drama naturally – but I thought that at least deserved a little chuckle."

"I'm sorry. I'm trying to figure out what happened."

"I figured." I slid into the chair from my desk and rolled closer to him. "What have you been able to ascertain?"

"Not much. There was a huge spike of energy right before it happened. It coincided with the noise. Before that, there was a slow build, but it was minuscule. We have nothing in place to alert on something that small."

"What happened back then?"

"They didn't have computer equipment like this. The souls were transported directly to the gate in those days. There was a receptacle on the right side. The scepters were plugged in, the souls sucked out, and then the scepters were returned to the reapers for another day of soul hunting."

"That doesn't sound like the most efficient system."

"It wasn't. A lot of souls escaped in those days for a variety of reasons. That's why you hear about old ghosts but newer ones are rare."

"Good to know." I studied the spiking line on the screen. "How long did the noise continue after I passed out?"

"Not long. It was different this time. I mean ... it was the same, but different. The buildup was shorter. The noise not as loud. I think you got a full dose because you were closer to the gate. No one else passed out."

That didn't make me feel any better. "Basically you're saying that I was weak compared to everyone else."

"On the contrary. I think it's because you're strong that you were affected. You saw into the past. I don't think anyone has ever been able to say the same ... especially when it comes to bearing witness to things that happened on the other side of the gate."

"So ... what do you think that means?"

"I don't know, but I'm going to find out. I owe those men that."

"You don't owe them anything. It's not as if you caused this."

"No," he agreed. "I didn't cause it. I didn't look for them either. I don't know that I could've found them, but I didn't even try."

Something occurred to me. "Did you stay here because of what happened? I mean ... was there part of you that always wondered if they would come back? I've been trying to figure it out. I don't understand why you stayed here all these years, never trying for advancement or anything. You didn't have to stay."

"I told you I assumed they were dead. What else was I to think?"

"Just because your head told you they were dead doesn't mean your heart agreed."

"Don't you know? The undead don't have hearts."

I didn't believe that. "You love as much as the next person. I've seen you with Brett. It's clear you guys are in love. Don't run that on me."

He sighed, clearly exasperated. "You have more faith in me than I probably deserve."

"I don't believe that either. That's why it just occurred to me. Part of you believed they would be back and you wanted to be here if it happened."

"Fine. Part of me – a very small part – believed they would be back. It made no sense, but I couldn't shake the idea. Does that make you happy?"

"Not really. It's just confirmation of what I already knew. You have a big heart."

"It goes well with your big mouth."

Six

Paris was on time and all smiles. For some reason, I found that disconcerting. Not the being on time thing. I admire someone who believes other peoples' time is worth as much as their own. There's nothing worse than someone who is perpetually late. It's as if he or she is saying, "I don't think you're worth making the effort to be on time."

The smiling made me nervous.

"I think we should start with a tour of the island," I offered, sliding a quick look to Oliver. He was still focused on the computer screen, compiling his data. It was Paris's first day, so I didn't want to overwhelm her with creepy hunches and suppositions. That couldn't possibly end well. "Have you ever been here?"

"I visited the island when I was a kid," Paris replied. "It's been a long time, though, and I obviously didn't see all the 'secret' stuff you guys have going on here back then."

"Well, it's not all that big, but there's a lot to see." I started moving toward the door, stopping long enough to give Oliver a look over my shoulder. "We'll be gone a few hours. You okay with that?"

Oliver offered a haphazard wave. "I'm fine with it," he confirmed. "Take your time."

I stared at him for a beat longer and then flashed a smile for Paris's benefit. "The island is bigger than it seems. We'll take my golf cart."

Paris brightened considerably. "You have a golf cart?"

"Yup. It's one of my favorite parts about this gig."

"I would've thought that was the guy I saw you with yesterday."

I was taken aback by the statement, and when I looked to her I found she seemed fixated on the eclectic cart rather than me as we ascended the stairs. I couldn't ascertain if the comment was a dig or innocent.

"Are you married?" I asked finally, changing the subject. It was time I learned more about her.

"I am," she bobbed her head. "His name is Heath. He just started a new business in Royal Oak, but we're still dealing with a few things on the west side of the state we have to sew up."

"Oh, yeah? I know a guy who owns a business in Royal Oak. What does your husband do?"

"He's working as an architect these days."

The way she phrased it made me believe her husband was the sort who jumped from career to career. That wasn't necessarily a good thing, but she didn't seem all that bothered by it.

"Well ... if you're ever downtown together and want a good cupcake, there's a bakery on Main Street called Get Baked. It's owned by a friend of mine."

"Who doesn't love cupcakes? My son is almost two now and he absolutely adores sugar. I have to watch my husband to make sure he doesn't load him up on sugar before bed."

I smiled. Now she sounded like a normal mother talking about her child. "Do you have just the one kid?"

"Yeah. Alvis. He's the light of my life."

Alvis? I ran the name through my head. "Like ... Alvis has left the building?"

This time the look she shot in my direction was cool. "Oddly enough, you're not the first person to make that joke. You kind of remind me of her, in fact ... but you're nowhere near as snarky."

That sounded like a challenge. "I can be snarky. Now that you mention it, I always thought I was the snarkiest person in the world.

Then I met another woman — my boyfriend's sister — and I'm pretty sure she's the snarkiest person alive. I couldn't even compete with a handicap against her."

"I'm pretty sure my friend has them both beat." Paris followed me to the cart and hopped in on the passenger side as I slid behind the wheel. "Did you grow up in Detroit?"

That was a conversation better left for another time. Still, I had to tell her something. "I was in Detroit for a few years as a kid. Then I moved to New Orleans. I'm back here now, and enjoying it a great deal."

"New Orleans! I've always wanted to visit. I've been in Michigan most of my life. Granted, I've hopped all over the state. We used to live on the west side before moving here. I like being here better. The buildings are great and there's a sense of history on this side of the state."

That was an odd thing to say. She seemed serious, though. "I read your file. You attended Covenant College?"

For a brief moment, something akin to worry flashed through the depths of her eyes. She recovered quickly. "I did. Are you familiar with the school?"

"Not really. When I was deciding where I wanted to go my junior year of high school, Covenant College was on the list. It had an interesting reputation."

"There's no doubt about that." Paris pursed her lips and kept her gaze forward as I pulled out onto the road. "Are you a reaper? You don't have an aura like a normal reaper."

I shouldn't have been surprised. Manning the gate was a paranormal endeavor. If Paris knew about the gate, it was likely she knew about other things as well. I sensed something in her now that I was able to focus ... and that something was magic.

"Are you a witch?" I asked, going for broke.

She nodded without hesitation. "I am. And you?"

"Bruja."

"It's basically the same thing except your influences probably lean heavily toward New Orleans voodoo and hoodoo, if I had to guess."

"It is largely the same ... and you're right. My grandfather sold his services as a brujo, and I learned from him. I can work root magic and earth magic. I'm even adept at some elemental magic. I'm really a hodgepodge of abilities."

"That sounds fun." This time the smile Paris flashed was genuine. "I've known a lot of magical people in my life. Some have been more powerful than others. I was intrigued when I realized Oliver was a vampire. I'm guessing he's the warm and cuddly type."

Yup. She was definitely interesting. "Most people, even those who understand about magic and the gate, don't really grasp the vampire thing. I'm impressed."

"I've known a vampire or two."

"Oh, yeah?" Now we were finally getting somewhere. "Did you deal with vampires at Covenant College?"

The second I circled back to the college, she stiffened. "I might have."

I wasn't sure what to make of her reaction. Covenant College had been in the news for a long time. Somehow — and no one could exactly say how — it had been completely razed within a few hours almost two years ago. One minute it had been there, students laughing and flirting on the lawns, and the next minute it was gone.

It hadn't burned. That, at least, would've made sense. Instead, the buildings simply disappeared and the entire parcel of land flattened into a grassy plain. No one could explain it. Even those magically inclined were at a loss. For some reason, I couldn't help but wonder if Paris knew more than what she was letting on about the school's downfall.

"You don't have to tell me what happened," I started, going for broke. "You don't know me yet. I could be untrustworthy and evil for all you know."

"Your aura isn't dark," she countered. "You're not an evil being. You're powerful, but you're not evil."

"Maybe I'm just good at hiding who I am."

"Maybe, but given what happened yesterday I don't think so. You were in a vulnerable position when I arrived. You were out cold on the ground. The guy with you was having an absolute meltdown and screaming at his father. At least I'm assuming that's his father. They look enough alike to almost be clones."

I smiled. Everyone noticed those strong Grimlock traits. "Yeah. That's his father."

"His aura is orange. That means he's a good person, if conflicted. You care about him as much as he cares about you. Feelings like that can't be manufactured and evil beings don't react that way when someone they care about is undergoing an emotional assault."

She had a point. "I see auras, too."

"Oh, yeah? We'll have to compare notes sometime."

"We will." We fell into silence as I steered toward the conservatory. If she was a witch, I figured she would be as interested in the plants and herbs. "I don't want you to feel you have to tell me about Covenant College. When you're ready, I'll be eager to listen. I've been curious about what happened there since I heard the news."

"I don't know that I have the answers you're looking for," she hedged, clearly uncomfortable. "I don't know exactly what happened."

"You know more than most, though, don't you?"

"I know a few things," she conceded. "What happened that night was dark, and it could've gone a way that would've scarred that land forever. Instead, it was reborn and the evil was eradicated. That should be enough to make most people comfortable."

Ah, but I wasn't most people. "You do realize that not everyone recognizes there was a faction of evil planted at that school?"

Her forehead wrinkled as she slid her gaze to me. "How do you know about the evil at the school?"

"Because I dug hard when I was making decisions about what I wanted to do after graduation. I knew magic would be involved. That's why Covenant College was on my list. But once I delved deeper, I realized that the school wasn't a good place where the occasional person dabbled in evil. It was the opposite. It was a bad place where the occasional person dabbled in good."

She barked out a hoarse laugh. "That's a very succinct — and very accurate — way to put it. Not everyone at the school was evil. I would never pretend otherwise. Not everyone was good either. And ... well ...

I made a few mistakes there. I thought some people were good but they turned out to be evil. Those decisions still haunt me."

"Everyone makes mistakes. You don't have to be fearful of mistakes. In fact, you don't have to be fearful of me either. I've read your aura. The core is pink. That means you're a loving and sensual person. You love the arts and are psychically gifted. The outer ring is lemon yellow. That indicates a fear of loss, which doesn't always mean a fear of death or change of lifestyle. A lot of people don't realize that. Your yellow indicates you could be afraid of losing yourself.

"The thing is, most people don't realize that if you're afraid of losing yourself you never will," I continued. "Those who are afraid are too careful. That means they want to be good ... so they'll be good."

"That's kind of simplistic," Paris countered, "but I like the way you think."

I smiled and gestured toward the front door of the conservatory. "I think you'll like this building best. That's why I picked it as our first stop. I know I was surprised when I first got a glimpse inside."

"Then I'm looking forward to it. I ... ." She frowned when her phone dinged in her pocket. "I'm so sorry. I told Heath not to bother me today. He's got Alvis. He's heading to the west side of the state to finish up our business there later in the day. He wouldn't call unless it was an emergency."

"Then you should definitely take it." I shuffled to the side as she answered the video call.

"Hello?"

Instead of a man, the face of a young girl filled the screen. She had long black hair, olive skin, and she looked to be in the middle of a freakout. "Aunt Paris? I want to come live with you. I know what you said last time I told you that, but I really mean it this time."

Paris's expression was hard to read, but she looked frustrated. "Sami ... I can't believe you called me today. I'm at my new job. I can't deal with your drama when I'm supposed to be professional."

The girl — she looked like a Sami — jutted out her lower lip. "Dad says I'm grounded for life because I met a boy at the library last night and didn't tell him it was a study date instead of a study group."

Paris heaved out a sigh and shot me an apologetic look. "Were you supposed to meet a boy?"

"No. I told him I was meeting Janet. She's the new girl at school. I didn't want him to beat his chest and howl at the moon like Mom says he will when I finally start dating. It was innocent."

I stirred. Howl at the moon? That was an interesting turn of a phrase. I couldn't read the girl's aura through the small phone screen, but there was something interesting about her. I couldn't quite put my finger on what.

"Sami, we've had this discussion before." Paris feigned patience. "I'm not your parent."

"You should be. You're so much more fun than Mom and Dad."

"I am," Paris agreed. "I want you to make sure to tell your mother that as many times as you can. It's always fun when she yells at me over video conference. Alvis claps because he thinks she's a marvelous performer."

Sami rolled her eyes. "I'm being serious. My life is over."

"Sami, you're almost fourteen. You always think your life is over. The thing is, it never is. There's no reason to get worked up over this because you're not even going to remember it in a few years. This boy, whoever he is, will barely be a blip in your memory."

"No, I think he's the one."

I had to bite the inside of my cheek to keep from laughing at the girl's tone. I remembered what it was like to be that age. Everything seemed important. She couldn't help being dramatic. It was her age.

"Well, I can't wait to hear more about him." Paris adopted a pragmatic tone. "You'll be down here in a few weeks. Your parents are bringing you to the city for your birthday. They told me they're making a full week of it. You can tell me about this boy then. I really do have to get back to work."

"But ... I need you to tell Dad he's being unreasonable. He grounded me. He said I can walk Trouble and that's it."

"Well, he's your father. Believe it or not, he loves you. You have to listen to what he says."

To my surprise, another voice took over the call.

"Ha!" A handsome man appeared on the screen and grabbed the

phone from Sami's hand. "I knew you would lead me to your phone. You're grounded from that, too."

Sami's screech reminded me of a conversation or two I'd had with my grandfather when I was the same age. I was fairly certain every girl in her early teens has the same conversation.

"Hello, Aric," Paris drawled, clearly amused. "How is life?"

"Paris." Aric seemed more intent on his daughter than on the woman on the other end of the call. "I knew she would call you the second I grounded her. She was trying to hide her phone, but I outsmarted her. Ha!"

"You can't take that phone away from me," Sami bellowed. "I'll die without it."

Aric wrinkled his nose. "Stop saying that. Hold up a second." He lifted a finger for Sami's benefit and then focused on Paris. "I'm sorry she bothered you on your first day of work. You know how she gets. Zoe is meeting with her editor this weekend and Sami is out of control. We're still set to visit next month. Even if she's grounded, we won't cancel our trip. Zoe won't allow it."

Paris's smile was soft. "I'm looking forward to seeing you guys. I really do have to go, though. This is unprofessional."

"Go ahead and namedrop my father if you think that will get you out of trouble. Tell your boss you were talking to a state senator. That always goes over well."

Paris slid me a horrified look. "I don't think that will work. I really have to go. I'll see you in a few weeks." She disconnected the call before Aric could comment further. "I'm so sorry. I promise that won't happen again. She's a teenager and she acts before she thinks."

I waved off the apology. "I know a few adults who do that." The fact that I was one of them was only a mild irritant. "You don't have to apologize. I didn't know you had a niece. I thought your file said you were an only child."

"I am. That's my goddaughter. Her mother is my best friend."

"Ah. That's why you're the bohemian aunt in her eyes. You're exotic."

"She's just at that age." Paris shook her head and shoved the phone in her pocket. "Now, show me the conservatory. I've read a few things, but I've always wanted to see it."

"Right this way." I had a few questions about Sami — mainly I wanted to know exactly what sort of paranormal she was because the energy crackling off her had been impressive for a video chat — but all frivolous thoughts disappeared when we moved toward the massive plant emporium.

Something was off.

"I ... huh." I moved my eyes from right to left, looking for ... something. Then I saw it. There, in the bushes to the east side of the building, a body jutted from beneath the green foliage. It was a man. I could see that from a distance, but the way the body was angled told me he wasn't doing anything constructive ... or sleeping off a bender. He was dead.

"Ugh." I slapped my hand to my forehead. "Not again!"

If Paris was bothered by the body, she didn't show it. "Who do you call in situations like this?"

That was a very good question.

Seven

It was indeed a dead body. Even the slim hope I had it was someone who'd lost his way, perhaps had too much to drink and passed out before managing to stumble, fell by the wayside when I touched the body. He was cold and stiff ... and long gone.

I contacted Cormack. I probably should've called the police, but I was nervous enough to go with my gut. He arrived thirty minutes later, Lily strapped into a carrier on his chest, and he looked grave.

"It's not the same as before, is it?" Obviously he was as worried as I was at first glance.

I shook my head. "It's not even remotely the same."

"Well, that's something at least." Cormack knelt by the body, using one hand to shield Lily's face. I found the effort sweet, especially because there was no way Lily would even understand what she was seeing. Still, he was a marvelous grandfather. "He's been here at least twenty-four hours."

"He has."

"We need to call Griffin."

I wasn't surprised by the declaration. "I figured."

"And I appreciate it. Someone could be missing this guy. I haven't heard any missing persons reports, but you never know. Griffin will have the most recent information."

"He didn't show up on your list, did he?"

Cormack arched an eyebrow and I could tell he hadn't even considered that. "No."

"That's strange, right?" Paris was surprisingly calm given the circumstances. She'd obviously dealt with much worse. She was on her knees and staring at the body. "All deaths are supposed to be recorded into the system. That's what I read."

"In theory, that's true," he confirmed. "It's not always true in practice. Sometimes things happen. We can't control everything."

"No. I would guess not." Paris dusted off her hands and locked gazes with me. "I think his neck is broken."

"What makes you say that?" I was genuinely curious.

"His head has turned completely around."

"Like in *The Exorcist*?"

She smirked. "You really do remind me of someone else I know."

I had no idea if that was a good or bad thing, but right now, it didn't matter. "Call Griffin," I prodded Cormack. "We need to figure this out. If something bad is about to happen ... ." I left the sentence hanging. He recognized the possibilities as easily as me.

"I'm calling him right now." He glanced ruefully at Lily. "I don't think Daddy is going to be happy to find you at a crime scene."

"WHAT DO YOU HAVE?"

Griffin saw me before Cormack when he parked in the conservatory lot. He was all business.

"We have a dead body," Cormack replied, drawing his son-in-law's attention.

Griffin frowned the second he saw Lily. "What is my baby doing at a crime scene?"

"Having a good time," I volunteered. "She's fine. Cormack made sure she didn't see the body."

"I don't care about that." Griffin tilted his head to stare at his daughter. She was wide awake. "Crime scenes were supposed to be our thing. I can't compete with the Grimlocks when it comes to magic, but I'll be the cool dad who shows her dead bodies. That was supposed to be my gift to her."

Cormack snorted. "I'm sorry. If it's any consolation, I don't plan to ever repeat this outing."

"That's a relief." Griffin ran his hand over Lily's dark head and pressed a kiss to it before focusing on the body. "He doesn't look homeless."

"You're the third person to mention that," Paris noted. "Do you have a regular problem with homeless individuals showing up out here and dying?"

Griffin didn't immediately respond. Instead he merely eyed her for a beat. That's when I realized she was a new face to him.

"This is my new assistant," I offered hurriedly. "Paris Princeton. She's well aware of the paranormal situation here. You can trust her."

Griffin nodded, apparently comfortable with the explanation. "It doesn't happen a lot, but it does happen. The island is largely isolated in the winter because of the weather. There aren't many people who visit. In the summer, things are different.

"The beach is a draw," he continued. "There's a golf range, the aquarium, the conservatory ... you know the drill. There are fireworks for the Fourth of July. This is a target-rich environment for an individual hoping to find some easy money. There's a lot of drinking that happens out here during the summer, too. Things sometimes get out of hand."

"That's sad." Paris's face reflected genuine regret. "I knew there were a lot of homeless people in the area, but for some reason I assumed they stuck close to the city."

"They do. The area around the casinos is especially thick. This area is popular in the summer. It is what it is."

"It's just sad." Paris blew out a sigh and then tilted her head. "What's with his clothes?"

The abrupt conversational shift threw me. "Nothing. They actually look pretty clean considering he was out here all night."

"Not that. They're dated. I mean ... these are polyester." She gestured toward his pants. "Like, really old polyester. And look at his shoes. I haven't seen rubber soles on loafers like that since ... well ... ever. I think I might've seen them in books at some point. I bet my grandfather wore shoes kind of like this. My mother always makes fun of his shoes when she tells stories."

I straightened and leaned forward, taking an extra few minutes to actually study his ensemble. "They are dated."

Paris nodded. "Incredibly dated."

Cormack moved closer for a look. "You're right," he said. "These clothes are old. They're not something you can pick up in stores these days. I don't even think you could get them in second-hand shops. Maybe in vintage shops, but even then I would think they were just for looks."

"Why is that important?" Griffin asked.

"Because yesterday we had five people return from the dead and they were all wearing dated clothes," I volunteered.

"They were all men," Paris added. "He kind of looks like he fits in with that group."

Realization dawned on Griffin's handsome features. "You think he's part of the group that disappeared. Why would he be out here? I thought they all appeared in the gate room."

"They did." Cormack was thoughtful. "We need to confirm that he's one of the missing men. Izzy, take a photo of his face and text it to Oliver. He's our best chance at getting answers without having to wait too long."

I nodded and lowered myself to the ground, my phone already out. I grimaced as I focused on the man's face. Thankfully his eyes were closed, so I didn't have to see him staring back at me. My hands were steady as I texted the photo to Oliver.

"It shouldn't take him long," I offered. "He was focused on the gate data from yesterday when I left, but he's a vampire. He can multi-task."

"I thought that meant he drank blood," Griffin argued, smiling at his daughter and doing a little dance that seemed out of place.

"What are you doing?" Paris asked, confused.

I knew what he was doing. "They're all in a competition to see who can make her smile first," I explained. "I'm convinced that she's not going to smile at all because she has her mother's personality."

Griffin scowled at me. "I'll have you know that my wife smiles all the time. She's not always dour. You haven't spent time with her when she's been at her best."

"That's true," Cormack agreed. "Aisling doesn't often withhold her smiles. She is a pouter, but she's always open for a good time. As a child, she smiled at me every single day ... even when she was upset. Lily is going to be the same way. Of course, Aisling smiled at me first, and I think Lily is going to be the same way there, too."

Griffin rolled his eyes. "Aisling smiled at her father. Lily is going to smile at her father." He increased his pace, sighing when the baby merely stared at him. "Of course, she really could be channeling her mother and enjoy torturing me."

Cormack snorted. "I wouldn't be surprised if she tortures all of us. Her mother will teach her that particular lesson well."

"Yeah." Griffin grinned at the baby. "Part of me can't wait until she starts talking and expressing her opinion. The other part realizes that she's going to be an unholy handful when that happens. What was Aisling's first word?"

Cormack pursed his lips, his expression telling me he was going back in time. "Well, let me see. Redmond's first word was 'no.' Braden's was 'mama.'"

My heart rolled at the information. Braden, out of all his siblings, struggled the most with the death of his mother. When she came back, only a shell of the person he remembered, he fought his siblings over her motivations ... and lost. He didn't often talk about his mother now that she'd died a second time. He especially didn't talk about the thing that came back in her form. When he was in a good mood, though, he would tell me stories about what she'd been like when they were children. He always lit up when relating those tales.

"Cillian's first word was 'story,'" Cormack continued, his lips quirking. "He loved books even then. We read to them every night, and that was his favorite time of day. He would demand story after story. Aidan's first word was 'no.' He was yelling at Aisling because she kept trying to take his favorite toy. And Aisling's first word was 'mine.' She uttered it the same day she tried to take the truck from him."

Griffin's face split into a wide grin. "I think that's still her favorite word."

"I think you're right."

"Lily's first word is going to be 'Daddy.'" He brushed his hand over the baby's hair. Her eyes were getting heavy. "We've already agreed on that, haven't we?"

Slowly, the baby's eyelids drifted shut.

"I don't think she agrees," Cormack countered. "It's going to be 'Grampy.'" He made a face once the word escaped. "Wait ... I don't like that. It makes me sound old."

Griffin chuckled. "Well, there's no way Grandpa is going to be her first word. It's too difficult."

"You don't know. She's gifted. It could be her first word."

"I'm guessing 'mine' is going to be her favorite word, too," I offered, exhaling in relief when my phone dinged. "It's Oliver. I read the text twice before sharing. "He recognizes him. He says his name is Ray Smith. He was one of the people who disappeared that day."

"Anything else?" Cormack asked.

I shook my head. "No." It was hard to read tone in a text, but I could practically see Oliver's stricken expression in my mind. "I think he's upset."

"Do you blame him?" Cormack pressed the heel of his hand against his forehead. "What are we going to do here?"

Griffin remained focused on the body. "His neck is broken. That doesn't necessarily mean he was murdered, but it doesn't point to a natural death either. We need an autopsy."

"We could call in a reaper expert," Cormack offered. "That might be the smartest way to handle this."

"It might," Griffin agreed. "But you called me on my official cell phone. There's a record — and I already mentioned to one of the guys in the bullpen that there was a body out here. I didn't think about it at the time. I assumed we were dealing with something else. I can't put that genie back in the bottle."

"So ... you're handling this officially?" Cormack looked horrified at the thought. "Do you know what that means?"

"It means the same thing it did yesterday." Griffin's tone was clipped. "You can't hide the fact that those men are back. You might be able to delay the world finding out, but it's only a matter of time until the truth leaks to the media. Those men deserve to go back to their families, even if the families they find aren't the same. I'm not going to just sit back and let you guys hide them away."

Cormack balked. "Did I say that's what was going to happen?"

"No, but you're not in charge. Those above you might try to make this go away, and you know it. I'm not going to play that game with you. I can't."

Cormack opened his mouth to protest and instead turned his attention to me. "What do you think?"

I hated being put on the spot. "I don't know what to think," I admitted after a beat. "I agree with Griffin that hiding this isn't an option. We might not have all the answers yet, but the people who lost these men ... well ... they deserve answers. This man didn't make it all the way back. He's still here and that can't be erased."

Cormack grumbled. "I didn't say I was going to hide things or try to erase them. I wish you would stop assuming things like that."

I held my hands up in capitulation. "I wasn't insinuating anything."

"You were, but we'll ignore that for now." Cormack planted his hands on his hips. It was hard to look manly and in charge with a baby strapped to his chest — especially as she wore a lavender onesie — but he somehow managed to pull it off. "Call in your team, Griffin. You're right. We need everyone working for answers. The only thing I ask is that you don't volunteer what happened here yesterday just yet. Explaining that ... ."

Griffin nodded without hesitation. "You don't have to worry about that. We're going to have another problem, though. You realize that as soon as word leaks that a man who disappeared sixty years ago has turned up dead — and he looks exactly as he did all those years ago — every conspiracy theorist in the world is going to descend on this island."

"I hadn't thought of that, but you're right."

"They won't immediately jump to conclusions about a death gate," Paris pointed out. "I mean ... that's not even going to be in the top ten theories. You're going to be dealing with aliens first. The public is hungry for stuff like that. They'll believe that somehow Ray Smith was scooped up sixty years ago, transported to outer space for experiments, and then returned to Earth."

Cormack looked legitimately horrified at the prospect. "Oh, geez."

"That's better for us," I countered. "Having people erroneously believe aliens are to blame than correctly assume reapers are doing funky stuff on Belle Isle relating to life and death is a good thing."

"I guess." Cormack stroked his cheek. "This is going to be a mess."

"It is," Griffin agreed. "There's no getting around that. I won't hide this."

"Would you if it kept Aisling safe?"

The question clearly grated the dedicated police detective. He planted his hands on his hips and glared. "Don't do that. Aisling isn't in danger here. I will do whatever it takes to keep my family safe. You know that. That's not what we're dealing with. I'm not going to institute a cover-up because it's more convenient."

Cormack's eyes momentarily flashed with annoyance and then he scuffed his shoe against the grass. "Fine. I guess that's fair. It's not as if you haven't covered up things for us in the past."

"And I did that to protect Aisling," Griffin confirmed. "I'll always protect her. I don't like that you're insinuating otherwise ... while wearing my child as a vest."

"I know you're loyal," Cormack offered. "I just ... this is going to be a huge mess. I don't even want to consider how easily this could fall apart for us."

"That's not my concern." Griffin straightened his shoulders. "This man died about twenty-four hours ago. He very well could've been murdered. That's my concern. The rest is your problem."

"Fine." Cormack threw his hands into the air, frustration wafting off him in waves. "I'll handle the ramifications. That's my job."

"Good for you." Griffin clapped his shoulder and then smiled fondly at his sleeping baby. "Take care of my daughter, too. This will probably be a late day if it goes as I expect. I can't volunteer that I know this guy disappeared sixty years ago. I still expect the information to be known by the end of the business day, tomorrow at the latest."

"I'll keep my granddaughter safe. You don't have to worry about that." Something akin to mischief glinted in Cormack's eyes. "I think she's definitely going to smile at me first now. She'll be angry at you for giving Grandpa a headache. I know my girl."

"Ugh. This family." Griffin retrieved his phone. "I'm calling this in. Prepare yourselves. There are going to be questions."

I slid my eyes to Paris. "If you don't want to deal with the police you can head back to the gate room. It's okay."

"Oh, police officers don't scare me." Her lips curved. "I've dealt with worse things in life. Trust me."

I had no doubt that was true.

Eight

"We have another problem."

Paris was somber when she approached me an hour later. Uniformed police officers and representatives from the medical examiner's office had arrived right on schedule and I'd spent the better part of the last hour answering questions with the sort of breathless nervous energy I hated. I figured it was better to put on a show than act calm and collected. That wasn't what was expected, and I didn't want to garner suspicion.

"What other problem do we have?" I asked, glancing around at the endless activity. "I'm not sure we can handle another problem."

"Well, maybe it's not another problem," she conceded, "but it is an additional wrinkle for this problem."

"Lay it on me."

"Fourteen men went missing through that gate. Five came back, ending up in the exact spot from which they disappeared. One has now turned up about a mile from that location. That leaves eight people unaccounted for. What if they were returned too but somehow missed their mark?"

"Oh, holy ... !" My eyes felt like saucers as I scanned the horizon.

Most of the police officers had congregated in this small area. That didn't mean they would stay here.

"I think we should search the rest of the island," she supplied. "And I think we should do it without an audience."

It made sense. "Yeah. I need to tell Cormack first so he knows where to find us if there's trouble."

"I'll wait for you by the golf cart."

PARIS WAS ON VIDEO CHAT AGAIN when I rejoined her.

"Sami, there's nothing I can do about your father," Paris explained pragmatically. "I'm not his boss. In fact, I'm not your boss either. You've got to learn to suck it up."

"But he's being an idiot," Sami whined. "He took my computer. He says he doesn't trust me not to talk to boys on it. He says that boys are sick and demented and that I'm not allowed to date until I'm thirty."

It took everything I had not to laugh. The teenager obviously couldn't see me, but she wasn't deaf. If she knew someone else was listening she would melt down even further ... which couldn't possibly be a pretty sight.

"Sami, he's been saying that since you were five and you announced you were going to marry that guy from that movie."

Sami sniffled. "Robert Pattinson. He was Edward in *Twilight*. I'm still going to marry him."

I made a face and spoke before I thought better of it. "Isn't *Twilight* the one where the vampires sparkle? All the girls were reading that when I was a teenager and I couldn't stop laughing. I mean ... vampires don't sparkle."

Sami jerked her head. "Who is that?"

"That's my boss," Paris replied. "I told you I was working."

"Well, I don't like her." Sami turned prim, which only served to make her funnier. "We don't know that vampires can't sparkle. I bet people would say that vampires can't be tan and walk in the sun either, but we both know that's not true."

"Very good point." Paris looked tired, but she didn't lose her temper with her goddaughter. "You'll have to deal with your father on your own while your mother is out of town. Either that or wait until she comes back and have a serious conversation with her."

Sami's expression was withering. "My mother doesn't have serious and adult conversations. Besides, she's going to side with him. She always sides with him. Most of the kids in my classroom can play divide-and-conquer games with their parents. I can't do that because you can't divide my parents."

"That's very true." Paris looked amused rather than sympathetic. "You're lucky, Sami. A lot of kids don't have parents who are as involved as yours. They love you."

"They're stupid." Sami's expression was dark. "When Mom gets home she and Dad will disappear into the bedroom and say they're reading. They won't be reading. They'll be doing ... other stuff. She won't have time to listen to me."

"That is not true." Now Paris's expression took on an edge. "They always have time for you."

"They always have time for each other," Sami pouted.

"They do always have time for each other. Believe it or not, you'll be grateful for that in a few years."

"But not now. Now they're embarrassing."

"I think they work hard to be that embarrassing ... and every time you melt down, it rewards them for their efforts. If you would stop reacting, they would stop doing it."

Sami's eyebrows drew together. "Do you think that's true?"

"I do."

"But then ... that means they only do it to annoy me."

Paris laughed. "I believe that you've just figured out one of the biggest secrets of your parents' marriage."

"Oh, well ... I'll make them pay for this." Sami was irate as she stood. In the background, a German shepherd hopped to its paws, as if readying for action. "They'll be crying and begging by the time I'm done with them."

"I'm sure they will. Good luck."

I waited until Paris disconnected from the call. "Do you think you should've told her that?" I asked as I climbed behind the wheel of the golf cart. "Now she'll have a leg up on them."

"Oh, she'll never get a leg up on them. Her mother is too smart for that and is two steps ahead of Sami. It's simply one of the family games they play."

"They sound interesting."

"They have their moments," Paris agreed. "I really am sorry that she keeps calling. With her mother out of town, she seems to have a lot of free time on her hands. Aric isn't as equipped to deal with Sami's outbursts as Zoe is."

"And Zoe is your friend."

"She's my best friend."

"Well, it's nice that you take the time to deal with her daughter when she's out of town. That's the sort of friends I want to have."

"Don't you have them now?"

It was an interesting question. "I guess I do, but I just moved to this area. My friendships are still works in progress."

"What about the Grimlock girl? I mean ... there's only one of them, right? That's basically what I figured out while listening to Griffin and Cormack snipe at each other. Cormack referred to Aisling as his only daughter and said Griffin was lucky he still had hands given what happened at the wedding."

I could picture the argument — I'd witnessed it several times — so all I could do was laugh. "Yes, well ... they don't mean anything by it. That's simply the way they communicate. If it came down to it, they would die for each other ... and everyone in that family would die for the baby."

"Oh, I already figured that out. That baby is the center of their world. That's how Sami was for us when she was born. She was the first baby in our group. She was special. She was also spoiled — still is."

"I think there's every possibility that Lily will be the most spoiled child to ever live. As for Aisling, I like her a great deal. We simply don't have the benefit of spending decades together like you have with your friend."

"It doesn't take decades. Sometimes friendships are forged hard and fast. I'll bet you'll find it works that way for you."

"Maybe for us, too."

"Maybe."

"We should start looking for bodies now," I offered. "Maybe that can be our first bonding exercise."

"Sounds like a plan."

WE FOUND NOTHING. It was both a relief and a worry.

"We obviously couldn't check every single nook and cranny on the island because there're simply too many places bodies could end up," I explained to Cormack. Lily was wide awake and playing with the button on his shirt. "We should consider that bodies might've landed in the water, too."

Cormack absently nodded. "I didn't think about the possibility that other bodies might've missed landing in the correct location until you mentioned it. It makes sense."

"Brett and I can search the island after dark," Oliver volunteered. "We'll be able to scent a dead body if there are any. As for the water ... I suggest we enlist the merrow. They hate each other and won't go out as a team, but they can split the territory. If the bodies are floating in the river, they'll find them relatively quickly."

"Merrow?" Paris leaned forward, her interest piqued. "You have merfolk here?"

"We do. I'll introduce you later. They're ... unique."

"That's putting it mildly," Oliver agreed. "We can search the island and surrounding waters in a few hours. That makes more sense than allowing you to blindly wander around."

I shot him a dirty look. "Thanks for your support."

"It's a fact, not an insult." Oliver turned his attention to Cormack. "I see the police are shutting down the bridge. That's a wise idea."

"Griffin was right about them figuring out the identity of our dead guy relatively quickly," Cormack replied. "Once that news spread they went into damage control mode. They don't want looky-loos on the island screwing up their crime scene."

"How are we going to get off the island?" Paris asked. "I have a toddler waiting for me and he's not going to understand police protocol."

"You'll be allowed to drive your vehicle off the island tonight.

There's a parking lot directly on the other side of the bridge. When you return tomorrow, you will park there and be transported over on a boat. This isn't the first time we've had to shut down the island."

Paris didn't look thrilled with the idea, but she didn't put up an ounce of argument. "I can see why keeping the island empty is important."

"Izzy, it's up to you if you want to spend the night on the island or at my house," Cormack supplied. "You need to make the decision quickly."

I'd purchased a vehicle several weeks before — it wasn't new but it was reliable — and I understood what he was saying. If didn't leave tonight, I would essentially be trapped. "I'll drive to the other side tonight. I want to stop by the reaper headquarters anyway."

"Why?"

"I want to see if I can find any information on the original incident in their library. I know it's a long shot, but information is power and we need it."

"That's not a bad idea. I'll be heading in that direction, too. If I hear anything of importance, I'll fill you in. For now, there's very little else we can do here. If Oliver and the others find bodies, that changes. Right now, we still have five survivors who don't seem to have answers and one dead guy who will never be able to answer questions."

"That's a very concise explanation of where we're at," Paris noted.

"Do you disagree?"

"No. We're stuck without more information. We'll have to work together to get it."

I'D BEEN TO THE LIBRARY AT REAPER HEADQUAR-TERS several times. There was no rule keeping me out. I still felt like an intruder when I slipped through the door.

The library was like visiting another world. A really quiet one with comfortable chairs, a warm fireplace and a gargoyle running the show. Yup, a gargoyle. His name was Bub. Word had it he'd been severely injured in a fight with the Grimlocks – he was an ally, not a foe – almost a year ago. I had no idea what a gargoyle was supposed to look like, but if Bub was any indication, they were scarred and slow-moving.

"Hello, Izzy." Bub moved between the aisles, his tail thrashing. I wasn't even sure it was a tail at first. Heck, I still wasn't sure. It could've been something else. If it was, I felt sorry for the female gargoyles. Sometimes bigger absolutely isn't better.

"Hello, Bub." I greeted him with a bright smile. He wasn't so bad. In fact, I kind of liked him. He was like a pet who talked … and you didn't have to walk him because he walked himself. "How is life?"

"I can't complain."

But he would. He always did.

"Life pretty much sucks, though," he continued. "All the reapers are in a tizzy because those people came back through the gate. I hear you were there. Was it neat? Was there a bright light? Did God send them back because they were annoying or something?"

The gargoyle was amusing, I had to give him that. "I didn't see what happened. The noise from the gate knocked me out."

"It knocked you out?" He didn't have eyebrows, but he arched some skin and it was fairly disconcerting. "That had to be some pretty powerful noise."

"It was."

"Did you see anything while you were knocked out?"

"Why? What are people saying?"

"That wasn't a denial."

"I just want to know what people are saying."

Bub chuckled. "All manner of things. You're a curiosity. The fact that you're dating the surly Grimlock is as of much interest as your magic. As for what they're saying about this, your name hasn't come up … other than to say you were there, that is."

Well, that was something at least. "Why did you ask if I saw something? I just told you I was out."

"I see more than most. I know that you're psychic. I'm guessing you saw something, because you're here. The library is a place for research. You're researching something."

"Maybe I want to look up the mating habits of gargoyles. Have you ever thought of that?"

He chuckled, the sound raspy. "I can tell you all you'd ever want to know about that topic if you're really that interested."

"I think I'll pass."

"So, tell me what you saw."

I told him. There was no reason not to. When I was finished, his expression was hard to read.

"Well, it sounds to me as if something came for them."

I was hoping for more help than that. "You don't know what's on the other side of the gate either?"

"No. Gargoyles don't go there."

"Why not? You obviously have souls."

"All creatures have their own form of afterlife."

"Even dogs and cats? What about rats?"

"All creatures." He smirked and shook his head. "I don't know much about this gate. Humans are the only creatures I know who are completely obsessed with death. The rest of us merely accept it as a fact and move on. Still, I've read enough about it to be intrigued.."

"What about when the men went missing? Were you around then?"

"Yes, but I wasn't working with the reapers. I was an independent contractor at that time. Up until recently, I didn't have much of an affiliation with anyone ... including my own kind."

"Your injury forced you to work for the reapers," I noted. "You don't want to be here, do you?"

"It's as good a place as any. I don't know where I want to be right now."

"You helped the Grimlocks." I'd heard the stories. I knew how much he gave of himself to save Aisling. "You didn't have to. You could've ignored what was right and let them die."

"What does that have to do with anything?"

"It's just an observation. I don't think you were nearly as uninterested in the travails of the reapers as you pretend. Even if you were, you had to have heard rumors."

"I heard a few things," he conceded. "Some said it was a cover-up. Others said it was an experiment gone awry. Still others said it was an accident. Most believed those men were long gone and never coming back. That's the one thing I can say with any degree of certainty. No one expected to ever see them again."

"So that means all the stories were wrong. Something else happened to those men. Something that absolutely no one considered."

"That would be my best guess."

Mine, too. I let loose a sigh. "Are there reaper history records? I'm talking books that keep track of what was going on with the reapers at any given point in time."

"You want to know what the reapers were thinking when it went down."

"Pretty much."

"I think I can help you, but I guarantee there won't be legitimate answers in the journals left behind. They're not that stupid."

"I still want to see what I can find."

"Then follow me. I know exactly where to look."

Nine

Cormack joined me in the library two hours later. I was surprised to find he still had Lily, although he'd shifted her from his chest to a handheld carrier. She was sleeping when he strolled into the library, but Bub, who had been lounging in front of the fire while I researched the incident, was suddenly on his feet. Initially I thought it was because he wanted to look good in front of the boss. I figured out I was wrong relatively quickly.

"The littlest Grimlock's baby is here." He announced it in such a way that I had to smile. He wasn't exactly awed, but he was clearly curious.

"Lily," I offered. "Her name is Lily."

"Not after the bad Lily, I'm sure."

"No, after the *real* Lily," Cormack volunteered. He placed the carrier on the floor and didn't complain when Bub scurried over to look at the baby. He didn't leave Lily unprotected, instead sitting in a chair directly next to her, but he also didn't reprimand Bub for invading the baby's personal space.

"She looks like Aisling," Bub announced after a moment.

"She does," Cormack agreed.

"She looks like all of you," I countered as I flipped through another report. "I know you get sick of hearing this, but you all look as if you came out of the same test tube." My eyes landed on Cormack. "I guess you're that test tube."

He chuckled. "Yes. They all do resemble me. That wasn't always good when they were in trouble as children ... and teenagers ... and, for that matter, as adults."

My lips quirked at the whimsical look on his face. As much as he complained about his children — and it was a regular occurrence — I knew he wouldn't trade even one of them.

"Was it hard for your wife?" I asked. "I mean ... the fact that they all looked like you. I'll bet she would've liked at least one of them to look like her, though that might've been difficult when she died because it would've meant you didn't want to look at your own children."

The words were out of my mouth before I realized how insulting and invasive they sounded. When I risked a glance in Cormack's direction I found Bub smirking and Cormack watching me with contemplative eyes.

"I didn't mean to say that out loud," I offered. "That was really rude. I mean ... really rude. I wasn't thinking."

The smile he offered was small but heartfelt. "You don't have to temper your words with me, Izzy. I don't want you to be afraid to say what's on your mind. That's not how we operate in my family."

It was nice to hear, but I still felt like an idiot. "I don't always think before I speak."

"None of my children do either. Well, Cillian does ... and occasionally Aidan. The other three are mouthy idiots."

"But you love them."

"I do. I'm quite fond of you, too. You didn't hurt my feelings, so don't worry about it."

That was a relief, but I still couldn't shake the unease washing over me. "What did the big boss say?"

For the first time since entering the library, Cormack's expression darkened. "He said that he had no knowledge of what happened to those men."

"Do you believe him?"

"I have no reason not to. We've known each other for a long time. As far as I know, he's never lied to me. Er, well, at least about something big. We've both told little white lies to get out of work occasionally, but that's to be expected."

It wasn't the little lies that concerned me. "I'm bothered by a few things," I admitted. I opted to be upfront with my concerns. "There are notations in the files back then, but I don't think there's a complete record of what happened. That seems to indicate they're hiding something."

Cormack shifted on his chair. "Be more specific."

"Okay, for starters, there were four council members who covered the event. They all had journals at the time. Those journals are in this library ... and all the pages in each journal that would've dealt with the disappearances have been removed."

He furrowed his brow. "What?"

"Here." I grabbed one of the leather-bound journals in question and turned it so he could see for himself. "The entire section on the disappearances is gone, completely ripped out."

Cormack's mouth dropped open as Bub made cooing sounds to entertain Lily, who was suddenly awake. If the baby was bothered by what she saw, she didn't show it. She merely watched the gargoyle cavort in front of her with unreadable eyes.

"And you say all the journals are like this?" Cormack asked when he'd finished checking the book for himself.

"As far as I can tell. Obviously it's possible there were other people involved in the investigation and they have journals, but I haven't made it that far yet."

"Right." Cormack tapped his chin and turned his eyes to Bub. "Has anyone been in here to read the reaper journals?"

"Not while I've been here," Bub replied, making a comical face for the baby's benefit. "Why won't she smile?"

"Because she's going to smile at me first," Cormack replied.

"She's not smiling at anyone yet and it's driving them crazy," I offered. "If you make her smile they'll deny it happened. You've been forewarned."

"He won't make her smile." Cormack was firm. "She's my granddaughter. She loves me best."

"I think it would be best if she smiled at Aisling first," I said, going back to my books. "That would make her feel less unsure about how Lily feels about her."

Cormack stiffened and I could feel his eyes burning holes into my skin as I stumbled. Well, crap. I couldn't believe I said that out loud. Today was clearly not my day. "I mean ... ."

Cormack extended a quelling finger. "Are you saying Aisling doesn't believe Lily loves her?"

"I'm saying that Aisling struggles with the fact that her mother came back from the dead with the express purpose of killing her, stealing her body and taking over her life. That skewed her opinion on mother-daughter trust. You have to know that."

"I knew that Braden was still having a few issues, though you've done wonders for him." He turned thoughtful. "Maybe I should insist on family counseling."

For another family, I would've thought that was a marvelous idea. For the Grimlocks? Yeah, not so much. "Do you have a therapist you absolutely hate? If so, go for it. You can drive her into the nuthouse. If not, I wouldn't recommend it. Your family is difficult under normal circumstances. Adding a therapist to the mix will only make things worse."

Cormack pursed his lips and then sighed. "I guess you're right. I don't know what to do about this. I didn't realize Aisling was still feeling insecure about the baby."

"Why do you have to do anything about it? She'll get over it eventually."

"I'm her father. It's my job to fix things."

That was a rather simplistic approach. "Perhaps when she was younger. She's an adult now."

"And she's still my baby. Just because she has a baby, that doesn't change."

Lily gurgled, as if agreeing.

"Isn't that right?" Cormack beamed at the baby. "I get to spoil my children as much as I want and no one can say a thing about it."

I rolled my eyes and shifted when I realized someone else was entering the library. I let out a breath when I realized it was Cillian.

"You're late," Cormack announced when he caught sight of his son. "I texted you twenty minutes ago."

"And I was conducting research." Cillian offered me a brief smile before focusing on his niece. "Hello, beautiful. Did you miss Uncle Cillian?"

The baby's expression didn't change, even when he made a funny face for her.

"You're going to smile at me first even if my face freezes like this," Cillian ordered, causing me to grin. He was the most laid back Grimlock. That didn't mean he wasn't keen to win. "I'm taking her back to Grimlock Manor, right?"

Cormack nodded as Cillian snagged the baby carrier. "Aisling should be on her way back to the manor. She said she's dropping off her souls and then taking Lily home, but … try to talk her into staying."

Cillian furrowed his brow. "Why? Is something wrong?"

"No. I just want to spend some time with her, make sure she's rested."

He had ulterior motives he didn't want to share. I could've given Cillian a heads-up, but I didn't bother. The Grimlocks often stumbled when working out their personal issues, but they always got back up. This time would be no different.

"I'll tell her, but I'm not going to make her stay. She bites when she feels weighed down by family pressure."

"Just … ask her to stay." Cormack slid his gaze to me, something unsaid lurking in the depths of his eyes. "As for Izzy and me, we're going to visit the returnees again."

That was news to me. "We are?"

He nodded. "I received clearance right before I texted Cillian. I don't want her in that room in case … well, just in case."

I understood what he wasn't saying. We still had no idea why the men had returned. They could be dangerous, especially now that they were being treated as lab animals and found themselves locked in a secure hospital ward.

"When are they going to be allowed to contact their families?"

"I don't know. I don't believe Renley can put them off much longer, but he seems determined to try. That's a mistake if you ask me. He's simply delaying the inevitable."

"What new information do you expect to get from them? I think they've told us everything they know ... or at least everything they seem to know. They might have more locked in their brains, but it's probably traumatic so they've shut it out."

"Or they were simply not meant to remember what happened to them," Cillian added. He was still making faces for his niece's benefit. The baby looked less than impressed.

"Or something else entirely is going on," Cormack countered. "It's possible they know more than they're saying and they're simply very good when it comes to acting."

I couldn't rule that out. "Maybe. That doesn't explain what you expect to learn from them. Whether by choice or happenstance, I don't think they're going to talk about anything important."

"I want to ask them about Ray Smith."

I was taken aback, although in hindsight I should've seen it coming. "You're not going to tell them what happened, are you?"

"I am." He nodded once. "I want to see their reactions. I also want to learn a little something about Mr. Smith. Maybe there was a reason he was separated from the rest of the group."

"There's also a chance his return was blown somehow and he was dropped in the wrong spot," I argued. "Have you gotten a cause of death from Griffin?"

Cormack turned grim. "His neck was broken, probably from a fall. He had internal injuries as well. He didn't die right away. It took an hour or so."

My stomach twisted at the news. "Could he have been saved if we'd found him right away?"

"Probably not, but we'll never truly know."

I dragged a hand through my hair and forced the melancholy to retreat. "I guess it can't hurt to talk to them. Maybe I'll be able to get a better reading off them this time."

"That's what I'm hoping for."

. . .

SECURITY IN THE HOSPITAL ward was much tighter. There were four guards posted outside the doors and two present inside, which made for a tense environment.

"Well, this is quite the homecoming," I muttered.

Cormack slid me a sidelong look. "I was just thinking the same thing. I didn't realize Renley had so many men in here."

"Can you do anything about it?"

"No."

We made our way to the far end of the room, to where all five men sat in chairs and talked in angry tones. Doug was the first to look in our direction as we approached. It wasn't warmth and welcome that I saw on his features.

"Get out," he ordered harshly. "I've already told your overlord that we will not cooperate until we're allowed to contact our families. If you think you can come in here and schmooze us, you've got another think coming."

His aura was a cloudy blue, which meant he was struggling. Trust wasn't high on his list right now. I couldn't exactly blame him for that. "We're not here to schmooze you," I offered. "We have a few questions."

"Oh, really?" Hank cocked an eyebrow. I'd taken the time to memorize each face so I would have no trouble recognizing the individual men — and any others who might pop up — and I offered him a bright smile, which he returned with an icy glare. "Why would we possibly answer any of your questions?"

"Because we want to help you," Cormack replied evenly. "I understand that you're frustrated — no, I really do — but I can't change that for you. I also understand what everyone is worried about, so I'm legitimately torn.

"I think you've been through enough and should be reunited with your families right away," he continued. "The fear is that once your miraculous return has been made public that it will turn into a media sideshow."

"That's already been explained to us," Manuel snapped. "I want to see my family. I don't even know if they're still alive."

"I don't even know that I believe this is the future," Doug admitted, gripping his hands together hard enough that his knuckles whitened. "For all we know, this could be some elaborate hoax. Maybe you dosed us with LSD and are playing a game."

"LSD is a drug from the sixties and seventies that causes hallucinations," Cormack explained to me. "It's not really in vogue now."

I had to swallow my laughter. "Did you just mansplain LSD to me?"

He balked. "I wasn't mansplaining. You're young. You can't know what LSD is."

"I hate to break it to you, but LSD is still a thing today," I told him. "Some people use it recreationally and some use it therapeutically."

"Which means we've been dosed with it," Doug crowed. "I knew it!"

"You haven't been dosed with LSD," Cormack shot back. "This isn't an experiment gone awry. You really were gone sixty years. I know that's difficult to swallow, but it's the truth."

"Maybe we would have less trouble believing it if we were allowed to see it for ourselves," Manuel pressed.

"I agree with that sentiment. I don't think it will be much longer. We're not here about you, though. We're here about Ray Smith."

Carefully, I watched the men for hints of distress ... or even curiosity. All five faces were blank, however, as Cormack broached the subject of their fallen companion.

"What about Ray?" Doug asked finally. He appeared to be the de facto leader of the group, although I wasn't certain if it was by design or something that merely happened upon their return.

"We found his body earlier today," Cormack replied. He clearly believed it was best to yank off the bandage rather than to peel it away slowly. "It was on Belle Isle, about a mile from the gate. It looks as if Ray died about the same time you men returned."

Doug's mouth dropped open. "Are you kidding me?"

"No. We really did find his body."

"But ... what happened to him?" Hank asked, his voice quiet.

"We're not sure," Cormack replied. "The coroner believes his injuries indicate he took a great fall. His neck was broken and he had internal injuries. I was hoping you men might be able to tell me something."

"We already told you that we don't remember anything," Doug exploded, his temper on full display. "We don't know what happened. We don't know where the others are."

"Wait ... ." Manuel held up his hand, his mind clearly busy. "If Ray came back at the same time, does that mean the others are back? Is it possible they landed in different places?"

"Anything is possible," Cormack replied. "We're checking on that. We're not sure what to make of any of this."

"Oh, well, that's comforting," Doug drawled. "I can't tell you what a comfort that is."

"I can't fix that," Cormack said matter-of-factly. "We need to know what you can tell us about Ray. We're trying to figure out the bigger picture, but it isn't easy. We're doing the best we can by you. I promise."

Doug rolled his eyes. "And we're just supposed to believe you?"

"That would be nice."

"Well ... we don't." Doug's edginess was on full display as he gripped his hands into fists and rested them on top of his knees. "We don't believe any of you. We want out of here. We're not answering a single question until you release us. Period."

Cormack opened his mouth, and I was certain he was going to run his usual domineering Grimlock routine. That was a big mistake as far as I was concerned. It would backfire spectacularly if he tried. I sent him an almost imperceptible shake of my head. We had to come up with another solution.

He held my gaze for a long beat and then nodded, his hand automatically moving to my back as he prodded me toward the door.

"I'm sorry life is difficult for you right now, gentlemen. Believe it or not, I am on your side. I'll be back to visit as soon as I can. If we find others of your group ... well ... I'll keep you updated. That's the best I can do."

"That's not nearly enough," Hank groused.

"It's all we can do. We all have rules we live by."

"Just get out." Doug flicked his hand in a disgusted manner. "We're done with you."

And just like that we'd been dismissed.

Ten

We tried for another ten minutes, but the men were adamant. Cormack waited until we were outside the room to ask the obvious question.

"What do you think?"

"I think they're angry."

"That goes without saying."

"I think they have a right to be angry," I added. "Have you considered how you would feel if you were in their position? I mean ... is there anything that would stop you from getting to your children if you found out you'd been separated from them for sixty years?"

Cormack sighed. "No. nothing would keep me from them. I can't even think about that."

I understood he was sympathetic, but I felt the need to hammer it home harder. "If you went missing when your children were little you would come back at a time when you had great-grandchildren.

"Imagine missing all the teenage years," I continued. "Imagine not being able to watch Aisling and Griffin fall in love ... or Lily's formative years. By the time you got back Lily would be an adult with children of her own. You would've missed everything."

He looked pained. "I get it. I don't agree with what's happening here."

"I know you don't. It's just ... this feels cruel. If my parents suddenly came back, if I found they hadn't died, I would burn this place to the ground to get to them."

He rested his hand on my shoulder. It was a very fatherly gesture. "I understand loss. It might not be the same way you understand it, but I get it. We are in an untenable position. How are we going to explain the return of these people?"

"I don't know. What does Griffin say?"

"They've identified Ray Smith. They're confused. There are a lot of ideas being bandied about. Most of them revolve around it somehow being a child of Ray Smith, or even a grandchild, but not him. A few people are suggesting it's a hoax."

"Like what? He disappeared sixty years ago, started another family, and now his grandchild volunteered to die on the island to mess with people?"

"Or maybe he was involved with the mob — this is Detroit after all — and he went into Witness Protection and somehow one of his enemies found his new family and killed his grandson before dumping him close to Ray's old stomping grounds as a message."

Oh, well, that was an intricate hunch. "Do you think they'll go with that?"

"I have no idea. Griffin is being careful not to put forth his own ideas. He wants to see this play out naturally. If these other men show up and it becomes public a whole different type of story will begin circulating."

"Aliens."

"Or government experiments. When something can't be explained, the human brain will grasp at anything for answers. We'll be in a pickle regardless."

"Those men didn't do anything to deserve being kept from their families. They're losing time and a lot of the people they left behind might not have much left."

"I agree with you. I'm not the one making the decisions, though."

"It just seems so unfair." I wasn't the type to turn petulant and pouty, but I couldn't stop myself this time.

"I always told my children life was never fair. I stand by that. The thing is, for them, they had a leg up on life because of my money and connections. That didn't stop them from losing their mother. That didn't stop her from coming back to terrorize them.

"Nothing that has happened to you ... or them ... or these men is fair," he continued. "We still have to do the best with what we're given and move on. We can't control what's happening to these men. We can try to find answers."

"Then that's what we're going to do."

BRADEN MET ME AT THE PARKING lot on the other side of Belle Isle. With the bridge closed, we'd have to take a boat across. I was fine with that, but I expected him to put up a fight. Instead, he gestured with his chin for me to join him in his BMW

"Hop in. We'll need groceries before we head over. There are no stores on the island."

I was surprised. "You're not going to give me grief about wanting to stay on the island?"

He shook his head. "You can't be away right now. If Oliver and the others find a body, you'll want to see it right away. I know you."

He did. We'd been together only a short time, but he knew me better than most. I found comfort in that despite the fact that I'd been leery of him at the start.

"Thanks." I gave him a quick kiss when I hopped in the car. He slid his hand around the back of my neck and deepened the exchange before pulling back to study my face. I felt self-conscious. "What? Do I have food on my face or something?"

"No. Besides, I'm pretty sure you haven't eaten since breakfast."

How could he possibly know that? As if on cue — and to prove him right — my stomach picked that moment to growl. "I might be a little hungry," I said.

"There's a cool neighborhood market around the corner. We'll stock up there in case we have to spend more than one night on the island. It's a definite possibility given everything that's going on."

"That sounds ... good."

"I'm glad. While we're shopping, you can tell me what went on with my father this afternoon. He's being a little ... funky."

That was an odd word choice. "Do you want to expound on that?"

"Sure. He wants Aisling and Griffin to spend the night at the manor again. He's volunteered his time to watch Lily all night so they can sleep, even though he took baby duty last night. Usually one night is his limit."

"He's just feeling overprotective because I let slip that Aisling is still struggling with being a new mother."

Braden's eyebrows hopped. "I thought she was over that. She's been sleeping. She looks ten times better."

"It's still difficult for her because she feels cut off from your mother. She remembers what it was like to grow up with her and she wants to emulate that person. She can't stop thinking about the person who came back, though, and she's afraid."

"That she'll be that sort of mother?" Braden looked horrified. "She won't. She doesn't have it in her."

"And she mostly knows that. Every once in a while, though, the fear returns. That's natural."

"Since when did you become a licensed psychotherapist?"

"Since meeting your family. It was a necessity."

He snickered. "I can see that." He gave the back of my neck a light squeeze and then moved his hand to the steering wheel. "My sister has always been difficult, but I don't want her worrying about nonsense. This should be a happy time. They have the baby; she and Griffin are content, and she's actually getting some much-needed rest. Worrying about stupid things is a waste of time."

"I think she knows that, but fear is a funny thing. She'll be fine. You don't have to worry about her. I probably shouldn't have said anything."

"Why did you say something? Usually you keep stuff like that to yourself."

"It slipped out when talk of Lily smiling for the first time surfaced again. I said it would be best if Lily smiled at her mother first. Your father asked why."

"Ah." Understanding dawned on his handsome features. "Sadly, she's going to have to find something else to bolster her spirits. Lily is definitely smiling at me first."

I shook my head. "Your family should be studied for posterity."

"You're a member of our family now, so you'd have to participate. Are you up for that?"

"I might be."

THE MARKET HE'D PICKED WAS CUTE. I'd driven past the building several times and ignored it because the exterior was rundown. I assumed the inside was the same. I was wrong.

"I love this place," I enthused as I filled my cart with fresh produce. "It's awesome."

Braden chuckled as he moved around me, ignoring the tomatoes and asparagus and going straight for the display of chocolates. "If we're going to have regular sleepovers at your place, you'll need better food. I can't have a tomato for a midnight snack."

"You should start eating healthier. Given the way your father shovels unhealthy foods into you, you're going start spreading at the middle once you hit thirty-five if you're not careful."

Braden's face was full of mock outrage. "I'm going to be trim and studly my entire life. You've seen my father. He still sends tongues wagging."

That was true. Cormack was a stellar male specimen even though he ate just as poorly as his children. There was every possibility his metabolism would pass on to his children ... just like his looks. I didn't say that to Braden, though. I didn't want to encourage him.

"You know what we should do?" I was delighted when I saw the bin of fresh okra. "I should cook some gumbo for you. Do you like gumbo?"

He followed my gaze and nodded. "I've only had it a few times but I was a fan. I don't like grits."

"Grits aren't in gumbo."

"I'm well aware of that, smarty." He lightly flicked the spot between my eyebrows. "I'm just explaining that if you're going to start cooking — and you totally should because a woman's place is in the kitchen — that I don't like grits. I know shrimp and grits are a southern thing. I like the shrimp fine. The grits, not so much. They taste like ass."

I shot him a dark look. "How do you know what ass tastes like?"

"I have brothers. They did gross things to me growing up ... like wipe boogers on my arm and fart in my face. I'm pretty sure I'm comfortable making the comparison."

He made me laugh. It was only one of the things I liked about him. "Your poor sister. Did you fart on her, too?"

"Of course. She wanted to be one of the boys. She was fine with it. Oddly enough, we were not allowed to fart on Jerry. He was far too finicky and would completely melt down if we tried."

I could see that. "Anyway ... back to the gumbo. I kind of want to cook for you now."

"Then cook for me." He slipped his arm around my waist and kissed my temple. "I'll never argue if you want to wait on me hand and foot."

I pinched his flank. "You are a total pain. I'm not waiting on you. I'll cook, and you'll do the dishes."

He made a face. "We should really consider getting you a maid."

"We'll muddle through." I started collecting ingredients and he disappeared into the interior aisles. When he returned five minutes later, his arms were laden with junk food, to the point my stomach hurt just looking at it. "What's all this?"

"Midnight snacks," he replied without hesitation. "We need all of this to survive the night stranded on the island together."

"It's not as if we're facing the zombie apocalypse."

"If we were, we'd head straight to Grimlock Manor. That place is so stocked we could ride it out for years. Plus there's a full bar."

He had a point. "What is all this stuff?" I was curious as I watched him unload items into the cart.

"Swiss Rolls from Little Debbie. Salt-and-vinegar potato chips. I got the kettle kind because they're my favorite. I probably should've asked if you preferred regular chips."

"Kettle cooked is fine." I furrowed my brow. "We're going to go into a sugar coma. You got Red Vines, peanut M&Ms, Rice Krispies treats and beef jerky. That's a weird combination."

"I have a refined palate."

"This is the sort of food children eat when their parents leave them alone for a few hours."

"And your point is?" His smile was impish. "We're without parental supervision tonight. We should live it up."

He was too geeked to deny. "Okay, but I'm not going to stay up all night entertaining you when the sugar kicks in. I'm going to bed at a decent time like a good girl."

"We'll see."

"WHAT DO YOU THINK?"

I was nervous when I dished out the gumbo. I'd used my grandfather's famous recipe, but cut down on the spices a bit. I could handle the heat, but Braden was used to blander food. I didn't want him up all night with heartburn.

A spoon clutched in his hand, Braden sent me a searching look. "I haven't tasted it yet."

"Oh, right." I remained standing, my gaze expectant.

"Sit down," he instructed, shaking his head. He looked as uncomfortable as I felt. "I'm going to love it."

"You don't know that." Something occurred to me. "If you don't like it I don't want you pretending otherwise. I would rather you tell me the truth."

"I'll tell you the truth." He averted his eyes at the last second when he delivered the line. I knew he was lying.

"You will not. You'll say you like it regardless." I felt defeated. I sank into the chair across from him and frowned. "I was so excited to cook for you."

Instead of being sympathetic, he looked exasperated. "Hey, I haven't even tried it yet," he complained. "You have to take a breath."

He studied me for a long moment once I fell silent. "Why are you suddenly so manic about this? I've never seen you react this way. Before you would've been all, 'I don't care if you like it' or even 'You'll like it or I'll kill you.' This self-conscious Izzy isn't the woman I fell for."

The simple statement was enough to shake me out of my doldrums. He had a point. "I have no idea why I'm so nervous." That was the truth. "You're right, though. It's not like me. I'm feeling ... out of sorts. I guess that's the best way to describe it. Everything that's going on has me thinking about fate. Do you ever think about that?"

He shrugged, noncommittal. "I guess I think about it ... not very often. Fate is one of those things that I'm not sure I believe in."

"Really?" I couldn't hide my surprise. "Your mother's soul found the strength to come back at the exact right time to keep your sister safe. Thanks to that, your sister managed to keep you from falling to your death. You don't think fate had a hand in that?"

He looked troubled. "I don't like thinking that my mother's death was predestined, and if I believe in fate, then I have to believe that there was absolutely nothing that could've changed the outcome. I prefer believing that we can change fate. Otherwise, what's the point in trying to be a better person or saving the people you care about? If everything is already determined, why try at all?"

It was a defeatist concept and yet I understood. "I never really thought about it that way."

"Believe what you want. I choose to believe that I can affect my reality ... and my happily ever after. That still doesn't explain why you're so manic about the gumbo."

"My father was an outstanding cook. He learned from my grandfather. I guess I wanted to be able to say I inherited something from them."

"Why?"

"Your father and I were talking about what he would do if he was one of the people who had disappeared through the gate, whether he would allow the council to keep him separated from his family if he were in the same position. It got me to thinking ... probably more than it should have. You're right, though. That's not me. I'm just letting things get to me when they shouldn't."

"I think we're all doing a lot of thinking. No one wants to die — least of all me — but I almost think it would be better than what's happening with these guys. I mean ... they went away for five minutes and came back to find that sixty years had passed. The people in their lives had no idea what happened to them. None. They hoped, dreamed and prayed for a miracle. Then they gave up only to find years later, years after they'd moved on, that their miracle happened ... but at a time when it was too late to enjoy."

"They haven't been informed that a miracle occurred at all. That's the part that bothers me."

"There's a lot about this that bothers me. It's too much. All I care about is keeping my family safe. That includes you."

I smiled, the emotion in his eyes warming me all over. "That's a really sweet thing to say."

"I'm a really sweet guy."

I couldn't stop myself from laughing. "Eat your gumbo. You're going to love it."

Eleven

He did indeed love the gumbo. He had three servings and only one Swiss Roll. We fell into bed early, into each other seconds after that, and into sleep well before midnight. I slept soundly ... until an alarm started ringing in my ear.

"Is that the fire alarm?"

Braden shifted next to me, confused. "What are you talking about?"

"That noise. Is that the fire alarm?"

"There's no noise, Izzy. You're imagining things. Or maybe you're dreaming them. Go back to sleep and pick a better dream. I suggest something about me." He absently patted my head as a form of comfort. "Goodnight."

I ran his words through my mind, figured he was right about me dreaming the alarm, and then I bolted to a sitting position. I knew better than to believe it was somehow imagined. "Son of a ... !" I viciously swore and tossed off the covers. "Get up!"

Braden wasn't a morning person. He liked his eight hours of straight slumber more than most. That's why I wasn't surprised that he was slow to react. "Come back to bed, Izzy. If you're a good girl I'll knock you out with my gumbo love again."

Under normal circumstances I would've smiled. These were not normal circumstances. "Get up!" I wasn't playing around. "Something is happening, Braden. The alarm ... I've heard it before. You're right. It's inside my head. It's a magical alarm of sorts."

Finally, he opened his eyes. "What are you saying? Is it the gate?"

I shook my head. "I don't think so. I've never alerted over the gate before. It's something else."

"What?"

"I don't know, but I intend to find out."

I FOLLOWED MY INSTINCTS, WHICH led me to my golf cart. I hopped in the passenger seat, allowing Braden to drive, and directed him down the dark streets.

"That way."

"Where are we going?" Braden was no longer sleepy. His alert eyes were trained on the road. "Tell me exactly what you sense."

"I don't know what I sense." That was true. Even as I reached out with my magic, the thing I brushed against was a void. I didn't know how to explain it. "There's something out here. We have to find it."

"I'm assuming because you used the word 'thing' that you don't believe we're dealing with a human ... or a returnee."

I hadn't even considered that. "Oh, um ... huh." That was stupid of me. Given everything that was happening, it made far more sense that another man had returned from beyond the gate than the notions I'd been entertaining.

"You're not leading us back to the aquarium," he offered, filling in the silence. "You don't sense it's one of the returnees, do you?"

I shook my head. "It feels like something else."

"Okay." He was resolute. "Tell me where to go. When we get there, I would appreciate it if you wouldn't run off half-cocked."

"I'll be fully cocked when I run off. There's no need to worry."

He grimaced. "Izzy, I'm serious. I know you're strong and capable, but I want to be with you. If something happens ... ." He trailed off. I imagined he was thinking about our conversation over dinner.

"I won't disappear on you, Braden," I reassured him. "I promise."

"I still want to be with you."

"I'm not going to stop you. Just ... chill."

Braden exhaled heavily and I had the distinct impression that he was trying to maintain his temper. I couldn't focus on him, though. I had to follow the warning signal in my head. "Turn here," I gestured when we were almost on top of another road.

Braden extended his hand to make sure I didn't inadvertently fall out of my seat as he took the turn hard. Then he put his foot on the gas pedal and pressed it to the floor. "Where are we even heading?"

I'd been asking myself that exact question. "It must be the old sawmill."

His forehead wrinkled. "What old sawmill?"

I fell back on my training. "It was built in 1905. It hasn't been used in years. There's talk of renovating it."

"I've visited Belle Isle a million times since I was a kid. I've never seen a sawmill."

"Then you're in for a treat."

His expression was dubious, but he didn't speak again. Perhaps he sensed the danger now, because he killed the headlights on the golf cart as we approached the ramshackle building. He hit the brakes and shut off the engine a hundred feet from our goal.

"I think we should call for help," he said suddenly, his eyes keen as they scanned the overgrown expanse. "I don't like this at all."

"It will take people too long to get out here," I countered, climbing out of the cart. "It's fine. We don't know if anything is even out here."

He grabbed my wrist before I could move too far away. "Oliver is on the island. Brett, too. Those weird merfolk are always hanging around. We don't have to do this right now."

On that he was woefully off the mark. "We do. In fact ... ." I sensed movement rather than saw it and swiveled quickly.

"Behind you!" Braden bellowed, abandoning his reticence and hopping to his feet. I could hear the soles of his shoes pounding on the ground as he raced to my aid.

The only available light came from the moon, which was big and new. I could still make out the creature's features ... and it was monster rather than man I was dealing with.

It was huge. It had to be almost seven feet tall. Broad shoulders ran directly into a misshapen head. There was no neck. I couldn't see a nose, which briefly had me wondering how it breathed. It boasted huge red eyes. They almost glowed, and it let out an unearthly scream as it reached for me.

"Izzy!" Braden was there in an instant, shoving me out of the way in an effort to take on the creature himself.

A lot of thoughts went through my head as I tumbled to the ground. The first was that he was willing to sacrifice himself for me, which was simply unacceptable. The second was that the creature had wicked blood-red claws to match its eyes and they were heading for Braden's throat. The third was that I was about to lose something very important to me and my heart ached at the thought.

I reacted out of instinct and ignored the disoriented feeling washing over me when I hit the ground. Instead of giving into the confusion, I unleashed a torrent of magic from my fingertips. Braden stood between me and the creature, but I didn't allow fear for his well-being to overtake me. Instead, I aimed the magic and prayed it wouldn't let me down.

"Duck!" I screamed, just to be on the safe side.

Braden's reflexes were strong and he did as I commanded. His head slipped lower and the magic barreled over the top of him, smacking into the creature's chest with a sickening thwack.

My body ached, my head hurt, and yet I prepared myself for a second magical barrage. I didn't see that I had a choice. The creature glared at me, another roar escaping. I delivered another crushing blow, putting my own anger and fear into the spell as I desperately tried to keep us safe. This time when the magic collided with the creature, there was an explosion of sorts and sparks flew in a million different directions.

The creature screeched again before falling silent. The red eyes widened, but all movement ceased. And then, slowly, it toppled backward. Those miserable eyes were vacant as they stared at the night sky. It didn't move again.

It took Braden a moment to regain his senses, and then he scrambled to me. "Are you okay?"

I nodded as I wiped the back of my hand against my forehead. "I'm awesome."

The look he shot me was dubious. "How are you really?"

"My back and butt hurt from the fall. Otherwise, I'm okay."

"I'll rub both for you later." He hooked his hands under my arms and tugged me up. "We need to call for help. There might be more of them."

I didn't believe that. I would know. That didn't mean help was a bad idea. "Place the call. I'll be okay."

Frustration lit his brilliant lilac eyes. "You and I are going to have a talk about self-preservation later. You've been warned."

He was stern enough that I laughed. I couldn't help myself. "We definitely are. What were you thinking charging in front of me?"

"I was thinking that you were in trouble and I had to help."

"That's what I was thinking. I guess we're a good couple, huh?"

It was obvious he was annoyed, but he managed a wan smile. "The best." He pressed a kiss to my forehead. "This is un-freaking-believable. My father is going to have kittens."

I couldn't wait to see that.

GRIFFIN AND CORMACK CAME TOGETHER. They both looked disheveled, as if woken from a deep sleep, and I instantly felt guilty. Braden was another story.

"At least you didn't wear your pajamas," he groused to Griffin, whose shirt was on backward, his hair standing on end.

"I sleep naked," Griffin replied. "That's what I was ... naked ... when you called. So was your sister."

"Don't make me kill you," Cormack warned, his eyelids heavy. "I don't have much energy, but I can manage that."

"You're the one who volunteered to take Lily duty two nights in a row," Griffin pointed out. "We didn't twist your arm."

"I wanted to spend time with Aisling. Pacing the hallways with Lily as she refuses to go to sleep was just an added bonus."

Griffin rested his hand on his father-in-law's shoulder. "I heard what you and she talked about. I could've told you that she was okay, still struggling a bit with what happened ten months ago, but mostly okay. She'll be fine moving forward."

"She *will* be fine," Braden agreed. "Oh, don't look at me like that. Izzy told me what you guys talked about, that Aisling is worried about being a mother because her most recent memory of our mother gutted her. She needs to remember that wasn't our true mother, because she risked everything to come back and save us. That's what's important, not what that ... thing ... did to us."

"That's very well said, Braden," Griffin offered. "She'll be fine. You guys need to stop worrying about her. That somehow makes it worse."

"That's my fault," I volunteered. "I just see her surface thoughts occasionally. I think it's when she's feeling weak. It's not very often. I only brought it up because I think she would be totally fine if the baby smiled at her first."

"No way."

Braden, Cormack and Griffin all shook their heads in unison.

"Lily is smiling at me first," they said at the same time.

Men. Seriously. They're so much work. "Whatever." I could do nothing but roll my eyes. "Shouldn't we focus on our actual problem right now?" I gestured toward the misshapen figure on the ground. "I'm pretty sure that's Ray Smith."

Three heads jerked in my direction.

"Ray Smith?" Braden was the first to speak. "That's not Ray Smith. It can't be. You said he looked the same as when he disappeared. That definitely doesn't look like the guy I saw in the photo."

"It's not." Griffin's gaze was heavy. "I saw the body. That's most definitely not the same guy."

"No?" I shifted closer to the body. "Then why is it wearing the same watch?"

Cormack moved closer and peered at the piece of jewelry in question. "That's an Omega stainless steel watch," he said after a beat. "It's vintage to the sixties."

"You recognize the watch?" Griffin slipped on a pair of rubber gloves and knelt next to the body, intent.

"My father had one. He wore it for years. He got it from his father as a gift. It lasted forever. I even bought him an expensive watch to replace it. He refused until it stopped running." Cormack's expression was hard to read. "This isn't a watch that someone could just stumble across, especially a ... monster."

"How could it be Ray Smith?" Griffin carefully shifted the creature's head to study what looked to have been a hairline at one time. "Does anyone know what this is?"

"It looks like Bub," Braden answered. "I mean ... what Bub would look like if he walked on two legs, that is."

That was an interesting comparison. "He is kind of rubbery." I reached out to touch the monster, but Braden slapped my hand away. "Hey!"

"He could be diseased or something," he snapped. "You don't want to catch what he has. I mean ... I'll still adore you, but it might have to be from afar."

Cormack cuffed his son. "That was lovely, Braden. Now I see why you've gone so long without a steady girlfriend. Try not to scare this one away. She's a keeper."

"I know she's a keeper. That's why I don't want her to touch that thing."

"You mean Ray Smith," I corrected. "He used to be a human being."

"And then he died," Griffin pointed out. He'd completely ignored the exchange between Cormack and Braden. "I saw the body. He was gone. This can't be him."

"Unless it wasn't really Ray Smith that came back," I noted. "He was already dead when he landed. Maybe that's because whoever sent him shoved something inside his body that couldn't survive the trip without a host."

Cormack made a face. "That's a cheery thought."

I turned to Griffin. "Can you check to see if the body is still at the morgue?"

"Yes, but not until tomorrow morning. It will look strange if I call tonight."

"Fair enough." I slid my eyes to Braden. "I guess that means we're going back to Grimlock Manor for the rest of the night. I want to be close when Griffin makes the call tomorrow."

"Okay." He slung his arm around my neck and focused on his father. "You'll have to call the home office to take care of this. It's not as if Griffin can call this in to his people."

"I know." Cormack pressed the heel of his hand to his forehead. "This is definitely something we don't want to hit the mainstream."

"I'll let you handle that," Griffin supplied. "I need to get back to my wife. I still have a chance at a solid four hours of sleep."

"Get to it. I'll handle this. All of you get out of here."

He didn't have to tell us twice. We were already gone.

THE ENTIRE FAMILY – MINUS GRIFFIN – WAS ALREADY in the dining room when Braden and I joined them five hours later. A few hours down and a hot shower completely revived me. I was starving.

"Good morning, lovebirds," Aisling teased as she shoveled blueberry pancake into her mouth. She looked bright and shiny. "I hear you had a busy night ... one that required my poor husband to be dragged out of bed."

"You don't look very sorry about that," I noted.

"Actually, I am sorry for him. I'm sorry for myself because I missed him. I'm just happy that I'm not the one losing sleep. Having a baby was a great idea. Now everyone spoils me."

Cormack snorted as he shifted Lily, who was on his lap and watching the activity with mild interest. I could never tell what was going on in her brain. It probably wasn't much given her age, but there was something about her that made me think she was brighter than most infants. She had ... something. It was a spark, and I was fairly certain she was empathetic, a power most reapers didn't have. She was going to grow into something special.

Right now she was just a curious lump on her grandfather's lamp. She was darned cute, though.

"You've always been spoiled rotten, kid," Cormack countered. "I don't know who you're trying to fool. The reason you weren't called out last night is because it wasn't necessary for you to be there. It had nothing to do with the baby."

"Yeah, yeah, yeah." Aisling waved off his statement. "I like my version better."

"You always do." Cormack shifted at the sound of footsteps near the door and focused his attention on Griffin. "What's the news?"

Griffin didn't even have to answer. His face said it all. "Ray Smith's body is gone. It looks like Izzy was right. They're treating it as further perpetuation of a hoax, but we know better. That thing that she killed last night was Ray Smith."

"So ... what does that mean?" Aisling asked.

"I have no idea," Cormack replied. "I just ... I don't know what to make of any of this."

Twelve

I lost my appetite fairly quickly, but Braden seemed intent on making me eat. Once we separated for the day — he had work and I had an idea — I perked up a bit. That lasted only until I found Aisling waiting for me in front of the house.

"Aren't you supposed to be sucking souls?" I asked as I headed for my car.

She nodded, her expression hard to read. "I am. My father is giving me special treatment. I have only two charges and they're both this afternoon ... at an assisted living center in the safest neighborhood around. I have time to burn."

That made sense. Cormack would've instructed Redmond to make sure Aisling was unlikely to run into trouble when he was doling out assignments. He would keep up that mandate long after Aisling had tired of being treated like a porcelain doll. "Why do I think you have a specific idea for how you want to burn this time?" I asked, wary.

"Because you know me well." Aisling's smile was mischievous as it split her features. "It's kind of interesting because I tend to dislike females a great deal. You're the exception."

I held her gaze for an extended beat. She meant the statement as a compliment but there was something telling about the way her lips twisted. "You're one of the boys," I said finally. "You've always felt that way and it's what you desired from the start. You didn't want to be treated differently from your brothers so you went out of your way to be one of them."

I usually didn't get off on psychoanalyzing people, but the Grimlocks were a cornucopia of dysfunction that somehow always managed to work itself out into a relatively healthy family dynamic. It was fascinating ... and often ridiculous. "You even found a best friend who was the best of both worlds. He allowed you to be a girl — even encouraged it — but he was still a boy, so you were clear when it came to doing decidedly female stuff that freaked you out. It wasn't that you didn't like females. You simply didn't want to give your brothers a reason to treat you differently."

She furrowed her brow. "No, I'm pretty sure I just find most women to be stupid."

I couldn't stop myself from laughing. She wasn't the best liar when she didn't put effort into it and she clearly didn't care if I believed her. "What do you want?" I opted to get to the heart of matters because I didn't have time to burn. "I have an errand to run and then I need to get back to the island."

"I want to go with you on your errand."

"Why? You don't even know where I'm going."

"You're going to see your aunt." She was matter-of-fact. "You feel out of your element and you want to see if she has any ideas about what's happening. I think that's smart. She knows a lot of things ... even if she keeps those things to herself when she shouldn't."

There was bitterness to Aisling's tone that set my teeth on edge. "That's fairly astute," I offered. "I *am* going to see Aunt Max. I feel as if I'm missing something in this scenario that I shouldn't. But I'm not sure you should go with me."

"And why is that?" Aisling frowned. "I can be useful. Whatever your aunt has said, I'm totally useful."

"I have no doubt that's true. My aunt really hasn't said anything about you." That was a lie, but I recognized that Aisling's paranoia would jump if she believed my aunt was talking out of turn. "I don't think it's a good idea because you're still mad at Aunt Max about your mother."

Aisling frowned. "That's not true. I'm perfectly fine about the fact that she helped my mother's soul cross over to help us and didn't say a word about it. Why would I be upset about that?"

There were a million reasons for her to be upset about it and I understood every one of them. That didn't mean I wasn't on my aunt's side. I also understood Aisling's emotions. There simply wasn't time to deal with them when we had so much going on.

"I think it's best if I talk to Aunt Max on my own."

Aisling held my gaze for a long moment and then shook her head. "I'll behave. I know this is a big deal. I have a few questions of my own. I won't ruin things for you."

She seemed sincere. She always had good intentions, but that didn't mean she could carry them out. "I don't know." I felt caught. Aisling was used to her family members capitulating to her whims. I didn't want to reinforce bad inclinations, but I didn't have time to argue with her.

"I'll be good." Aisling mimed crossing her heart, and I knew I was about to make a mistake because there was mischief lurking in her eyes. "I just have a few ideas and I think Madame Maxine is the best one to bounce them off of."

As long as she didn't bounce anything else — like a brick — off my aunt, we were probably fine. I was going to give in ... so I did it. "Fine. The second you get out of line, though ... ." I left the threat hanging.

She didn't look worried. "I'll be on my best behavior."

Sadly, I knew that wasn't saying much.

MAXINE SAT ON THE small settee in the middle of her store, what looked to be a catalog on her lap. She was jotting down notes when we entered. Her smile was pleasantly bland ... until she realized who we were.

"Izzy." She broke into a wide smile and stood to offer me a hug. She seemed delighted to see me. She'd tried to keep me with her after the death of my parents — we were always tight — but my grandfather put his foot down. Even though they didn't always get along, they pretended to for my sake. I appreciated the effort on both their parts.

"Aunt Max." I was legitimately happy to see her. She had a soothing presence and would listen for hours as I told her my woes. "How are you?"

"I'm fine." Maxine's gaze was keen as she slid it to Aisling, who was loitering about five feet behind me. "Hello, sourpuss. You look pretty good for giving birth six weeks ago. I see you're one of those women who got her body back right away ... which essentially means all the other women in the world hate you."

Aisling merely shrugged. "My father had the cook make healthy stuff and didn't tell me. I'm a little disappointed myself, if you want to know the truth."

Maxine snorted. "Right. I'm sure you've been quiet as a mouse and not chasing after Angelina to show her how great you look."

Angelina Davenport was Aisling's nemesis — that's the word she used — and she'd been nothing but a pain the few times I'd met her. In truth, I could see Aisling happily taunting Angelina with her physique. Unfortunately we'd been too busy to wedge that in this week.

"I'll see her when I see her," Aisling replied. She was keeping her distance, making sure not to get close enough for Maxine to touch her. That was clearly on purpose, but I didn't chide her for it. If Aisling was uncomfortable, we would all hear about it until the end of time.

Maxine stared at her for a long moment before turning back to me. "I take it you're here for a specific reason."

"You could say that." I sat on the couch. There was no sense being uncomfortable for what was sure to be a long conversation. "We have a situation."

Maxine didn't bother to hold back her sigh. "Don't you have a situation every week now?"

"Pretty much." I saw no reason to pretend otherwise. My life had turned into one big drama. "This one is different." I launched into the tale, leaving nothing out. It was a relatively long story, but I managed to condense it. When I finished, she was thoughtful. "So ... what do you think?"

"I think you guys have definitely been busy," she replied after a moment's consideration. "I don't even know what to make of this. I mean ... really. How did a man who returned from the dead manage to die within seconds and then turn into a monster? I don't even know what to make of it."

To my surprise, Aisling's hand shot in the air. It was as if she were in a classroom and wanted to be teacher's pet.

Maxine arched an eyebrow. "Yes, pouty wonder. Do you have something you would like to add to this conversation or do you merely have ants in your pants?"

Aisling licked her lips, making me realize for the first time that she was nervous. I should've figured that out sooner. This was a big deal for her ... and apparently she really did have something on her mind.

"What are you thinking?" I asked.

"I'm thinking it's a revenant."

I wasn't expecting that. "I ... you ... a revenant?" All I could do was draw my eyebrows together. My initial reaction had been to shut down that idea, but I honestly couldn't.

"A revenant, huh?" Maxine didn't shut her down either. "That's ... interesting."

"I know a little about them," Aisling admitted, taking a tentative step forward. She still wasn't close enough for my aunt to touch — a deliberate choice on her part — but she was getting bolder. "I thought maybe that's what came back with my mother's face."

Sympathy washed over Maxine's soft features as she nodded. "I can see that. What did you find?"

"There's a lot of conflicting information about revenants. Some think revenant is an interchangeable word for ghost. Others think vampires are revenants. There is one faction that thinks they're different.

"Revenants originated in Western European folklore," she continued. "Cillian and I talked about them one afternoon, but he wasn't nearly as keen on the idea so I let it go. When I heard what happened to Izzy and Braden last night, revenants were the first things that popped into my head."

"And what do we know about revenants?" Maxine asked in her most reasonable voice. "Are they blood-suckers, like vampires?"

"They can be. In this particular case, I don't know what to believe. I can't figure out why Ray Smith looked normal when his body was found and then he turned into a monster when he came back from the dead. That doesn't make sense because if they were revenants, they would always look like monsters."

I'd been thinking of the monster phenomenon myself and had a few ideas. "Unless the monster was hidden inside for a specific reason," I offered. "Maybe someone wanted to send Ray back like a Trojan horse or something. You know, hide what he really is from the outside world with a simple glamour spell or something. I'm guessing he wasn't meant to die. Something happened during the exchange that caused him to inadvertently die."

"That makes sense," Aisling mused, rubbing her cheek. "Maybe it was as simple as a glamour, like you say. I've read about them. I thought maybe the thing that came back with my mother's face was using a glamour at first ... but I didn't tell anyone I was thinking that."

"We all had different thoughts about that creature," Maxine offered, calm. "It's nice that all the research you did wasn't for nothing. It's helping us now."

Instead of being grateful for the words, Aisling was suspicious. "Oh, don't shine me on," she groused. "I'm being serious here."

"So am I." Maxine was firm. "You've grown quite a bit ... even though you're still a massive whiner. I can tell. You've still got that look about you. I blame that on your father for spoiling you rotten. It's too late to beat out of you, so I'm opting to ignore it."

Aisling didn't bother to hide her eye roll. "How awesome for you. You really are a magnanimous soul."

I had to bite back a chuckle at her dry tone. I wasn't particularly worried about taking my aunt's side. She could take care of herself. The same could be said for Aisling. Neither of them needed an assist if they wanted to go after one another. They wouldn't even draw physical blood.

Mental blood was another story.

Maxine ignored Aisling's dig. "I don't know that I believe it's a revenant, but it is an intriguing prospect. Any ideas how we test it?"

"That's why I wanted to come with Izzy," Aisling replied. "I figure that should be your job. I already did my part."

"Yes, and it was obviously taxing." Maxine's eyes twinkled as she glanced at me. "I'm not sure how to test for a revenant, but I can do some research. I'm assuming you've got Cillian on this."

"I sent him a text," Aisling confirmed. "He promised to see what he could find, but I thought you might know more about revenants. You're supposed to know all and see all, right?"

If she was offended by Aisling's flippant tone, my aunt didn't show it. She remained calm, which I appreciated.

"I don't know much about revenants because we so often deal with different things here. In truth, wraiths could be considered revenants. I mean ... they're kind of dead because they're soulless."

I found the hypothesis fascinating, but Aisling was already shaking her head. "No. Wraiths are alive. They might be soulless, but they're alive. That's the whole point of becoming a wraith. You give up a soul to prolong your life."

"There are different ways to live, though," Maxine pointed out. "If Ray Smith hadn't landed wrong — at least in theory — then he would've been alive. I'm guessing the thing inside of him would still have been an issue. I mean ... that kind of explains why he's back, doesn't it?"

She was in the middle of the sentence when something occurred to me and I straightened. My mind was a hodgepodge of possibilities and I was suddenly worked up. "Oh, geez." I fumbled for my phone in my pocket, several different urges fighting for supremacy in my head. "Oh ... and I can't believe I didn't think about this before. Stupid."

Maxine's gaze was curious when it landed on me. "What?"

"Yeah, share with the class," Aisling demanded. "You can't just freak out like that for no apparent reason. We need answers."

Maxine smirked and nodded. "Totally. We need answers."

They were an odd double-team duo, but I didn't have time to focus on that. "You just said it yourself," I reminded them, my stomach tightening as my anxiety built. "Even if Ray Smith would've lived, there would've been a revenant inside of him ... or whatever it is that we're dealing with. His experience was unique because he ended up dead."

"So?" Aisling made a face. "That still doesn't explain why you're so worked up."

I feigned patience. "He's not the only one who came back. Five other people did, too. They were alive when they landed, so if there was a plan, it's probably still in the works."

The color drained from Aisling's face as realization smacked her upside the head. "Oh, geez."

"Who are you calling?" Maxine asked.

"Cormack." I was grim. "We need someone to talk to the guys in the hospital ward. I'm starting to think — even though I was against it at the time — that it's good the reaper council kept them under wraps. At least now we don't have to look for them."

"That's something," Aisling agreed. "It's not much, but it's something."

Cormack picked up on the third ring. He sounded harried. I laid everything out for him in a precise manner.

We were already too late.

"If only we'd put this together ten hours ago," he muttered, his tone dark.

My heart skipped a beat. "What do you mean?"

"They're gone."

"Gone?"

"They attacked the guards outside the door," he explained in measured tones. "I don't know if they transformed before doing it. We're searching for the security footage now. All five of the men are missing and two of our reapers are down. It was a bloody and terrible death."

I felt sick. "So ... what do we do?"

"I want you over here right now if you can manage it. I want to see if you get a reading off the scene."

That made sense. "Okay. I can manage that." I remembered I wasn't alone fairly quickly. "I have Aisling with me. Can she come?"

If Cormack was curious about why I'd teamed up with his only daughter, he didn't show it. "Bring her. I'll make sure she isn't late for work."

That was something. "What do you think we're dealing with?"

"I have no idea. Just get here. We should have the footage by then and it will provide some answers."

"We're on our way."

Thirteen

The reaper headquarters bustled with activity. Aisling carried herself with an air of authority that I found amusing. She strode right past the security guards, practically daring them to stop her, not stopping until she was next to her father.

"I was kind of hoping they would give me grief," she admitted, glaring at the guards. "I haven't fought with anyone in weeks. I'm starting to get that itch."

Cormack was in the middle of a conversation with a man I didn't recognize, but he took the time to slide his daughter a look. It wasn't disappointment reflected there. It was fondness and amusement.

"Track down your buddy Angelina," I suggested. "She seems the sort who will fight with you."

"Oh, that's still coming." Aisling's expression darkened. "I don't need to seek her out. The universe keeps shoving us together. It will happen when it's meant to happen."

"Yes, and I already have bail money earmarked for when it does," Cormack said, offering me a smile before gesturing toward the man in front of him. "This is Drake Windsor. He's the head of the medical department."

Oh, well, that was good. I had so many questions I didn't know where to start. "What were they?"

Drake appeared surprised by the question. "I'm sorry. I don't understand."

Cormack cleared his throat. "I haven't mentioned the new premise yet. I thought I would wait until after we reviewed the security footage."

I wasn't in the mood to wait. "The more I think about it, the more I think our revenant idea might be correct."

"*My* revenant theory," Aisling corrected. "It was my idea."

Cormack's lips quirked. "Since when do you conduct research?"

"I didn't do it for these guys," she reassured him. "I was researching revenants for another reason."

He blinked twice and then nodded. He didn't need to ask why she was looking up revenants. "I'm not opposed to the idea. I've never really given revenants much thought. I thought they looked like normal humans ... only slightly different. At least that was my assumption."

"Our guys did come back looking like normal humans," I pointed out. "Ray Smith died looking like a normal human. He only changed after ... well, after he died."

"I think they were always dead," Aisling countered. "I think they died the second they crossed the barrier and something was done to them over there to change them."

"What?" Drake asked, curiosity etching across his distinguished face. He was one of those men whose age was impossible to guess. He could've been forty or seventy.

"How am I supposed to know?" Aisling asked, agitation flashing. "I've obviously never been on the other side of the gate. They're clearly not the same people they were when they crossed over."

"They're not," I agreed. "I don't necessarily believe that crossing the gate results in instant death. I mean ... remember the wraith? I know you were preoccupied with other stuff at the time, but he crossed over and returned. He was different, but still alive.

"We've already talked about the wraiths," I continued. "They're not dead simply because they don't have souls. We don't know that these men are without souls either. All we know right now is that Ray died upon arrival — which I'm guessing was an error — and then he turned into a revenant.

"What if these other men are still alive?" I was starting to warm to my topic now. I'd done a lot of thinking on our drive from Royal Oak to headquarters thanks to the thick traffic. "What if whatever was done to them isn't supposed to trigger until their deaths? That would mean they're perfectly fine until the end ... and then we have to deal with the monsters after the fact."

"That's a nice idea," Cormack countered. "But it doesn't explain why these so-called normal men killed two guards on their way out. You haven't seen the bodies yet. They were ... ripped apart."

He was grim, which made me nervous. He had seen death his entire life. If he was bothered by this, it had to be bad.

"So, let me see the bodies," I suggested.

"Okay." He gestured toward a door on the other side of the hallway. "They're in there." When Aisling moved to follow, Cormack shook his head. "You stay out here."

"No way." Aisling was instantly on the attack. "I'm an adult ... and you agreed to let me return to work. This is part of my job."

"This is most certainly not part of your job. You have souls to collect ... and I believe you have to travel to St. Clair Shores to do it. You should head there now to make sure you're not late."

Aisling's eyes narrowed to lavender slits. "I want to see them."

"No, you don't."

"Yes, I do. This is my hunch. I've seen death before."

"Not like this." Cormack held his youngest child's gaze for what felt like forever before heaving out a sigh. "What if I have a cupcake bar for dinner tonight? Will that convince you that seeing the bodies is unnecessary?"

All of Cormack's children had a price. Well, at least when it came to things like this. They could easily be swayed with food and I could practically hear the gears in Aisling's mind working.

"I want a chocolate fountain, too," she said finally. "And I want cupcakes with sprinkles ... and gummy worms ... and Twix."

He sighed again. "I'll make it happen."

"Fine." She was morose as she straightened her shoulders. "I guess that means I should head to my charges."

Cormack managed a cheeky smile and extended his hand toward her. "It was a pleasure doing business with you."

Aisling merely stared at his hand.

"Aisling, you're going to work," he growled. This time he sounded serious. "You don't want to see what's in that room. It will give you nightmares."

"Oh, I don't want to go in there any longer." The smile she let loose was mischievous enough that even I was worried. "I don't have a way to get to my charges. I rode with Izzy. That means I need a vehicle ... and I'm guessing you have one."

The dark look that flitted across Cormack's handsome features was enough to have me biting the inside of my cheek to keep from laughing. I had to avert my gaze because I knew that if I watched Aisling too closely I would start chuckling , which would infuriate Cormack.

"I brought the BMW," he complained. "Can't you take an Uber?"

"Do you want me to get raped and killed? You've seen the stories about those guys lately. It's not safe."

Cormack glowered at her. "You've never been afraid of Uber drivers."

She merely held out her hand expectantly. I had no idea why Cormack was even pretending to put up a fight. It was obvious he was going to acquiesce to her demands.

"Fine." He dug into his pocket and dropped a set of keys in her extended hand. "If you wreck that car I'm cutting you off for life. You've been warned."

Aisling didn't look particularly worried. "I'll see you for dinner. Don't forget my cupcakes."

"I wouldn't dare."

I remained silent for a full minute after she departed. I was just about to suggest we head toward the bodies when he finally spoke.

"I really have created five monsters," he lamented. "They're spoiled rotten, each and every one of them."

"I think they're fine." I meant it. "They might be spoiled, but they're giving souls. Besides, you were going to give Aisling whatever she wanted no matter what it was. It wasn't that you didn't want her to see death, but because you were afraid Lily would pick up on the horror in her mother's mind. You didn't want to point that out to Aisling because that might be more than she can deal with now. You were going to kowtow to her every whim no matter how you pretended otherwise."

Instead of smiling, Cormack frowned. "Do you know everything?"

"Yes."

He laughed. "You're kind of like one of my children."

"Although not nearly as spoiled. When am I going to request something special for a dessert bar?"

"What did you have in mind?"

"Have you ever had beignets?"

His smiled. "Only in New Orleans. I'm sure I can make arrangements for them. My children may talk big, but if there's sugar involved they'll eat anything."

I already knew that. "Let's see these bodies, shall we?"

His expression turned grave. "I'm warning you, it's not pretty."

THE BODIES MOST CERTAINLY WEREN'T pretty. In fact, I couldn't remember the last time I'd seen anything this bad.

"Wow." I held it together and managed to refrain from making a face, but it took effort. "That is ... wow."

He wasn't wrong about the bodies being ripped apart. They were on two gurneys, but I wasn't sure the correct pieces had been put together.

"I don't understand." I was breathless as I circled the first gurney. Meeting the gaze of the dead security guard was difficult because there were a million different horrors reflected in his open eyes. "How did they manage to do this?"

"That's a very good question," Drake intoned. He'd trailed us into the room even though I wasn't certain his presence was necessary. I didn't need a cause of death. That was obvious. "It takes a great deal of strength to dismember a body. You usually need some sort of tool. They didn't have access to anything that would've been any help."

"How fast did this happen?"

"We don't know," Cormack replied. "We know that at twenty-two-hundred last evening the duty nurse looked in on her patients as she normally did. The ward was locked down at that time, the guards positioned outside the door, and things were quiet. When a different duty nurse returned at six hundred hours, this is what she found."

I nodded as I crouched so I was at eye-level with one of the bodies. "Is anyone in this part of the building overnight?"

"Not normally. I mean ... there are people in the building. There's never a time when it's empty. That doesn't mean there are many people here. We're talking researchers who are night owls ... janitors ... and a few other people. No one saw anything. No one heard anything."

"After killing the guards, they had to make their way through the building," I noted. "How did they manage that without anyone seeing them?"

"I don't know. We're heading to look at the security footage next. They're bringing it down. I'm not sure why it's taking so long."

My fingers were shakier than I would've liked as I extended them toward the nearest head. I was hoping to catch an image of what had happened. Actually, I didn't want to see what had transpired, but I needed to see it. Figuring out what we were up against was of utmost importance.

"What are you doing?" Drake started in my direction, as if he meant to stop me, but Cormack shook his head.

"She knows what she's doing."

"You can't touch the bodies." Drake was adamant. "We need to see if there's any evidence to collect."

That was an absurd statement. "You already know what happened," I reminded him. "There's really only one option here."

Drake squared his shoulders and fixed me with a pointed look. "We don't know that an outside force didn't enter the building, kill the guards, and then remove the men."

Strangely enough, I hadn't even considered that. I'd jumped to the same conclusion as Cormack ... and it wasn't necessarily the right conclusion. "Is that possible?"

Cormack looked uncomfortable at the question. "I don't know. I didn't consider it."

"Can outsiders get into the building?" I didn't want to think of the men as monsters. It appeared I had no other option until now. The good doctor had just given me one, though, and I was almost grateful.

"They shouldn't be able to," Cormack answered. "The thing is, this shouldn't have been possible either. I guess we can't rule anything out. I'll message the security office and tell them we need footage of each exit and entrance. We need to be sure."

I turned back to the body. "I still have to touch him. I need to see."

"See what?" Drake's eyebrows drew together. "I don't understand what it is you're trying to do."

I looked to Cormack for help. I wasn't certain how much I was supposed to volunteer about my abilities.

"Izzy is not a normal reaper," he replied, choosing his words carefully. "She's the new gatekeeper on Belle Isle. Her skill set is ... different."

The explanation wasn't enough to placate Drake. "Different how?"

"Just different." Cormack was firm. "I'm authorizing her to touch the body. If you have a problem with that, take it up with Renley."

"You can be assured I will." Drake was stiff. "I don't have the authority to stop you, young lady. Do what you're going to do."

I didn't need his permission — heck, I didn't need Cormack's permission because I would've done what I wanted regardless — but I was glad to have backup. "It shouldn't take long." I exhaled heavily and pressed my fingertips toward the mangled man's temple. The images that immediately assaulted me were of the bloody and horrific kind.

"Oh, geez." I didn't pull away. I'd been down this road enough times that I knew it wouldn't change the outcome. I would definitely see the images — and hear the screams — for weeks to come. "Oh, man."

"What do you see?" Cormack asked, his voice gentle. He didn't touch me, which was good. I didn't want to inadvertently transfer the images to his head. They would be in mine long enough that I would have to refrain from holding Lily for the foreseeable future.

"It's a mess," I said. "The guards were caught completely unaware.

They were already under attack before they realized there was a problem."

"Did you see who did it?"

That question was harder to answer. "I don't know." I licked my lips, searching. "I saw blood ... and there was screaming ... and I saw a flurry of movement. I saw two of the men — Pat and Stan — and they looked normal. As for the others ... ." I was at a loss.

"Just give me the basics," Cormack prodded, ignoring the haughty look on Drake's face. It was obvious the doctor wanted to say something derisive but was fearful enough of Cormack that he didn't push matters.

That was for the best.

"It was dark," I replied. "There was limited light in the hallway. Keep in mind, I saw things from the guard's perspective. He was fine ... until he wasn't. I don't know what killed him. I don't know if it was man or beast. It happened so fast. He was gone within seconds."

Apparently giving up on his effort to remain disassociated from me, Cormack rested his hand on my shoulder. It was big ... and warm ... and soothing. I was glad for his presence. "You don't have to touch him any longer, Izzy. It's not necessary."

He was right ... and I felt like an idiot. "Oh, yeah." I drew my hand away and pushed myself to a standing position. "All I can say with any degree of certainty is that the first noise they heard was from behind them. That means it came from the ward, not the hallway in front of them."

"That doesn't necessarily mean that another force didn't come from that direction," Drake persisted. "Multiple forces could've been working together."

"They could have," Cormack agreed, lifting his eyes to the door when it opened and nodding at the man who poked his head inside. "Danny, did you get the footage we're looking for?"

"No." Danny looked resigned, as if embarrassed and worried. "The cameras are wireless and something disrupted the feed moments before the attack. The cameras have a backup system, but it didn't kick in for five minutes. By that time, this was already done and there was no one in the hallways. We've been over the footage five times. There's nothing."

Cormack visibly sagged. "Five minutes? Are you saying all of this happened in five minutes?"

"That's what I'm saying, sir. We don't know how. We don't know anything. There's no way for us to ascertain what door they went out or if they were altered when they left. We have absolutely nothing."

Cormack pressed the heel of his hand to his forehead and tracked his eyes to me. "This can't be good. I mean ... are revenants capable of this?"

"I don't know. I don't know enough about revenants to even hazard a guess."

"Do we know anyone who has knowledge of revenants?"

I shrugged. "I don't even know how to figure that out."

"I can only think of one way." Cormack was grim. "I'll have Cillian start digging. We need someone with unique life experience ... and I just don't know where to look."

I risked a glance back at the bodies and shuddered. "We'd better find out quick. We don't want this to start happening with the general public. It will send the city into a panic."

"Which means the residents will arm themselves and things will only get worse when they start firing guns into shadowy corners," Cormack agreed. "We need to solve this before that happens ... and fast."

Fourteen

I t turns out there was only one person on the payroll with a knowledge base expansive enough to help us. I was ridiculously impressed — and a little awed — when Paris was shown into Cormack's office. By that time, Redmond and Braden had been pulled from their work details. They were being added to reconnaissance teams to search for the missing men. Before that happened, we needed a little magical help.

"Revenants, huh?" Paris looked more intrigued than worried. "I guess I should've considered them from the start, but they never entered my mind."

"Have you dealt with them before?" Cormack asked.

"No, but I've done a lot of research," Paris answered. She was matter-of-fact. "There was a time I thought it was possible revenants were attacking a friend, but it turned out to be run-of-the-mill zombies."

Redmond snorted. "I had no idea zombies were ever run of the mill."

Paris was blasé. "You'd be surprised. I've seen them several times now and they're really only terrifying the first time ... and maybe the second time. Actually, now that I think about it, I was terrified each time. They were only a problem when we were trying to figure out how to kill them."

"And what did you hit upon?" Redmond was clearly amused. Honestly, if I was reading his expression correctly, he was also turned on. Paris had ten years on him, but she was exotic-looking. Besides, Redmond was the sort who didn't discriminate based on age. He would sleep with anyone.

"She's married," I blurted out before Paris could answer, earning a speculative eyebrow from my assistant.

Redmond balked. "I wasn't doing anything."

He was full of it. "And she has a child."

Cormack snorted and shook his head before dragging a hand through his hair. I'd never seen him looking this disheveled. He was always so put together. "Let's forget about Ms. Princeton's dating status for the moment. I need to know more about these revenants."

"And I want to know how the zombies were killed," Redmond added.

"Fire," Paris replied simply. "My friend magically set them on fire. They were easy enough to take down after that."

"You have a friend who can set magical fires?" Redmond looked impressed. "Is she single?"

The mirth in Braden's eyes at the question was enough to have me send him a pointed look. He instantly turned serious.

"Stop being an idiot, Redmond," he chastised. "We have dead people to deal with. It's time to get serious."

Redmond didn't bother to hide his eye roll. "Whatever."

For her part, Paris looked caught, as if she would rather be anywhere else. That surprised me. Finally, when she spoke, it was with gravitas. "Listen, I know what's in my file," she started. "I'm well aware I have two files, in fact. One is very basic and the other, the secret one, goes into greater detail regarding my past."

I was taken aback. "Wait ... you have two files?"

She nodded without hesitation. "I've lived a very colorful life. I told you that."

Actually, she'd avoided questions when I asked. Her non-answers, however, were enough to fill in some of the blanks. "You were there when Covenant College was razed, weren't you?"

"Kind of," she hedged, clearly uncomfortable. "I wasn't lying when I told you I didn't know how that happened. That is the truth. We didn't do that. We were there for the run-up to those events, but ... that was something else."

"What?" Redmond was awed.

"A lesser god," Paris replied. "And, before you ask, I have no idea how to find him. He shows up occasionally because he's interested in my friend."

"And who is this friend?" Cormack prodded.

Paris stubbornly jutted out her chin and folded her arms over her chest. "That's none of your concern. It doesn't matter. She has nothing to do with this."

"I'm not saying she does." Cormack appeared calm, but I could feel the agitation wafting off him. "I'm curious as to whether she'll be able to help us with this. By your own admission, you've only researched revenants. We need someone who has dealt with them before."

"And that is not my friend." Paris was firm enough that I believed her. "She's dealt with a lot — sometimes with me and other times on her own — but she can't help us with this."

"And you don't want to call her in," Braden surmised.

"Not really," she admitted, rueful. "They've been through enough. It's been a quiet year and a half — at least for the most part — and they deserve a break. I'm not going to call them in unless there's a reason ... and we're most certainly not there yet."

I had so many questions. This friend that she talked about in quiet and reverent tones had to be powerfully magical. I wanted to meet her, pick her brain, and maybe even compare notes. That clearly wasn't going to happen until Paris felt more comfortable with us. She wasn't going to betray her friend. Quite frankly, I would never ask her to do so. It was unfair. We had to focus on our own problems.

"Here's what we're dealing with." I told her everything, not omitting a single detail. When I was finished, Paris's face was lit with intrigue. "Well, that's ... interesting." She pursed her lips. "It certainly sounds like revenants from all I've read. The thing is, they're not all that common on this continent. They're a Western Europe thing."

"Well, they're here now," Cormack responded. "We have to deal with them. Does anyone have any suggestions?"

"It sounds to me as if Izzy managed to eradicate one already." Paris, ever the pragmatic sort, never changed her inflection. She attacked the problem from a clinical perspective that I admired. "If she took out one, she can take out the others. In fact, if we work as a group we should be able to handle the problem without losing a single soldier."

"We have to find them," Redmond pointed out. "Do you have any suggestions as to how we do that?"

She instantly started nodding, taking me by surprise. I was hopeful. "You do?"

"They wanted to go home," she reminded me. "That's all they wanted. I have no idea why Ray Smith returned to Belle Isle. The gate might be calling to them, although that seems unlikely.

"Listen, they were obviously sent here for a reason," she continued. "This wasn't a naturally-occurring event. Someone set a plan in motion. We don't know who. I'm not even sure it's important to know who at this point. We simply need to find the other men and either capture or eliminate the revenants. I mean ... it would probably be beneficial if we can catch one of them alive, but the most important thing is getting them off the streets.

"There are people out at Belle Isle right now," she said. "If the revenants show up there, we'll hear about it. We need to hit other locations. The most obvious are the homes of our missing men. It might be a natural instinct for them to return there even if they've become monsters."

"What if they're not there?" Cormack challenged. "This could be a waste of time."

"It could be," Paris agreed. "The thing is, we don't know where else to look anyway. We might as well start there."

"We need addresses," Redmond said. "They shouldn't be too hard to track down."

"We need multiple addresses," Paris corrected. "We need the addresses of the homes these men lived in at the time they disappeared and the addresses of where their loved ones live now. They could be at any of those locations."

"That's going to be a lot of locations," Cormack muttered, paling slightly. "I didn't think about that, but you're right. It makes a lot of sense."

"We need those addresses and you're going to need more teams. I don't think we can wait to start checking."

"No." Cormack was resolute. "We'll start now. I'll give you three addresses and you can head out. I'll keep in contact if I have updates."

I smiled but it was only a reflex. "That sounds like a plan."

"TELL ME ABOUT YOURSELF."

Redmond didn't argue when Braden directed him to sit in the back seat of his truck with Paris. In fact, he seemed eager to get her in a confined space, and he immediately started peppering her with questions as we headed toward one of the older Detroit neighborhoods.

Instead of being put out or annoyed, Paris looked amused. "You really are wasting your time," she offered. "I'm married — happily so — and I'm quite a bit older than you."

"That's okay." Redmond's smile was wide and impish. "I love older women. I think they're great." He made a weird cat sound and batted his hand. "You have no idea how fond I am of cougars."

"Oh, geez," Braden muttered under his breath as he navigated onto a narrow street. "Leave her alone. She's not interested in you. She has a baby."

"I like babies."

"She also has a husband," I added.

"And a friend who can shrivel your junk until it looks like raisins," Braden supplied. "I mean ... if this woman can conjure fire out of nowhere to burn zombies to a crisp, she can handle you without a problem."

"Geez." Redmond made a face. "You guys are absolutely no fun. Why can't you just chill out? All I'm trying to do is get to know her better. I'm really not going to hit on her."

"He's fine," Paris agreed. "He's not offending me or anything. In fact, I'm flattered. As for my husband, he has nothing to worry about. I'm completely in love with him and Alvis."

"Alvis?" Redmond's forehead wrinkled. "Is that your husband's name?"

"No. That's my son."

"As in 'Alvis has left the building'?"

Paris let loose a defeated groan. "Ugh. I really should've listened when people told me not to use that name. I had no idea it would turn into this."

I laughed despite the serious situation. "He'll be fine. You can call him Al and he'll charm women left and right."

"He's a bit away from that ... at least I hope."

"And what about your friend?" Redmond clearly wasn't letting it go. "Is she single?"

"No. She's most definitely married — has been with the same guy since we were in college — and she has a daughter. If my friend doesn't kill you and her husband somehow misses — which is unlikely — I know a certain teenager who will make you wish you'd listened to your brother about the raisin comment."

A picture, unbidden, pushed itself to the front of my brain. I thought about the dark-haired girl who kept calling Paris. It made sense. There was power emanating from that girl even though she was miles away. If I could feel her from this distance, she had to be something special.

Still, it was none of my business.

"What other things have you fought?" I asked. It seemed a safe enough topic. "You mentioned zombies, and I know you're familiar with vampires."

"I'm familiar with a lot of things. Sphinxes, evil witches, ghosts."

"Gods," Redmond added. "I'm dying to know how you met a god."

"Not me. My friend."

"You never met him? How do you know she wasn't lying about meeting him?"

"Technically I did meet him. I didn't talk to him much. He was much more interested in my friend ... and her family."

"But what sort of god?"

"Does it matter?"

"I'm simply curious. What was his name? That's all I want to know."

A small smile played at the corners of Paris's lips. "Bob. His name was Bob."

"A god named Bob?" Redmond was obviously dubious, as was I. "That doesn't sound right."

"It's not. That wasn't his real name. My friend couldn't pronounce his real name and she didn't take the time to try to learn to. She renamed him Bob and it kind of stuck."

"She re-named a god?" Redmond's eyes lighted with delight. "Okay. I definitely have to meet this woman. I don't care if she's married. She's clearly my soul mate."

"Oh, her soul is already joined with another." Paris's smile was whimsical. "I'm sure you're charming, but there's nothing you can do to entice her. Sometimes souls join once and never separate. That's what happened to her."

There was something poetic about the statement. I was stirred enough to glance at Braden and wasn't surprised to find him watching me with contemplative eyes.

"This is the address," Paris noted, leaning forward and turning to the business at hand. "This is Doug Dunning's house. I guess we'll find out soon enough if our idea holds water."

She was right. It was time to get serious. Talk of her magical friend could wait.

"WELL, THIS DOESN'T LOOK GOOD."

When no one answered the door, we decided to let ourselves into the Dunning house. It was a risk, but Braden and Redmond seemed up for it, both of them whipping out lock-picking tools as if this wasn't the first time they'd attempted something of this sort. Instead of pointing out I could use my magic to open the door, I decided to let them compete — because it was clearly what they wanted to do — and five minutes later we were inside. Luckily, nobody saw us.

The scene that greeted us in the living room was enough to chill me to the bone. I was in complete agreement with Redmond for once. "It definitely doesn't look good." I rubbed my cheek and stared at the overturned coffee table. There were items strewn about the room, huge holes in the couch where stuffing spilled out. Something very bad had clearly happened here.

"There are no bodies," Paris noted. She was all business. "There's a little blood in this corner, but no bodies."

I shuffled closer to check for myself and grimaced. "That's not enough to kill someone but it is enough to worry me. That didn't come from a small wound."

"No," Braden agreed, sliding around me to look closer at the stain on the floor. "Paris is right. There are no bodies. We have to treat that as a good sign."

"Unless the revenants eat bodies, like cannibals," Redmond countered, earning a stern glare from his brother. "What? I was just thinking out loud."

"Well, stop doing that!"

"I agree," I supplied, moving to the kitchen. The room was equally disturbed. "I don't want to think about the bodies being eaten. I'm choosing to believe there was an attack and somehow the family members managed to fight off the creature. Maybe they're at the hospital or something."

"That's possible," Braden agreed. "I'll call Griffin to see if he's heard anything."

"Don't do that." Redmond shook his head. "He'll melt down if he thinks Aisling is out in this."

I could see that. "She's not out in this," I reminded him. "She's fine."

"Besides, he has to get over that," Braden added. "He knew what Aisling was when he fell in love with her. It's not as if that's suddenly going to change."

"I bet he was hopeful that would change when she got pregnant," Redmond countered. "He's not the Neanderthal type, but if she chose to change her career he wouldn't offer up a word of argument."

"She won't do that ... and he knows it," I offered. "He loves her for what she is. He didn't marry her with the expectation of changing her.

They're fine." I meant it. My eyes were plaintive when they locked with Braden's somber face. "You need to call him. Then we need to search this house from top to bottom before heading to the next on our list. We have to keep looking. If they're all like this ... ." I couldn't finish the statement.

"We don't know that anyone died here," Braden reminded me as he dug in his pocket for his phone. "We shouldn't get ahead of ourselves. It won't do anyone any good."

He was right. Still, I couldn't shake the growing fear that clung to me like a shadow on a sunny day. "We can't stay here. We have to keep moving. Put Griffin on the hospitals. There's a chance, if we move fast enough, that we can stop one of these attacks before it happens."

That's all I could think about now.

"Okay." Braden was sympathetic as he squeezed my shoulder. We both knew what it was like to deal with decimated families. Neither of us wanted that. "I'll make the call. You guys conduct the search. We'll hit every address until we're certain."

He was trying, but the words didn't make me feel better. I couldn't escape the feeling that we were already too late.

Far, far too late.

Fifteen

W e checked every house. We went into every bedroom, bathroom and closet in those houses. They were all empty.

Some of the houses were messy, like the first. Others were desolate and quiet, not a thing out of place. Those houses were even more disturbing for some reason.

"My father is assigning reapers to watch all the houses in case someone comes back," Braden offered as we parked in front of Grimlock Manor later that evening. We'd separated at reaper headquarters, Redmond returning to work and Paris gathering her son before they joined us for dinner.

"That's good," I offered. "Maybe we'll luck out and one of them will come back."

"But you don't think that's going to happen, do you?"

I shook my head. "I think they're either dead or ... something else has happened to them."

"Like what?"

That was the question. "I don't know. I want to talk to Cillian, maybe attack that library your father has upstairs after dinner. There must be something in there about revenants."

Braden was quiet, so I shifted my eyes to him and almost laughed at his downtrodden expression.

"What?"

"That just doesn't sound like the sort of evening I had in mind," he said.

"Oh, yeah?" It had been a long and terrible day, and yet I was feeling playful. "What did you have in mind?"

"Well, I thought we would steal some extra cupcakes from Aisling's cake bar and have them in the big tub for starters. There's nothing better than bubbles ... cupcakes ... and you."

It was a sweet sentiment. "Maybe we can do one hour in the library and then do the cupcake and bath thing after," I suggested.

"Oh, are we compromising?"

"Maybe."

"Then I agree to your terms." He leaned over and planted a kiss on me before resting his forehead against mine. He looked as exhausted as I felt. We all hoped we would be able to find some survivors. With each house we hit, with each empty room, those hopes faded. Now we were all numb.

"I'm kind of excited for Paris to see your house," I said, pulling back to stare into his eyes. "She'll enjoy it ... and I want to meet her son."

"Alvis?" Braden's lips quirked. "I like kids. I'm sure Alvis will fit right in. As for Paris, I find her interesting."

I narrowed my eyes. "Like your brother finds her interesting?"

He chuckled. "No. I only find you interesting that way." He poked my side, causing me to squirm. "I'm more intrigued about this magical friend of hers. If she was involved in that whole Covenant College thing ... well ... they say there were some mighty powerful forces involved in the razing of that school."

He might have better information than me, I thought. He was closer to the action. I'd researched the downfall of the college, but information was difficult to come by. Maybe he knew more than I did.

"What did you hear?"

He tucked a strand of hair behind my ear and leaned back in his seat. "There were a lot of rumors. I mean ... a lot. Some people believe what happened at the college was because of aliens."

It took everything I had not to roll my eyes. "We both know that's not true."

"No, but that doesn't mean the paranormal ideas were any easier to swallow. For starters, there are a lot of people who believe witches hypnotized farmers to yank down the buildings and then plant grass over them. There are others who believe the buildings were sucked into the ground, like a hellmouth opened up or something."

"What do you believe?"

He worked his jaw. "I don't know," he said finally. "Paris's assertion that a god was involved makes a lot of sense. I saw the photos. One day the college looked like a normal campus. There were buildings ... and students ... and tons of frat parties where you just know nubile young women had been partying in skimpy clothes two days before."

I flicked his ear. "Keep on track."

His grin was charming and made me feel as if I was the only one in the world for which it was intended. He had a way of making me go warm all over, and this was one of those times.

He sobered after a moment. "The photos of what happened that following day were ... I don't know how to describe them. All the buildings were gone. It wasn't like a natural disaster. There weren't shells of buildings left behind ... or broken glass on the ground ... or even abandoned parking lots. The entire space was covered with rolling hills, trees and even an endangered bird habitat."

I tilted my head, considering. "An endangered bird habitat? How does that happen?"

"I have no idea. I don't remember the name of the bird they found. I only know it was endangered, which meant they couldn't have re-built the school even if they wanted to. There are federal protections in place over the bird."

Oddly, that made sense. "That had to be the god. I wish I knew which one it was."

"Do you know all of them?"

"I've researched a few. I don't know that anyone knows all of them." I rubbed my palms over my jeans as I considered our quandary.

"I don't really blame Paris for not trusting us with her friend's secret. She hasn't exactly seen us at our best and ... well ... she's loyal. I hope she'll trust us enough to introduce her friend at some point."

"I don't know. Her friend sounds scary."

I laughed at his serious expression. "People might say the same about your sister."

"And they would be right." He slid his arm around my neck and tugged me close enough that we stared into each other's eyes. "I almost wish we hadn't invited Paris for dinner. Then we could raid the kitchen, steal all Aisling's cupcakes and hide in my bedroom all night. That sounds better than putting up with my family for five hours."

"It won't be five hours."

"It will feel like five hours."

He wasn't wrong about that. "We'll survive."

"Yeah." He gave me another kiss. "Besides, there's nothing better than cupcakes."

"Your dad is going to do a beignet bar for me one day. Those are better than cupcakes."

"Oh, you're cute." He tapped the end of my nose. "Beignets are good, but cupcakes are better."

That sounded like a challenge. "I guess I'll have to cook beignets for you."

His eyes sparked. "I could live with that."

I wasn't the domestic sort, but I could live with it, too. "I guess we have a plan for whenever this is over."

He was serious again as he smoothed my hair. "We do. As for all of this ... we'll figure it out."

"How can you be sure?"

"I don't see that we have a choice."

PARIS WAS DELIGHTED FROM THE second she walked through the front door. She couldn't stop exclaiming over the fancy tile, ornate crown moldings and the out-of-control decorations that practically screamed the Grimlocks were a family with endless money at their disposal.

"This place is amazing," Paris enthused as I led her toward the drink cart.

Alvis wasn't what I expected. He was blond, had huge cheeks and bright blue eyes. He looked nothing like his mother.

"Hello." Redmond, who was sitting on the floor in front of Lily's carrier, abandoned her and switched his attention to the toddler. "You must be Alvis."

The boy wasn't exactly shy, but his eyes were full of suspicion when they landed on Redmond. "No," he announced, extending a finger in Redmond's direction. His reaction was enough to have everyone laughing.

"He figured you out, Redmond," Aisling offered. She looked to be in a good mood, her skin practically glowing, and I couldn't help but wonder if she'd done something to her father's car. She always looked her best when she got to torture one of her male relatives.

"Don't listen to her," Redmond said to Alvis. "She doesn't know what she's talking about. I happen to be tons of fun."

Alvis narrowed his eyes. "No," he repeated.

Paris looked embarrassed by her son's reaction. "I'm sorry. That's his favorite word. He only knows ten of them and that's the one he lets loose the most."

"Don't worry." Aisling smiled kindly at the boy as she planted herself on the settee. "I expect Lily will be the same way when she starts talking."

"I expect Lily's favorite word is going to be 'mine,'" Cormack countered, grinning at the little boy as Alvis's gaze switched to him. "Hey, buddy. If you come over here, I have some licorice."

Braden made an exaggerated face. "That's the offer of perverts the world over, Dad. You can't say things like that."

Cormack balked. "I didn't mean ... ." He trailed off. "Huh. Now that you mention it, that probably wasn't the right thing to say."

"Oh, you think?"

Cormack made a big show of ignoring Braden and focusing on Alvis. "Sorry about that, buddy. You're a cute little thing, huh?"

"He doesn't look like you," Redmond announced. He almost looked disappointed. "Is that what your husband looks like?"

"Not that much." Paris was rueful. "I was blond when I was a kid. I'm guessing his hair will darken as he ages."

"I think he's cute as a blond." Aisling smiled at the boy, who had been glued to his mother's side until he finally focused on her. Then, out of nowhere, he took a step in her direction. The smile he graced her with was adorable.

"Oh, he likes you." Paris beamed at her son as she watched him toddle toward Aisling. "It usually takes him an hour or so to warm up to new people, but he already likes you."

If Aisling was surprised, she didn't show it. Instead, she waited for him to get close and then hoisted him up on the settee so he could get comfortable next to her. "Just wait for the cupcake bar," she enthused. "You'll get so sugared up people will mistake you for a Tasmanian devil."

"Not everyone thinks that's a good thing, Aisling," Cormack noted.

"It's fine." Paris waved off the comment and turned her full attention to Lily. "This must be your baby." She smiled at Aisling before kneeling next to the infant. "I guess those Grimlock genes are too strong to be overruled, huh?"

Cormack chuckled. "They're fairly strong. Aisling was a cute baby, and Lily looks just like her."

"Wrong." Braden appeared on my left and handed me a drink. "Lily looks like me. I'm the handsomest and she's the prettiest, so it only makes sense that she's taking after me."

Cillian and Redmond snorted in unison.

"Please." Redmond rolled his eyes. "If she looks like anyone, she looks like me."

"She definitely doesn't look like me," Griffin offered as he strolled into the room and headed straight for his wife.

"That won't hold up in court," Aisling teased as she accepted his kiss.

"I guess I'll have to keep both of you then." Griffin shifted his eyes to Alvis and smirked as the toddler openly stared at his wife. "Who is this?"

"Paris's son," Braden volunteered. "She's Izzy's new co-worker."

"Ah." Griffin grinned and nodded at Paris before focusing on Alvis, who was completely enamored with Aisling. "It looks as if I have some competition for your affections, baby."

"Usually I would say you have nothing to worry about, but he's pretty cute." Aisling smiled at him before sobering. "What about you guys? Did you find anything?"

I shook my head. "Every house was empty. Some of them looked as if a fight had gone down inside. Others ... they were quiet and abandoned."

"We don't know that anything happened to anyone yet," Cormack cautioned. "It's possible the mess you saw is because one of the returnees melted down when he couldn't find what he was looking for."

That was a nice thought, but I didn't believe it for a second. "We found blood in one of the houses."

"Yes, but not enough to suggest that whoever was inside is dead. We can't jump to conclusions."

"No, but we'd better come up with feasible hunches," Aisling argued. "We need to be sure that these revenants aren't somehow infecting people. This could be the zombies all over again. We don't want to take on an army of the undead."

Cormack rolled his eyes and rubbed his forehead. "Here we go."

Aisling ignored the sarcasm. "I don't want to remind you of the obvious, but I was the only one who believed in the zombies, and things were pretty much out of control before you guys finally came around to my way of thinking. We don't want that to happen again."

"But you don't want to remind us of the obvious," Redmond drawled, amused. "We've already told you that we're sorry, Ais. You're intellectually superior to us in every way."

"We should've believed in the zombies," Braden said. "Can you please forgive us?"

The little show made me laugh. I knew it would be even worse if Cillian and Aidan were present. Speaking of them, ... "Where is everybody else?"

"Jerry and Aidan had tuxedo fittings," Cormack volunteered. "They're coming, but won't be here for dinner. I've been instructed by Aidan to make sure I save him at least five cupcakes. Jerry insists they're both on diets to make sure they fit into their tuxes for the big day, but Aidan promised death if he missed the cupcakes, so ... ."

"So you'll save cupcakes for him," I surmised.

"I already set some aside in the kitchen. Aidan's favorite color is blue, and there was a peach one with rainbow waves or something on it that I know Jerry will love. I also put another ten in a safe place so they both have plenty to choose from when they arrive."

And there it was again. He was more than father of the year. He was father of the millennium. He doted on each child in a specific way. He would know that Aidan was feeling smothered by wedding plans and want to soothe those frazzled nerves as much as possible. Sure, Cormack's idea of soothing was food — which I wasn't a fan of endorsing — but he did his very best by each child. I couldn't help but marvel at how he always managed to carry it off.

"What's a cupcake bar?" Paris asked.

"Oh, you're in for a treat," Aisling enthused as she poked Alvis's stomach, causing him to giggle. "It's basically a mountain of cupcakes in every color. And there are so many things to put on the cupcakes you won't be able to stop with just one."

"Cake!" Alvis clapped his hands, causing everyone to laugh.

"It looks like he learned a new word," Redmond noted.

Paris smiled fondly at her son. "He'll probably be bouncing off the walls when it's time to go to bed tonight, but one sugar buzz won't hurt him."

She had a rude awakening in her future if she thought it would be just the one sugar buzz, but I kept that to myself.

THE CUPCAKE BAR WAS INDEED a big hit. Cormack asked about Paris's husband — his name was Heath and he was on the west side of the state closing up their old home because they'd sold it and would be closing in a few days. Paris was clearly in love with the father of her child. Redmond feigned bitter disappointment for a bit, but ultimately let it go.

After four cupcakes, I was feeling stuffed and moved outside to get some air. I opted for the backyard. It had been a mess of late because a professional landscaper was putting in a lily garden — not for the baby, but for the mother they'd lost — but it was finally open again.

The air was pungent with the smell of flowers and I smiled when I saw the huge batches of multi-colored lilies. Each child had selected a different color to memorialize their mother. Cormack also added one. Aisling and Griffin even picked a special lily to plant in their daughter's honor. The garden was massive ... and unbelievably beautiful. It took my breath away.

I walked to the closest section and leaned over to study the blooms. Because the Grimlocks did nothing small, Cormack went all out when it came time to order flowers to make sure they had the best stock money could buy. He'd spared no expense ... and it had been worth it.

I loved my parents. I didn't remember them as much as I would've liked, but I still loved them. My loss was different from the Grimlocks' loss. The children were all older when Lily "died" in the fire. The second time they lost her was almost more painful. The garden was a way to put that pain to good use.

I was just about to head back inside and gather Braden for our research session when the overhead sky lit with lightning. Storms weren't in the forecast and it was too early in the season for heat lightning.

So, where had this come from?

I watched again as the lightning flashed. It was close — right on the other side of the garden close — and the hair on my arms stood on end as I took a step back toward the house. The storm had seemingly come out of nowhere and felt dangerous. Being outside to bear witness to it was probably a bad idea.

I stepped under the protective overhang a few seconds before the rain started. It was heavy, sounded and smelled normal, and yet I remained unnerved.

Another flash of lightning had me staring at the far end of the garden. It was longer than it was wide, each Grimlock's addition to the garden being showcased in a different area. Another flash caused my heart to jump.

I told myself it was a normal storm, yet I had trouble believing it. Where was the thunder? Why had it come out of nowhere?

I watched it for a long time. Nothing happened. It didn't abate. I finally went inside. Even once safe from the elements, though, I couldn't shake my unease.

Something didn't feel right. Things were going to get worse before they got better. I don't know how I knew that, but it felt like an inescapable fact.

The ride was about to get rough.

Sixteen

I woke before Braden, which wasn't unusual. He was a heavy sleeper. I could've poked him until he opened his eyes — he wouldn't have minded — but instead I got up. I was restless.

Instead of hanging around the room and risking disturbing him, I headed out. Grimlock Manor was so massive it had various wings. Braden was in a wing with Redmond, which seemed unnecessary because they were the only two still living in the house with their father, but they were tight and I got the feeling they were creatures of habit. They liked being around one another.

I headed for Aisling's wing of the house. Technically it belonged to her and Aidan, and they both had their own places. Aisling and Griffin essentially spent half their nights under Cormack's roof these days — with his full blessing — because of the baby. Aisling was worried she thought like a man and that would make her a poor mother. That was on top of the fear that rooted in her heart when an abomination with her mother's face came back and tried to kill her.

In truth, Aisling was nothing like that woman. Everyone saw it but her. She claimed she was over it, but occasionally a furtive fear took hold and she couldn't shake it. I had no doubt she would settle eventually. Until then, she wanted her father and brothers close ... and they were more than happy to oblige.

I heard a voice in the hallway, causing me to slow my pace. It was early and the Grimlocks liked to sleep in until at least seven o'clock. I couldn't help but wonder what would have them up so early. Then I realized the voice was coming from the nursery.

I stopped in the door and poked my head in, grinning when I saw Griffin with the baby. He had her on the changing table, was clearly unaware that I was present, and was having a conversation with her.

"You couldn't have waited thirty minutes before you started shrieking, huh?" He didn't sound upset. "You get that from your mother. Thirty more minutes and everybody would've been happy. You're too demanding to let that happen, though."

The baby gurgled as he coated her with more powder than was probably necessary.

"I just know you're going to turn all my hair gray before you're five," he continued, oblivious to the fact that he had an audience. "I bet your grandfather had a full head of dark hair before your mother came along. That's what he says anyway."

I left them to their father-and-daughter bonding and continued down the hall until I heard additional voices. These came from Aisling's room, which gave me pause. If Griffin was in with the baby, who was she talking to?

"I don't see why he's being such a pain. There's nothing wrong with peach-colored tuxes." Jerry had one of those voices that is not only distinctive but carries. He'd clearly taken advantage of Griffin's absence from the bedroom to bend Aisling's ear about his upcoming wedding.

"I think peach tuxes are a great idea," Aisling enthused. "You look great in peach."

"Right? Although, let's be honest. There's no color I can't carry off."

"Avocado green."

"Oh, I wore pants that color once and I don't think I looked nearly as bad as you pretend."

"You looked like something that had been thrown up."

I felt guilty eavesdropping, but there was no way I could move past

Aisling's room without her seeing me. Instead, I decided to suck it up and at least offer them a morning greeting. Aisling didn't appear surprised when I poked my head in.

"Good morning."

She smiled brightly. Her hair was a mess, sticking up in a variety of directions, and she was dressed in an oversized T-shirt. "Morning. What are you doing up so early?"

"I couldn't sleep." I shuffled into the room because it seemed to be expected. "I saw Griffin with the baby. He's dousing her in powder."

"Yeah, he goes overboard." Aisling snickered evilly. "He thinks if he puts enough powder on her she won't smell like crap. He thinks she should always have that new baby smell. I warned him things are going to get worse before they get better and that he's wasting powder, but he doesn't care."

She wasn't worried, so I figured it wasn't my place to lodge my opinion. A little extra powder never hurt anybody. "What are you guys doing?" I eyed the open magazine on Aisling's lap. "Are you talking about wedding stuff?"

"We are," Jerry confirmed, patting the bed. "Come join us. If you agree on the peach tuxes, I think Aidan will have no choice but to give in."

I acquiesced out of sheer curiosity, and when I got comfortable next to Aisling and she tapped the page so I would know exactly what they were looking at, it took a great deal of effort to hide my horror.

"Oh, well, those are ... distinct."

Aisling wriggled her eyebrows, letting me know that she was in agreement. That begged the question of why she was encouraging Jerry to bully Aidan into what could only be described as pastel nightmare formal wear.

"They're awesome." Jerry's gaze was on the catalog, so he missed our exchange. "I look good in peach. Tell her I look good in peach, Bug."

Jerry was the only one who could get away with saddling Aisling with a nickname like "Bug." I'd heard the story of when they were kids and she tried to save ants from her brothers and a magnifying glass — and I was still confused how the nickname came into being

— but their friendship was so warm and hilarious that it somehow fit.

"He looks awesome in peach," Aisling said automatically. "That should be his official color."

"Oh, don't be ridiculous." Jerry made a face. "You know that powder blue is my official color. But that's too ridiculous for a wedding. It will make everyone think of Easter ... and I don't want people hunting for eggs when they should be admiring me."

"That's a very good point," Aisling agreed. "Send Aidan in here and I'll tell him the peach tuxes are a good idea. Go get him now."

Apparently eager to get his way, Jerry was on his feet in two seconds. "We'll be right back."

I watched him go, curious, and then turned to Aisling. "You don't really like that tuxedo, do you?"

She squinched her face up into a hilarious expression. "Of course not. They're godawful. I like messing with Aidan, though."

Ah. I should've realized that was what she was doing. I assumed she was simply telling Jerry what he wanted to hear. "Aidan should have a say in what he wears for his own wedding," I offered. I wasn't sure why I felt the need to stick up for him, but he was often overpowered by Aisling and Jerry, so I felt he needed the backup.

"Oh, you don't have to worry about Aidan," she reassured me. "He won't wear a peach tux no matter what. It will cause a big fight ... which will be funny. I'm always in the mood for watching other people fight."

I could see that. I was about to ask her how often Jerry and Aidan fought — I'd witnessed a handful of loud arguments and I wasn't sure if they were normal or simply wedding-related — when Jerry returned. He almost looked giddy when he hopped on the bed.

Several seconds later, Aidan strolled in, looking anything but happy.

"I don't even want to know what you guys are plotting so early in the morning," he groused, dragging a hand through his onyx hair. "I knew spending the night here was a bad idea."

"You shouldn't have eaten so much sugar," Jerry said pragmatically. "You crashed hard and I was too drunk to drive. It's really on you."

"Yes, it's all my fault." Aidan offered me a half wave and then focused on his twin. "Jerry says you have something important to tell me and it's going to change our lives. I have a feeling it's going to tick me off more than anything else, but lay it on me."

Aisling was a master at manipulating her brothers. She kept her expression neutral so as not to tip her hand. "Jerry and I have been talking about the wedding and I happen to agree with him on a few things."

Before she could add to the statement, Aidan extended a warning finger. "I don't want to hear the word 'peach' come out of your mouth. I'm warning you now that I will melt down if you try to talk me into those tuxes."

He sounded serious, but Aisling wasn't deterred.

"You know how good Jerry looks in peach," she started. "How can you deny him the chance to be the handsomest groom who ever lived? I mean ... look how pretty he is." Aisling grabbed her best friend's chin and held it in such a manner that Aidan could look nowhere else. "You'll ruin his life if you don't reach for the peach rung of perfection."

"Oh, shut up." Aidan rolled his eyes. "You're just doing this to see if you can get a rise out of me. You're not even good at pretending you're serious. Jerry, she's playing you. She thinks the peach tuxes are ugly."

Jerry turned huffy. "She does not! She knows I look good in peach. Why are you trying to ruin my wedding?"

"It's my wedding, too, and I'm not wearing peach."

I knew inserting myself into the conversation was a risk, but I couldn't stop myself. "Why not let Aidan wear the colors he wants and Jerry wear the colors he wants? I'm assuming Aisling is standing up for Jerry because of the way the family dynamics shake out. She can get a peach dress to match his tux and then all the others can wear dark tuxes to match Aidan. It will probably look nice with the contrast of colors."

If looks could kill I'd be dead from the glare Aisling shot me. It was clear she had no intention of wearing peach.

"That's a fabulous idea," Aidan agreed. "In fact ... I can't believe we didn't think of it before. Jerry, it makes sense that you and I would have different color tuxes. Aisling will look great in peach."

"Wait a second ... ." Aisling shifted and I was certain she was about to change tack. Whatever was about to happen was bound to be hilarious. I never got a chance to see it play out, though, because Griffin chose that moment to return, and he looked harried.

"Everyone needs to get down to the backyard," he announced. His tone was no-nonsense. "Something has happened."

I furrowed my brow. "In the backyard?"

He nodded, his gaze immediately going to his wife. "It's not good."

NO ONE BOTHERED GETTING dressed. Instead, we raced down the stairs and through the house as a group. By the time we made it to the back patio, the others were already there. Even Cillian and Maya had spent the night because the scholarly Grimlock was up late researching revenants. The look of horror on each of their faces was enough to cause my heart to constrict.

"What happened?"

Braden swiveled when he heard my voice. There was palpable relief on his features. "I thought something might've happened to you when I woke and found you were gone. Are you okay?"

I was understandably confused. "I'm fine. I didn't want to wake you. I ended up with your sister and watched her torture Aidan."

"Just as long as you're okay." He gave me a quick hug and I could feel the defeat weighing him down.

"I don't understand." Slowly I turned to look over the backyard and my chest tightened when I saw the reason for the hoopla.

The lily garden was gone. The extravagant memorial they'd all worked so hard to build had been destroyed in the night. It wasn't just destroyed, though. It was burned. All the pretty blooms were melted, the stalks blackened and the cultivated earth between the rows had been burnt black.

"What happened here?" I was breathless as I stepped forward, rage rearing up and grabbing me by the throat. I didn't know Lily Grimlock. I'd never met her. I knew her children, though, and the grief they felt was so real it almost swallowed them whole. The garden had been a catharsis for them, a healing, and now it was destroyed.

"We don't know," Cillian replied, his voice raspy. "We were just alerted by the butler that something had happened. As far as we can tell, no one heard anything."

I thought about the lightning from the previous evening. "Maybe it was the storm."

Cormack slid me a curious look. "What storm?"

I was taken aback. "It stormed last night."

Cormack glanced at each of his children in turn. "I didn't hear a storm last night. Did anyone else?" When everyone shook their heads, he turned back to me. "Did you hear a storm?"

"I didn't hear it. I saw it. I was out here for a few minutes after all the cupcakes. I needed some fresh air. There was a lot of lightning."

"But no thunder?" Cillian queried.

"No thunder." That had stood out to me, too, but I'd discarded it. "I thought it was just one of those freak storms that pop up."

"Obviously not." Cormack moved his hand to Braden's shoulder. "It's okay. I'll order the lilies again and we'll get someone out here to fix this."

Braden didn't say anything, but I felt his despair. In an effort to offer comfort, I moved to his side and linked my fingers with his. "I know a lot about plants," I offered. "There might be a way for us to save these. I'll call my grandfather. He knows quite a few root spells. There's a chance we can fix this."

Braden's eyes were stormy when he turned them to me. "It won't be the same."

"Nonsense," Cormack chided. "They're flowers. They can be replaced. Izzy is correct. Flowers are resilient. I'll get the gardener out here this afternoon."

"I would wait," I countered, focusing on the closest plants. They looked sick. "I'm not sure what happened, but I think we should wait just in case."

"Do you think this has something to do with the revenants?" Aisling asked. She had Lily in her arms and looked worried.

"It's possible," I replied. "We don't know enough about them to say definitively. We need to hit the research hard today. I'm needed back at the gate, but a lot of books were delivered to the new library the other day. I'll start with those."

"And I'll head back to the main library," Cillian offered. "Izzy is right. We should probably wait to fix the garden until we're absolutely sure the revenants aren't to blame. We don't want to put much effort into it if it's going to happen again because the revenants are still here."

"Fine." Braden's voice was tight. "What should the rest of us do?"

"Look for the revenants," Cormack replied. "The home office is sending out reaper replacements to pick up our charges today. The rest of us — with the exception of Aisling — will be out in the field looking for clues. I don't know what else to do."

Aisling stirred. "Why am I the exception?"

Cormack inclined his head toward the baby she clutched against her chest. "You know why. Also, I think it's best if everybody spends the night here until we're absolutely sure this threat is eradicated. We're stronger together."

What he didn't say is that he wanted to make absolutely certain there were plenty of bodies around to protect Lily. He didn't want his children separated in a crisis, and he was willing to put his foot down to make sure he got his way.

Aisling looked as if she was about to mount an argument, but it died on her lips when Griffin slipped out the back door to join us. If possible, he looked even more upset than he had mere minutes before.

"Do I even want to know what bad news you're going to drop on us?" Aisling asked, resigned.

"Probably not, but you have to hear it." Griffin slid his arm around his wife, as if offering her solace before the storm. "I just got a call from the precinct. They have a homicide for me. It's the neighbor who owns one of the houses you guys searched yesterday. I know because I jotted down all those addresses in case something popped."

"A neighbor?" Cormack's eyebrows flew up his forehead. "Across the street or directly next door?"

"Next door."

"How long has he been dead?" I asked, my mind working overtime. "I mean ... was he dead when we were there yesterday?"

"He's been dead at least sixteen hours, so I think odds are good. I have to head there now. I'll know more when I get on the scene."

"It has to be the revenants," Redmond offered. "It's too much of a coincidence otherwise."

"It's definitely the revenants." Cormack's expression promised retribution. "Whatever this is, whatever the plan, it's starting to kick into overdrive now. We need to figure this out ... and fast."

"We'll get dressed and head out," Braden offered, "We'll start searching. The problem is, we have no idea where to look."

"Aisling isn't going out, is she?" The question was out of Griffin's mouth before he thought better of it, and he cringed when his wife shot him a death glare. "I just mean ... someone has to watch Lily."

"Aisling will be with me," Cormack promised. "I can't guarantee to keep her in the house all day because ... well, you know how she is. She won't be alone, though, and I'll have guards with us to watch her and the baby."

"Now wait just a minute." Aisling was livid. "I'm not some special case and I absolutely refuse to be treated differently."

"You are a special case," Cormack countered. "We're not going to argue about this. It's done. You're with me and the rest of you are in teams. I want to be informed the second you find anything. We need to track these creatures — whether they're revenants or something else — as soon as possible. We can't afford to wait."

That was the one thing everyone could agree on.

Seventeen

Braden put on a brave face, but I could tell the destruction of the garden bothered him. All the Grimlock children loved their mother — and in some respects Aisling was the one sporting the biggest open wound — but Braden carried the most weight where she was concerned. When the soulless being returned and tried to ingratiate itself with the family, he automatically believed her lies. The others were more leery, and Aisling was downright hostile. The garden was supposed to be a new start and now it was as if they were going through all of it again.

Redmond promised he would keep an eye on his brother before leaving. I believed him. That didn't stop me from worrying about Braden. He seemed lost when I left. We all had jobs to do, though, and that included me.

The island was still shut off to traffic, so it took me longer to get to work than it would've on a normal day. I'd forgotten to schedule time for travel, so Oliver and Paris were already at their desks when I joined the fray.

"Nice of you to join us," Oliver said dryly. "I hope we didn't interrupt your morning snuggle or anything."

I kind of wanted to smack him. "Something happened," I countered, figuring it was best to fill them in sooner rather than later. "Actually, several things happened."

I caught them up, leaving nothing out. They were incapable of understanding what the loss of the garden meant to the Grimlocks, and I didn't want to spread around the family's private business. Paris offered her condolences anyway, which only made me like her even more.

"The flowers looked melted?" Oliver drew his eyebrows together and I could practically hear the gears of his mind working. "I guess lightning could do that, but it sounds as if that storm was something other than normal."

"It definitely wasn't normal. I should've said something last night. I don't know why I didn't."

"That wouldn't have saved the flowers," Oliver argued. "Even if you called all of them out to look at the weird storm, what were they going to do? There was no way you could've known what was going to happen."

That was true, but it didn't make me feel any better. "We need to figure out exactly what we're dealing with. I'm talking about why they came back ... how they were infected ... and anything else that might be pertinent."

"Perhaps that's not what's important," Paris argued, her expression thoughtful. "I mean ... it's not my place to tell you what to focus on. I'm much more interested in why they were taken than why they were returned. To me, that's the real mystery."

I was flummoxed. "I don't understand what you're getting at."

"Has the gate ever malfunctioned before? I mean ... was sixty years ago the one and only time it malfunctioned? Is this the only gate that has malfunctioned? Why did it happen when it did? It seems to me those are the questions we should be asking."

She had a point. Unfortunately, I had no answers. I looked to Oliver for help. "What about you? You've been around a long time. Have you ever heard of the gate malfunctioning any other time?"

Oliver shook his head. "No, but the higher-ups are not exactly forthcoming when it comes to this stuff. I told you before that they never provided appropriate answers for the first instance. I always assumed it was because they didn't know. Or, as I mentioned previously, that somehow all those men died during the incident and I was spared because I was a vampire. I thought it was possible — perhaps even probable — that they were simply covering up an error on their part."

"We can't rule that out," Paris noted. "If they did cover it up, they might know what's happening now and not want to own up to past mistakes. It would hardly be the first time something like that happened."

She wasn't wrong. I pursed my lips and started to pace. "Well, let's look at this rationally. We've always assumed that the reaper hierarchy understands the function of the gate. We've been told how it works, but now I'm starting to wonder if it's true.

"I mean, think about it," I continued, warming to my topic. "We've been told you can't cross over and come back. That's supposedly a death sentence. It makes sense because otherwise people would be crossing the threshold willy-nilly when questions about the other side propelled true believers to prove their ideas of what happens when you die.

"Theology and certain belief systems have survived over the centuries because people want to believe there's something else out there. They want to believe we go on ... and with our loved ones at our sides. Without that belief, without a chance to be reunited with those we love most, despair would take over and the world would be different ... and not in a good way."

"That's all very well thought out," Oliver remarked. "There's a lot of truth in it. Something else has been occurring to me, though, and it circles right back to what you said. Was the gate discovered? Was it created? Is it man-made? Angel-made? Demon-made?

"If you think about it, had someone stumbled across the gate years ago — we're talking when Detroit was barely more than a trade station — how could they possibly know what it was? The entire reaper mythology is based on a story, and I'm starting to wonder if that story is true. What if this entire thing is a fraud that has been perpetuated for centuries?"

Well, that was a sobering thought. "I don't think it can all be made up." I chose my words carefully. "Lily Grimlock passed over and then came back to save her children. There's obviously something else out there."

"I'm not saying there's nothing else out there. I'm saying that the stories, the history, might be different from what we imagined. What if a group of people stumbled across the gate, tried to go through it, and really did see something on the other side? How else do you explain how they even knew what they were dealing with?"

The deeply philosophical discussion was starting to give me a headache. "None of it really makes sense when you break it down."

"Which means Paris could be right. Maybe we're looking at this the wrong way. Perhaps we should be focusing on why the men went missing and the actual history of the gate. I'm talking the true history here," Oliver said.

"That sounds great. How do we do that?"

"We talk to people who have a strong sense of history."

"And who would that be?"

"The oceans were once much larger than they are now. They were inhabited by creatures that had the run of the realm. These are creatures that never forget their history and continuously pass it down to future generations."

I understood what he was getting at. "The merfolk."

"They know more than we do by virtue of what they are. It can't hurt to tap that resource."

"Which one would be more willing to talk?"

"Collin is the obvious answer, but Claire is the one to go to. She might be bitchy, but she's a fountain of information ... and she's studied theology. She's your best bet."

I shifted my eyes to Paris. "Do you want to meet some merfolk?"

She nodded without hesitation. "Absolutely."

"Then we should head to the gardens. That's where we'll find Claire."

CLAIRE O'REILLY WAS INDEED AT THE gardens, and she wasn't in a good mood.

"I'm busy," she announced as we approached her.

I was used to her attitude and didn't back down. "We're all busy. I think we're dealing with something a bit bigger than your ... whatever that is." I gestured toward the plant she was studying.

"It's a rare lily. They're difficult to care for — and this one is struggling — but I'm determined to save it. There are only seven plants left and when they're gone, there's no bringing them back."

I made a mental note to ask her about the Grimlock lilies once things had settled down. "We need to know if you can answer questions about revenants."

Claire was surly, but the look she shot me was full of curiosity. "Revenants? Why do you want to know about them?"

"We believe that's what we're dealing with, but we can't be sure. No one has ever crossed paths with one."

"That's probably not true." Claire dusted off her hands on her shorts and stood. "Revenants are more common than you realize. But ... if you're asking about them now, you must think those who returned aren't what they originally appeared to be."

"You're correct."

"Ah, well, I expected that." She let loose a sigh. "Come along. We'll go to the cafeteria. I need a drink, and I expect this is going to be a long talk."

She had that right.

I'D NEVER BEEN TO THE CAFETERIA in this building and I wasn't impressed. It basically consisted of three tables and a coffee machine. It was clearly for the volunteers, not paying guests.

Claire was at home. She collected three bottles of water from the small refrigerator, doled them out, and then sank into one of the chairs. I didn't particularly like her, but she did most of the work in the garden, and I knew it had to be tiring.

"Revenants are not what you believe," she started. "Although ... I guess I don't know what you believe. Why don't you tell me and we'll start there?"

"From what I've read, revenant is a term that's been used for a variety of different things over the years," I replied. "Some people refer to ghosts as revenants, but I don't think that can be true because ghosts are non-corporeal. Revenants have to be corporeal."

"You're correct on that. Revenants have bodies. What else?"

"Some think revenants are vampires. Others, zombies. I think they're something else entirely." I told her about Ray Smith, the creature I'd fought ... and killed. When I was finished, she was bobbing her head.

"You're definitely dealing with revenants." She almost looked excited. She had a weird personality. If she was this excited, it couldn't be good. "Revenants are not vampires. In fact, they're essentially backward twins of vampires. They're not zombies either, but they do have a few things in common."

I sat back so I could get comfortable and listen. It was best to let her relate the information on her own terms.

"Vampires can be born or bitten," she continued, taking on a far-off expression. "Many people believe that vampires originated in Transylvania, which is what fiction books have told us. That is not true. Vampires have been around since the dawn of time in one form or another.

"The original vampires were much stronger than the ones we deal with today. They weren't born at that time. They were created. In a nutshell — because we don't have much time for an origin story, no matter how fascinating it is — demons started evolving into different creatures. Some drank blood, ate flesh and had no souls. Others became monsters of a different sort. That doesn't matter for the purposes of this discussion. What does matter is that somewhere along the line, they started to evolve.

"Because vampires evolved from demons, people assume they're soulless. That is not true. The original demons who transformed did not have souls. When they started procreating — something most demon lines don't do — the offspring were born with souls."

She was right. This was fascinating. "Did the vampires completely separate from the demons at some point?"

"Yes, and they did it quickly. Once vampires realized they were different, they started to think of themselves as superior. At the time, that wasn't true. The demons were still stronger. But because the demons weren't procreating, their numbers waned and the vampires grew stronger.

"There was a time when a certain sect of vampires started a push to revert to the old ways. Those vampires thought the entire race had grown soft. While it wasn't necessary for them to kill to survive, some of them liked it. That's where revenants come in.

"This faction wasn't large, but it was strong," she continued. "They went back to eating human flesh. They went back to killing mercilessly. As an interesting side effect, they were drawn to members of their own family or others who shared common blood. I've never heard an appropriate explanation for why.

"The thing is, revenants didn't procreate. I'm not sure why. There are numerous stories. Some say their carnivorous ways made it so they couldn't perform. Others said they merely lost interest. We all know how men are, how sexual appetites work, so I tend to believe the former. I don't know it for a fact, though."

"Is that important?" Paris asked.

"For this story it is," Claire confirmed. "Revenants couldn't procreate, so they had to multiply in other ways."

I was finally starting to catch on. "They had to create revenants from things they already had, which is exactly what happened to the people who were swallowed by the gate."

"Exactly." Claire nodded. "Revenants threatened to take over for a time. When the human race was weak, in times of plague for example, they would take out entire cities and turn them into followers. The other paranormals realized they were a threat and banded together to eradicate them."

"Obviously that didn't work," I muttered.

"Perhaps not the way you're thinking, but it did work," Claire countered. "The gates were public by that time. And before you ask, I don't know how the gates came into being. I don't know that anyone does. At a certain point, they were simply there ... and located in almost every major city.

"Back in those times, the population was more spread out," she explained. "Reapers came into being, but a lot of souls were missed. It wasn't until centuries later that the current system came into play.

"While I know a decent amount about reaper history, they guard their secrets well. We all have questions about the gates and where they came from. You're wondering if the men in that room sixty years ago were specifically targeted. I would have to say they were."

"But why?" I asked. "There's a big gap in your story."

"That's because I don't have all the answers you seek." Claire turned rueful. "I wish I did. No one person understands everything. What I know is that the revenants were hunted by huge groups of paranormals, all working together.

"When they tried to flee to the seas, we attacked from the water and they were boxed in. It was a coordinated attack. We knew that if we didn't cull their numbers, at least make a huge dent, we all would eventually fall victim to them.

"They were vile, hateful and disgusting creatures. They offered nothing to this world, so we sent those we couldn't kill to the next."

Something sizzled in the back of my mind. "You forced them across the gate."

"We forced them across *all* the gates," she corrected. "Remember, revenants were taking over the world. It wasn't happening in just one area."

"Didn't you wonder what was on the other side?" Paris asked. "I mean ... how did you know that you weren't empowering them even more?"

"We didn't. No one knew what was on the other side of the gates. There were rumors that angels actually descended from Heaven to explain the function of the gates to a chosen few. Obviously those stories were met with derision, but for all we know they could be true. All our ancestors knew was that if they managed to push the revenants across, they were unlikely to return."

"You're saying they were willing to damn the next world as long as this one was free of the evil," I mused. "I mean ... I get it. It was a huge risk."

"It was," Claire agreed. "It seemed to work, though. Revenants haven't gotten a foothold in centuries. Sure, a few were missed. They were easy to hunt down and eradicate after most of them were gone, though. Through the years, a few have popped up here and there, but nothing has happened like what occurred here the other day.

"You say they didn't look like dark creatures when they reappeared," she prodded. "Revenants didn't regain their human features like vampires. The original demons were a mixture. Some looked human, others didn't. The vampires eventually all resembled humans. It was a quirk of evolution that allowed them to walk amongst the humans. The revenants were not that lucky."

"So something happened to them on the other side," I deduced. "They were turned into revenants, but they can pass as humans."

"At least until their human forms are killed," Claire agreed. "I'm not sure what's going on there, but if the revenants have figured out a way to look human and cross back through the gates, we all could be in a lot of trouble."

The implications of the statement were chilling. "You're talking about another potential war."

"Yes, and the paranormal cultures are nowhere near as united as they once were. If this is happening now, we need to get ahead of it. If they come over in mass numbers, half the paranormal and human populations could be wiped out before the world realizes what's happening.

"If this is a test, we need it to fail," she continued. "I'm going to guess we don't have much time, so if you're going to figure things out, it had better be fast."

Oh, well, that wasn't daunting or anything.

Eighteen

C laire gave me a lot to think about. More than I was comfortable with, frankly, and I was at a loss until Aisling called and suggested lunch.

"I thought you were grounded."

The words were out of my mouth before I remembered who I was talking to. She took the slight fairly well, all things considered.

"Do you want to eat the best Mexican food you've ever had or not?"

That was a difficult question. "Mexican sounds good," I hedged. "I won't get in trouble with your father if I meet you, will I?"

"Ugh. The more time you spend with Braden, the more you act like him. It's ridiculous."

"I happen to like your brother."

"I know. It's your only flaw. Otherwise you're the first woman I actually like enough to have lunch with."

Oddly enough, I recognized that as a compliment. I figured her relationship with her father was Aisling's problem, so I opted to give her what she wanted — which I was guessing was a solid two hours away from her father — and acquiesced. "Give me the address and we'll meet you there."

I could practically see her preening over the phone. "Maybe you're not quite as bad as Braden after all."

"I just hope I don't live to regret this."

"You won't."

I wasn't so sure but I was already knee-deep in trouble, so why stop now?

AISLING WAS ALREADY SEATED AT a corner table when Paris and I entered the restaurant. I didn't mention I would be bringing a guest when we'd talked, but she didn't look upset. Instead she waved and sipped a margarita while dipping a chip in salsa and chatting amiably with a well-dressed man.

I kept my gaze on the man as I slid around the table to claim my seat. He didn't look familiar, but that didn't necessarily mean anything. Aisling had lived in the area her entire life and knew many people.

"This is Dan Sterling," Aisling offered by way of introduction. "His son went to high school with me. He owns this place."

Oh, well, that made sense. "It's nice to meet you." I extended my hand, which he took with a pleasant smile, and searched for something innocuous to say. "How obnoxious was Aisling when she was in high school?"

Dan chuckled. "She was ... a spitfire. I guess that's the best word to describe her."

"I was definitely a spitfire," Aisling agreed. "I was also awesome."

"You were that, too." Dan squeezed her shoulder before focusing on us. "What can I get you to drink, ladies?"

"I'll have an iced tea," I replied.

Paris bobbed her head. "The same."

Apparently our answers didn't please Aisling, because she made a face. "We're in Mexican Town. You're supposed to have margaritas."

"We're on the clock," I reminded her. "Not all of us snuck out of our father's house and can play hooky all afternoon."

"Stop saying that." She extended a warning finger. "I'm an adult. I can do whatever I want."

That was bold talk. "Where does your father think you are?"

"Taking a nap."

I had to bite the inside of my cheek to keep from laughing. "Well, that's just ... so you."

"I know." She sipped her margarita again. "I had to have an Uber meet me on the corner. Otherwise he would've heard me trying to sneak out of the house in one of his cars. He put security on the garage when I was a teenager."

"My understanding is that he did that because you wouldn't stop stealing his cars," I pointed out.

Her eyes flashed. "Do you have to remember absolutely everything?"

"I have a good memory. Sue me."

"Yeah, yeah, yeah." She focused on her drink and took another sip. "I haven't had a margarita since before I found out I was pregnant with Lily. You have no idea how good this tastes."

"I'm glad you're enjoying it." I picked up the menu and flipped it over to review the offerings. It looked like standard Mexican fare. "Do you want to tell me why you called us here?"

"It's nothing nefarious. I just wanted out of the house and figured you were due for lunch."

I read between the lines. "You tried Jerry first, didn't you?"

"Hey, you were second on my list."

"That's because Jerry and I are the only ones who won't narc on you for skipping out of the house."

"This is true." She leaned back in her chair and regarded me with serious eyes. "Did you find out anything good this afternoon?"

Ah. That's what she really wanted. I should've realized that being under house arrest wasn't the only reason she was antsy. What happened at Grimlock Manor the previous evening, the destruction of the garden, weighed heavily on her. More than anything, she wanted her family safe. She figured I was the key to ending this, so she wanted to dig inside my head for information.

"As a matter of fact, we did." I told her everything I could remember from our conversation with Claire. I combined most of it into a streamlined tale, so it didn't take long to recite. When I finished, she looked intrigued.

"Well, that's more than we had before you left the house this morning." She tapped her fingers on the table in time with the cantina music playing in the restaurant. "What do you think it all means?"

I'd been trying to put it together myself. "I believe most of it. I'm sure the lore changed a bit over the years, but the bones of the story are important, and I think she's mostly right."

"You believe the revenants were forced through the gates?"

"I do. I also believe that the reaper hierarchy is leaving out huge sections of information when it comes to the discovery of the gates. I mean ... haven't you ever wondered where the gates initially came from? Were they found that way? Did the reapers discover something else and force the gates into the form we see now? Who decided where to place the gates? Who decided the reapers should be the ones to administer them from the start?"

Aisling worked her jaw. "You know, I hate to say it, but I never really thought about any of that before you brought it up. I was taught reaper history as a kid. My father treated it as fact, so I believed him."

"Your father wasn't lying to you. He was simply repeating what he was told. I wonder how much of that story is true."

"I don't know. We could ask him. Not now, because he thinks I'm taking a nap, but later tonight."

"I'll ask, but I'm not sure he can fill in the blanks. I'm not sure any one person can."

"Renley should be able to," Aisling countered. "He's the head of the entire Detroit office. He should know the specifics about our gate."

"Do you think he'd be willing to share the information?"

She shrugged. "Sure. Why not?"

"Because he's part of the team that kept the missing reapers on the down low for years. I mean ... shouldn't the story of fourteen missing cadet reapers have been widely known in certain circles? Why didn't anybody know about it? Your father clearly had no idea. Sure, it was before his time, but his father would've been around then, right? Why didn't he pass along the story to his son?"

"Huh." Aisling tapped her finger against her chin. "You know, the more you talk, the more questions I have. I feel like an idiot because I didn't think to ask any of this earlier, but ... it is what it is. You must have an idea of what you're going to do to find answers on these revenants."

I'd given that a lot of thought, too, and nodded.

"Well, share your plans with the class," Aisling ordered. "I'm dying to hear what you're going to do."

"Me, too," Paris added. "An hour ago you had no idea what you were going to do."

"I'm going to ask a revenant."

Paris's face remained blank. "Ask a revenant what?"

"What's going on. What's on the other side of the gate. Why they're here now. What they want. There's no end to the questions I have."

"And you just expect a revenant to answer these questions?" Paris asked.

"Once we catch and persuade him that he'll die if he doesn't."

Aisling brightened considerably. "So, you're saying that you're going on a revenant hunt. I'm in."

I immediately started shaking my head. "No, you're not."

"Yes, I am."

"Your father thinks you're upstairs sleeping. You can't go running across the county, because he'll melt down if he goes up there and finds you've escaped."

"I left a note."

"You left a note?" I was incredulous. "How will that make things better?"

"I didn't want him to think I took off and left the baby. It will be fine. He'll only be angry for a little while."

"You sound awfully sure of yourself." Something I couldn't remotely say about myself. "How do you know he'll get over it?"

"He always does. He'll be fine."

I didn't believe her for a second, but I didn't see that I had many options. If I called to tattle on her — something I was absolutely loath to do — she would turn the tables on me. There was no way Braden would simply look the other way if he found out I was running head-long into danger.

"You did this on purpose." I was resigned. "You knew that I would have no choice but to take you with me once you made me complicit in your escape."

Instead of denying the charge, she patted my arm. "Don't get morose. Your face will freeze like that if you do and then you'll start looking like Braden. Nobody wants that."

"Your father is going to kill me," I muttered.

"He will not. The worst he'll do is ban you from the breakfast bar tomorrow. It's an omelet bar, so that's going to suck, but if you cry enough he'll give in. Trust me. I know exactly how to manipulate that man."

Sadly, I knew she was telling the truth. "Whatever. Let's order our food. If this is going to be my last meal, I want something really good."

"That's the spirit."

BECAUSE I THOUGHT OF HIM AS the leader of the group, we headed to Doug Dunning's house. It was the first we'd visited the previous day, the one that looked as if a fight had gone down in the kitchen and living room. It appeared vacant when we parked one block over and watched for signs of life.

"Are we just going to sit here?" Aisling was in full whine mode. She'd booted Paris from the passenger seat — something I told Paris she didn't have to take, but she was too nice to argue — and made catty comments for the entirety of the ride.

"We're going to sit here," I confirmed, leaning my head against the rest and staring at the house. "The revenants were drawn home. Claire said that's normal. They were always drawn to people who meant something to them in life."

"They're gone now," Aisling pointed out. "They've already taken what they're looking for."

"We don't know that they've taken everybody. They might come back if they missed someone. I mean ... maybe someone was out of town or on vacation."

"Good point." She rolled her neck and shifted her eyes to a house two driveways down. There was a "for sale" sign on the lawn and several people standing in the driveway.

AMANDA M. LEE

Slowly, as if all the oxygen was being stolen from the vehicle, Aisling moved her face closer to the window. Her eyes were wide and she was so rapt I thought she'd caught sight of a revenant. My heart skipped a beat at the prospect.

"Do you see something?"

"I do." She bobbed her head. "I see the world's worst real estate agent."

I was confused. "What does that matter? I ... ." Whatever I was going to say died on my lips when I finally focused on the willowy brunette in the driveway. "Oh, geez. No!" I barked out the order even as Aisling shoved open the door and hopped toward the sidewalk.

"What's going on?" Paris asked, clearly confused. "Is that someone she knows?"

"Yes." I used my anger when pushing open my door and it bounced back hard. "We have to stop her before she draws the wrong kind of attention to us and the police are called."

Paris's eyes went wide. "Why would the police be called? Wait ... isn't her husband a police officer?"

"A homicide detective. Thankfully we don't have to worry about that with these two. What we do have to worry about is a litany of insults and some minor hair-pulling. There's a better-than-average chance that the cops will be called because we're dealing with a feud that is so old and convoluted that several arrests have been made over the years."

Paris obviously didn't understand my distress, but she hurried to keep up with me. "Who is she?"

"Angelina Davenport." I was grim as I raced down the sidewalk. "She's the devil in Kate Spade knockoffs."

"She sounds delightful."

"Then clearly I'm telling the story wrong."

Aisling was already in full insult mode.

"This house is haunted," she announced to the young couple standing with Angelina. "Seriously. There's a ghost inside. Your real estate agent doesn't want to tell you because she's afraid to lose the sale, but I believe in being honest. She's ugly and this house has murderous ghosts living inside."

Angelina's expression reflected controlled rage. She was obviously caught between a Grimlock and a hard place. "You'll have to excuse Aisling. She's recently escaped from a mental institution — untreated syphilis drove her crazy before her time — and the police are on the lookout for her. If you give me a minute — please feel free to look around the house while I deal with this issue — I'll be with you shortly."

The couple, both sunny and bright, looked conflicted.

"She's lying," Aisling countered. "She's not even really a real estate agent. Her pimp makes her dress up like one so she can turn tricks in various houses and he doesn't have to shell out the thirty bucks for a dive hotel room. She can't even bring that in per trick because she's so bad in bed. I mean ... she's professional, but the clients should really be paying her."

Angelina gritted her teeth and held it together. I had to admire her determination to keep the deal moving forward. "Just go inside. I'll take care of this."

"Are you sure?" The woman looked frightened. "If the house really is haunted we should probably look at something else."

"The house isn't haunted," Angelina reassured her. "I'll be five minutes behind. Feel free to look around."

The couple exchanged a weighted look and then shrugged before heading toward the front door. They were obviously confused, but not enough that they wanted to rock the boat. They looked excited as they gestured at a pretty garden before sliding through the front door.

Once they were out of sight — and more importantly, earshot — Angelina let loose her pent-up rage. "I'm going to kill you!" She reached for Aisling's hair, but the youngest Grimlock, expecting the move, easily sidestepped her.

"I can't believe your pimp lets you moonlight as a real estate agent," Aisling taunted as she hopped away from Angelina. "You must really be coming up in the world."

"I'm going to rip your hair out and shove it down your throat," Angelina threatened.

Aisling didn't look worried in the least. "Bring it!"

I felt as if I was babysitting two children who knew better than to fight but I lacked authority to stop them. My frustration was on full display when I stepped between them. Angelina wasn't as coordinated as Aisling, so when I extended my hand toward her chest I caught her unaware and she tumbled backward. That only served to make Aisling laugh like a loon.

"Oh, why didn't anyone get that on camera?" she lamented. "I could've put that on YouTube and made a million dollars from advertising. You don't suppose any of these houses have security cameras, do you?"

"Knock it off," I hissed. I really didn't care that I would be getting myself in trouble by turning her in. It would be worth it to be rid of her. "We have serious things to worry about. We don't have time for this."

"Of course we have time." Aisling planted her hands on her hips. "Angelina and I haven't fought in eight months."

Paris stirred. "I thought your baby was six weeks old. Doesn't that mean you shouldn't have fought for ten and a half months?"

"She didn't know I was pregnant the last time she attacked. That one was on me."

"It definitely was," Angelina huffed. "I can't believe you just messed with my job like that. There are rules to the war, Aisling. You can't mess with my job."

"You messed with mine," Aisling shot back. "You didn't care that you interrupted me on the job."

"You work for your father. It's different. I have a real job."

The sun was starting to set and the bright light meeting the horizon was giving me a headache. "Who cares who ruined whose job?" I snapped. "You guys are freaking adults. Why don't you act like it? I mean ... you're almost thirty, for crying out loud. You shouldn't be doing things like this. We're trying to save people's lives and all you care about is messing with your high school nemesis. It's stupid ... and immature ... and it makes me want to lock you in the car."

"You can't do that." Aisling sounded pragmatic. "I'll die because it's too late in the season and I'll sweat to death. Also, stop being such a baby. You really are starting to sound like Braden."

"You really are," Angelina agreed, picking herself up off the ground.

She dusted off the seat of her pants. "I want to institute a rule about messing with people's jobs, Aisling. You work for your father and can't get in trouble. I don't have that luxury."

"Oh, whatever." Aisling's earlier glee had fled. "This has been a total bummer of a fight. I can't believe you ruined this for me."

Her eyes were on me. "We're supposed to be hunting for monsters," I reminded her. Angelina was in on the family secret, so there was nothing stopping me from stating the truth. "There are more important things than ... whatever this was."

Aisling threw her hands in the air. "You clearly don't get me."

I clearly didn't, because I felt like shaking her until she shut up. I didn't get the chance, because Angelina was suddenly pointing at something at the end of the street.

"Monsters like that?" Her voice was squeaky.

Confused, I turned to stare in that direction. Sure enough, four rubbery monsters had appeared from ... somewhere ... and they were stalking directly toward us with promises of mayhem illuminated in their red eyes. "Oh, well, crap."

Aisling and I turned to each other.

"This is your fault," we blurted out.

It didn't matter who was to blame. A fight was upon us and it was going to take all of us to come out of it alive. I should've thought better about my plan.

Nineteen

Where had they come from?

That's all I could think as my heart pounded and the blood rushed through my ears.

"Oh, what are they?" Angelina made a face that would've been hilarious under different circumstances. "They look like trolls or something. Why can't your family be normal?" Her furious gaze landed on Aisling.

"They're not trolls," Aisling shot back. She was calmer than I expected, even though now seemed like a good time to panic. "Don't be stupid. Trolls live under bridges and can be distracted by billy goats. These are something else entirely."

"Oh, well ... if you say so." Angelina rolled her eyes. "I'm not sticking around for this. I'm going inside with my clients to keep them from looking out the windows. If you kill these things, move the bodies right away. I'm not kidding. If you cost me this sale, Aisling, I'll make you pay in ways you can't even fathom."

"Oh, suck a lemon." Aisling shifted so her back was to Angelina and she faced the revenants. "Do you think that's four of the people who returned or did they make more?"

That was the question. "I think they made more," I answered

without hesitation. "I think that's the Dunning family. I'm not sure which is Doug — or if he's even amongst them — but I'm pretty sure those are the people he left behind."

The more I thought about it, the more the idea made me sick to my stomach. "We should've protected them." I meant to keep the last bit to myself, but it escaped.

"We should've done a lot of things differently," Aisling noted as she strode to the center of the yard and grabbed the "for sale" sign planted there. "The longer we dwell on what could've been, the longer we'll falter at ensuring what should be. That's not the way to get ahead."

"That's very pragmatic," Paris noted, her hands clenched into fists at her sides. "What are you going to do with that?"

Aisling was studying the sharp edges of the sign, the ones that had been buried in the ground until a few moments before. "I'm going to stab one of them."

"With a sign?" Paris's eyebrows flew up her forehead. "I don't think that's going to work."

"Yes, well, I forgot to bring my sword. Sometimes you simply have to make do with what you have at your disposal."

"You have a sword?" Paris was stunned. "Why would you possibly need a sword?"

"You'd be surprised how many times I've needed a sword." Aisling didn't hesitate as she headed toward the sidewalk. She was going after the revenants rather than allowing them to come to us.

"Wait." Something horrible had occurred to me. "I think you should sit in the car and let me handle this fight."

Aisling snorted. She was almost directly in front of the first revenant. "That's not going to happen."

"If you're hurt ... or if something worse happens ... ." I left the sentence hanging. I couldn't even think about how the Grimlocks would react if something were to go wrong.

"I won't get hurt." Aisling seemed sure of herself as she stopped in the middle of the street. "Hello, jerkfaces." She beamed at the creatures as they growled and continued to advance. "This is going to hurt."

There was no hesitation when she slammed the bottom of the sign into the first revenant. She'd obviously been in a fight — or ten — over the course of her life. She'd come to fight and that's exactly what she did.

The revenant's shrieking — the noise weak and brittle as well as shrill — shook me out of my reverie. Obviously there was no turning back now. We had to fight.

My fingertips glowed green as I ignited my magic. I sent a bolt directly at the shortest revenant, which saw the barrage coming but didn't have time to duck. The powerful ball hit it square in the face, causing it to grunt, and then the magic exploded. The revenant fell backward, a stunned look on its face. It stared sightlessly at the sky as I fervently hoped that the creature's small stature was due to the fact that it was previously a grown woman and not a child. For some reason, that bothered me more than anything else.

Paris had pulled a glowing knife from her pocket at some point — I couldn't wait to press her on that — and was engaged in battle with the revenant on the far right of the group. Her technique wasn't great, but she was the tenacious sort and didn't give up a single inch as she battled the creature.

Aisling was still grappling with her revenant. The sign did its intended job and injured the creature, but it was still putting up a fight. Aisling looked to have the situation in hand, so I focused on the last revenant. He — and I honestly had no idea if it was truly a he or a she, I just had a feeling — was huge. He was twice the size of the first revenant I'd put down.

"Back up," I warned, my fingers igniting for a second time. I wished I'd thought this out before we started attacking. The goal was to question a revenant. The little one would've been the easiest to take into custody. Now I was stuck with the big one, and he looked less likely to cooperate. "You don't have to die if you simply turn yourself in."

I wasn't sure the revenant could understand me — it didn't look like the sort of creature who understood things — but when it started laughing like a deranged clown on steroids I realized that I'd been underestimating them from the start because of their looks.

"Fine. Be a pain. I can't stop you." Paris and Aisling hadn't yet killed their revenants, but I figured I could take out this one and then help one of them subdue their creature. "You're going to regret not listening to me."

I conjured the same ball of green magic — it had worked so well the first time — and didn't hesitate as I sent it toward the revenant. He was expecting it, and dodged to the right. I didn't realize until the last second that he was coming directly for me in a rush after evading my attack and I had to put up my hands in defense.

The revenant and I collided with enough force that the oxygen was momentarily knocked from my lungs. I managed to keep on my feet and extended my hands in front of me. The glowing magic turned to an orange flame, and I poured as much energy as I could into the effort as I planted my hands against the creature's chest. His eyes went wide — there was still something human lurking there and it hurt me to see — and then his entire body went up in flames.

I scrambled to increase the distance between us and landed with a thud on the curb. Momentarily jarred, I watched the revenant lift its head to the sky and scream ... and then it was gone. Once the fire got a foothold, it burned quickly, leaving nothing but ash.

"Well, I guess we know fire also works," I muttered. I stared blankly for a full thirty seconds and then remembered Aisling and Paris weren't done fighting. When I turned to help, it was already too late to warn them to take one alive.

"Die, foul hell beast!" Aisling almost looked as if she was having fun as she shoved the sign into her creature's neck. It was a true blow, and the monster gurgled before its eyes rolled back into its head. Aisling looked satisfied as it rolled to its back and stared at the darkening sky.

I swiveled to check on Paris and found her sitting on the ground, a smudge of dirt on her cheek. She was still holding the dagger, which no longer glowed. She looked dazed.

"Oh, no." I stalked in her direction and stared at the body on the ground. "Is it dead?"

"Better it than me," Paris groused, shooting me a dirty look.

"I didn't mean that. It's just ... we were supposed to catch one, not kill them all."

"Oh." She pursed her lips. "Well ... I kind of forgot."

Aisling's face was dirty thanks to the revenant's blood splattering during their fight. "I guess we need to find more of them."

That sounded like an absolutely horrible idea. "I think we need to get back to Grimlock Manor before your father realizes you're gone."

"We can't do that."

"Why?"

"We can't leave these bodies here. We need to call my father and tell him what happened. He'll send a cleanup crew."

Well, crap. I hadn't even considered that. "Or maybe we could burn them." That sounded like a promising idea. "I burned the one and it turned to ash. No muss, no fuss."

"Normally I would agree. These things are ... different, though. They need to run tests on them. I don't like it either, but we have to call my father."

My stomach gave a pronounced heave. "He's going to yell at us, isn't he?"

"Oh, you have no idea."

CORMACK WASN'T THE ONLY ONE WHO YELLED when we returned to Grimlock Manor.

"You're both grounded!"

He started out the extravaganza with a bang.

"I hate to state the obvious, but you can't ground me," I pointed out, sinking into one of the chairs in the parlor and accepting the drink Aidan poured me. He looked more amused than concerned. Of course, he didn't have a lot of skin in the game. All the Grimlock males enjoyed watching their sister get in trouble. Their first concern was her safety. When it was obvious she was fine, they turned to torturing her as means of entertainment.

It was the Grimlock way.

"Oh, you're definitely grounded." Cormack's eyes flashed with annoyance. He'd made sure to hand Lily off to Jerry so she couldn't bear witness to him yelling at her mother. Jerry refused to leave entirely, though, and swayed back and forth as he patted Lily's back and watched the show.

"Listen ... ." I was about to go off, explain that I didn't need a father figure, when Aisling shot me a pointed look before stepping directly in front of her father.

"You can't ground Izzy and you know it," Aisling argued. "I know you like her and think of her as the well-behaved daughter you never had, but you have to suck up the disappointment. She's just like us. That's the reason Braden fell for her in the first place."

"Oh, don't bring me into this," Braden complained, his gaze furious as it landed on me. "I think she should definitely be grounded. In fact, I think it's time to dust off the cell in the basement and lock her in there until she repents."

He'd offered me an intense hug when he saw me and then he'd held me at arm's length since. He was obviously angry. Like ... really, really angry. Part of me wanted to apologize until he gave in and forgave me. The other part wanted to knock his head against the wall until he admitted he had no jurisdiction over me. I wasn't a child who needed to be scolded.

"Now there's a good idea," Cormack enthused. "There's only one cell, but we can fit two cots in there. Aisling and Izzy will have each other to talk to. It's the perfect solution."

"Oh, stop blowing smoke." Aisling dragged a hand through her hair. She was filthy and bedraggled from the fight, but her spunk was on full display. She had no intention of letting her father wear her down. "You're not going to lock me in that cell and you're not even all that angry."

"Oh, I'm angry." Cormack's gaze was dark. "You have no idea how angry I am. I'm so angry that ... no, I can't even think of another word that conveys how angry I am. Do you have any idea how I felt when I went to your room — with the tea set your mother insisted I buy when you were eight — and found you missing?"

"I left a note."

"That's not the point!" His voice boomed so deeply it echoed throughout the room. "I thought you were taking a nap and relaxing. Instead I find you were fighting monsters. What happened?"

When no one immediately responded, I glanced up and found him staring directly at me. "Oh, you're going to blame this on me, aren't you?"

He nodded without hesitation. "You knew I had her under house arrest. When she showed up at the scene — I still don't know how you ended up there, Aisling, and managed to find Izzy on top of that — you should've called me. I would've immediately come down and handled her."

"That's not exactly how it happened," I hedged, darting a quick look in Braden's direction as I searched for support. The look he shot me said I wouldn't find it there. I let out a sigh, resigned. "We had lunch in Mexican Town first."

"Lunch?" Cormack was incensed. "I can't even ... you ... both of you." He mimed tugging at his hair. "I don't even know what to say to you two. I can't believe you did this. I really can't.

"You're a mother now, Aisling," he continued, his voice laced with disappointment. "You left your child with me so you could have Mexican food and fight monsters. What if something had happened to you?"

"Nothing happened to me." Aisling made an exaggerated face. "I wasn't in any danger. I had everything under control from the start. Tell him, Izzy. I was totally fine."

"She was totally fine," I echoed perfunctorily. "Of course, we wouldn't have been out in the open the way we were in the first place if she hadn't picked a fight with Angelina and told her clients the house was haunted and Angelina was moonlighting as a real estate agent on orders from her pimp."

Cormack's expression remained stony. Redmond, Cillian, Aidan and Jerry all snorted in amusement thanks to the visual I'd painted. Hope welling, I glanced at Braden ... but he was still a morose monster. Apparently we wouldn't be making up any time soon.

"What was Angelina doing there?" Cormack asked, his tone weary. "I mean ... how did she get wrangled into this?"

"It was a coincidence," I volunteered. "She was showing the house across the road. Aisling went after her. The revenants arrived a few minutes later. I'm not sure where they were. They just came out of nowhere and attacked."

"Well, that's disconcerting," Cormack growled. "It's too bad you killed them all. We really could've used one for questioning."

I shot Aisling a pointed look. "I told you."

"Hey, I had a real estate sign as a weapon. I only cared about saving myself, not questioning those things. Excuse me for worrying about self-preservation. I have a daughter, after all." As if to prove it, she strode across the room, ignoring her father's glare, and collected Lily from Jerry. The second the baby was in her arms, she looked up at Aisling's dirty face and immediately grinned before cooing. It wasn't exactly a laugh, but it was close.

"Did you see that?" Aisling was in awe. "She smiled at me."

I couldn't help but be relieved. That was exactly what Aisling needed. And, frankly, it couldn't have happened at a better time.

"No way." Braden slid out of his chair, gave me a wide berth, and crossed to the baby. "She's supposed to smile at me first."

"No, she's supposed to smile at me first," Redmond countered. "I'm the best-looking Grimlock."

"In your dreams," Aidan scoffed as he stroked Lily's soft head. "That's so cool that she finally smiled, though. Now she'll do it all the time."

As if to prove him right, Lily smiled again, this time at her mother's twin brother.

"She smiled at me!" Aidan pumped his fist in the air. "That means I win the bet."

"It does not," Cillian shot back. "Aisling won the bet ... but she didn't bet because she didn't believe she would win. I guess that goes to prove you should have more faith in yourself."

Aisling's eyes were glassy as she held Cillian's gaze for a moment. Then she turned to her father. "I'm not sorry I went out. Everything turned out fine. You can't control me forever. I'm not a child."

"You're my child," he shot back, although the anger he'd been hoarding appeared to have evaporated. "You're in big trouble, Aisling. You're not getting any dessert ... and I have homemade ice cream and fresh cookies, so you're really going to miss out."

My stomach heaved at the notion. I loved ice cream. "Oh, man."

For a split second, I was certain I saw amusement reflected on

Cormack's features. He shuttered it quickly, though, and all I caught a glimpse of when I looked a second time was annoyance. "No ice cream for you either, Izzy," he ordered.

"Whatever." I blew out a sigh and watched as Aisling tickled her daughter, who grinned at Cormack when he leaned closer. Maybe the entire thing was worth it after all. Then I caught Braden's gaze again and found him glaring hard enough to cause me to gulp.

Twenty

Cormack was determined to hold strong and ban Aisling and me from dessert. He held out until Redmond and Cillian started taunting their sister with cookies dipped in ice cream, which made Lily smile. She was in her grandfather's arms when it happened, so he turned into a big ball of mush and acquiesced.

Aisling managed to hide her smile until it was just the two of us at the ice cream bar, and then she was full of herself. "I knew he wouldn't be able to hold out," she muttered, clearly proud of herself.

While I was happy for the ice cream, I had other things on my mind, including the fact that Braden refused to meet my gaze. I didn't see his anger dissipating anytime soon.

"Don't worry about Braden," Aisling offered when she realized I was staring at her brother. "He won't stay angry. He never does. Although ... if any of my brothers are going to hold a grudge over the long haul, it's him. It shouldn't be more than a few days, though."

That wasn't what I wanted to hear. "I don't even understand why he's angry." I blurted out the words even though they weren't true. "I was simply doing my job."

Aisling arched an eyebrow as she dished a huge dollop of hot fudge onto her sundae. "Your job is to monitor the gate. You didn't have to go after the revenants. You know that's exactly what he's going to say to you when he finally decides to start yelling."

Yes, and he had a point. That didn't mean I was going to acquiesce to his demands and suddenly turn into a wilting flower who needed a chaperone on dangerous outings. "He's being a butthead."

"He's king of the buttheads," she agreed, her eyes turning to the door as Griffin walked in late. The look on his face was as dark as the one Braden sported. "And here comes second in command for butthead dominance." She let loose a sigh. "I was hoping to get through a few bowls of ice cream before he showed up. This won't be good."

"You're in big trouble," Griffin announced, hands on hips. "I mean ... huge trouble. If there was an Olympic event for getting in trouble, you would have the gold, silver and bronze medals around your neck right now."

Aisling, never one to back down, smiled. "Look, everybody, it's the most magnificent cop and husband in all the land. Doesn't he look handsome?"

Cormack snorted. "And now you know why I don't feel all that bad about backing off regarding your punishment. He's going to do far worse to you than I ever could."

Aisling looked the exact opposite of afraid. "Yes, but I know his secret tickle spots. He'll be putty in my hands."

"Think again." Griffin's tone was grave. "I'm angry. I mean ... I'm Hulk angry."

"And funnily enough I still like you when you're angry," she drawled.

As if on cue, Aisling's brothers – even Braden – started growling and flexing their muscles. It was a routine I'd never seen before.

"What was that?" I was beyond confused.

"Aisling was obsessed with that old television show about *The Incredible Hulk* from the seventies," Cillian explained. "She used to growl like him when she was a kid. It's something we all used to do when she started growling at Dad."

"Yes, and it's no cuter now than it was then," Cormack argued. "In fact, it's beyond ridiculous."

Actually, I found the scene endearing. Now wasn't the time to point that out, though. "I think I'm going to sit down." I clutched my bowl of ice cream tighter and tried to skirt around Aisling in an attempt to get away from her. She was having none of it.

"You didn't get any sprinkles." She dumped a huge spoonful in my bowl, her gaze never wandering from Griffin's face. "There're whipped cream and cherries over there. You should definitely add those."

All I wanted to do was flee. Apparently that wasn't going to happen, because Griffin cut off my avenue of escape.

"You're in trouble for taking her with you," he announced, pinning me with a murderous glare. "I can't punish you like I can her, but I'm definitely ticked."

I risked a glare at Braden and found him watching the exchange with something akin to triumph. Griffin didn't have to worry about punishing me. Braden was doing a bang-up job of it on his own.

"Don't threaten her," Aisling snapped. "She's not to blame. If you want to be angry with someone, be angry at me."

"Oh, I'm angry with you." Griffin snagged a gummy worm from her bowl. "But I have plenty of anger to go around." As if to prove it, he shifted his attention to Cormack. "I'm angry with you, too. In fact, you might want to start running now."

Cormack shook his head and shifted Lily so he could hold her more comfortably. "I'm terrified. Whatever will I do?" he drawled.

Griffin opened his mouth, a nasty response at the ready, but then his gaze dropped to his daughter ... who was smiling again. Apparently now that she'd broken the seal she couldn't stop.

"Hey, she's smiling at me." He forgot his argument with his wife and moved closer to the baby. "Look at that. I won. She's smiling at me."

"She's been smiling nonstop for an hour," Redmond offered, morose. "You're not the first recipient of her smile. That honor goes to your wife, who apparently amused the crap out of her because she was filthy and whiny when Dad started yelling at her."

"Yes, proving she's a true Grimlock. Lily seems delighted when everybody yells at one another," Cillian volunteered. "It would almost be funny if it weren't so tragic."

Griffin deflated upon hearing the truth. "Oh, geez. She really is her mother's daughter."

Aisling's eyes lit with delight. "She is," she agreed. "If you want to get in good with her, you have to stay tight with me. That means no yelling."

"I didn't agree to those terms." Even though he was putting up a modicum of fight, it was over. I could sense that Griffin was in full retreat. The baby's smile had defeated him, too. "I'm just going to wait until we're alone later to explain my disappointment."

Aisling mock saluted and then went back to piling things on top of her ice cream. "I look forward to fighting and making up. I shall pencil you in for ten."

"Ugh." Cormack made a disgusted sound as he shifted, shaking his head when Griffin reached for the baby. "Have your dinner first. She's fine."

Oddly enough, that's the moment I realized everything was fine with the Grimlocks, that everything had gone back to normal – except for one thing. I glanced at Braden again, but his features showed no sign of softening.

Ah, well, it was only mostly over. I still had a battle in front of me. I was about to launch my first offensive to get into his good graces when the butler approached, a cordless phone in his hand. He immediately handed it to Cormack, who pressed it to his ear and began talking.

It didn't take long to realize that something horrible had happened. Cormack was on his feet, Lily clutched tightly against his chest as his face went unnaturally white. No one said a word until he was off the phone, and then the deluge of questions began.

"Shut up ... all of you." Cormack used his most authoritative voice. "I will tell you what happened. Don't interrupt."

"Well, this can't be good," Aisling muttered, clearly distressed.

"It's not," Cormack confirmed. "We had guards at several of the revenant homes. We were watching in case the revenants returned. At three of those locations, we lost contact with the security teams at almost exactly the same time. The home office dispatched backup. When they arrived, they found all of the security team members dead."

My stomach twisted into a big ball of horror. "Are you serious? How many men?"

"We're down six men. There were two at each location."

"But … ." My mind raced. "We need to get over there. I need to see if I can sense something." I discarded my ice cream bowl on the table. I'd lost my appetite. "It's a long shot, but I might be able to figure out what happened."

"Then we'll go," Cormack confirmed, immediately shaking his head when chairs began scraping against the floor. "Not all of us. I want most of you to stay here and keep researching. And, before you say one word, Aisling, you will be part of the contingent that remains."

"I'm fine with that," she supplied, her eyes on me. "I have information to share with those who stay behind. Besides, it's not as if I can help. I'm not magic."

"You're going to tell them what I learned from Claire?" I asked. I figured that's what she was talking about, but I wanted to be sure.

She nodded. "You can fill in the bigger gaps later. I'll give them the basics."

"Okay."

"Good." Cormack shifted Lily into Cillian's arms. "Braden and Izzy will come with me. If we learn something, we'll call. Otherwise, I want everyone locked down in this house. Does everybody understand?" He paused for a beat. "Aisling, if you're about to say something snarky, I would advise against it. I'm not in the mood."

"When has that ever stopped me?" she challenged.

Griffin slapped his hand over her mouth before she could continue. "Go. I'll handle her. Just … be safe. Always look over your shoulders. These things are apparently sneaky and strong. We don't want to lose anyone."

I SAT IN THE BACK SEAT OF CORMACK'S Maserati Quattroporte. It seemed a safe bet. Braden slid into the passenger seat and met my gaze long enough to nod. There was no warmth in the gesture, so I didn't know how to read it. I only knew I felt bereft.

When we arrived at the first scene, it was buzzing with activity, but there were no police. That's the first thing I noticed. All the emergency personnel were low key and dressed in street clothes.

"Why aren't the cops aren't here?" It was a stupid question, but I was feeling slower than normal.

"This isn't a job for the police," Cormack replied. "They can't do anything to stop this. What's happening here is our responsibility."

I couldn't really argue with that, so I moved around him and headed straight for one of the bodies on the street. I took a moment to study the houses that were packed in on both sides of the older street — there was very little space between the houses — and was surprised to find an absence of curious faces in the windows.

"Why aren't the neighbors watching?" I asked, accepting the rubber gloves shoved in my direction by one of the reaper paramedics. He was dressed in gray rather than white. "Thanks, but I don't plan to disturb your crime scene. I do need to touch the bodies, though."

The paramedic opened his mouth to argue, but Cormack shot him a firm head shake.

"Give Ms. Sage the room she needs to operate," he instructed. "If you have a problem with that, take it up with the head office. I've been cleared to do whatever I deem necessary on this scene."

The paramedic snapped his mouth shut and nodded.

I circled the body twice before dropping to a knee. The body was in bad shape, blood coating the man's face and chest. I had no idea how he died. The only thing I could be certain of was that it was a hard death.

"You don't have to do this if you don't want to," Braden offered, moving closer to me. Concern etched lines in his face and it was obvious he had more he wanted to say. "I mean ... no one will think less of you if you choose not to look inside his head. It doesn't always have to be you."

That was almost laughable considering the circumstances. "If not me, who?"

"We can figure out what happened without you having to emotionally batter yourself. We basically know how this happened anyway."

"Details are always helpful."

"Not at the expense of you getting a good night's sleep." He leaned forward to make sure nobody except me could hear what he was about to say. "I won't pretend I'm not angry, but I don't want you punishing yourself. It'll be okay."

Even though I told myself I wasn't worked up about his insistence on giving me the cold shoulder, the simple declaration was enough to loosen some of the worry that had been gripping my heart. I never wanted to be one of those women who got her self-worth from a man. That didn't mean I wasn't greatly relieved to know that he didn't plan on holding a grudge forever.

"I have to look." I forced a smile for his benefit. "I have to see. We're assuming the same thing happened at this house that happened at Dunning's. Once I get confirmation of that, I won't have to check the others. We have to be absolutely sure."

He held my gaze for an extended moment and then sighed. "Okay. Just don't stay in there longer than you have to. See what you need and get out. I'll make sure you get the ice cream you missed when we get back to the house."

The statement was so absurd, so out of the blue, that I had to fight the urge to laugh. "I thought you were angry with me."

"I am. Well ... was. It doesn't matter. Nobody should go without ice cream from the ice cream bar. It's a special treat ... and the gummy worms are delightful."

On instinct, I reached over and squeezed his hand. "I'll be as quick as I can. Don't worry. This is hardly the first time I've had to do this."

"I won't be able to stop myself from worrying, just like you won't be able to stop yourself from poking your nose in dangerous places. He leaned forward and pressed his forehead to mine. We're just going to have to learn to accept annoying things about each other."

This wasn't the place for the conversation, but I enjoyed the words all the same.

"All right, knock it off," Cormack growled, shaking his head. I'd almost forgotten he was watching over us. Apparently he'd witnessed everything that just went down, and he didn't look impressed. "Seriously, between you two and Aisling and Griffin, I'm going to lose all my hair before the end of the year. I don't understand why everything must be so dramatic."

"You raised us," Braden offered, taking a step away from me and positioning himself next to his father. "Maybe you provided the drama gene. Have you ever considered that?"

"No. It was definitely your mother."

The exchange was normal, cute, and almost sweet. It relaxed me enough to extend my hand and touch the guard. Almost instantaneously, I was transported to his final moments. What I saw was confusing ... and chillingly violent.

"Oh, geez." I jerked my hand away after two minutes of contact. I'd seen all that was necessary. In fact, I was certain I'd seen more than was necessary. My hand was shaking when Braden moved behind me and helped me to my feet.

"What did you see?" Cormack asked. He almost looked pained to ask, but we were here for information.

"First, the revenants are doing something with the souls," I offered after I'd collected myself, running the scene through my head again just to make sure I'd seen what I thought I'd seen. "I'm not familiar with sucking souls, but Braden has described what happens and I'm almost positive that the revenants took the souls of your guards."

"Took them?" Cormack's eyebrow winged up. "Did they absorb them in a scepter?"

"No."

"Then how did they take them? You need a receptacle for the souls. Otherwise they can just take off."

"They didn't have time." I was chilled by what I saw. "They seemed confused when they emerged from their bodies. The revenants were on them right away. They ... ate ... the souls. That's the only way I can think to explain it. They sucked them into their mouths ... and they shared what they got as if it were a huge meal."

Cormack's features twisted as he shifted his gaze to Braden. "Well, I guess that could explain why our people didn't show up on the lists of the dead. We know from personal experience that reapers are no different from humans when it comes to collecting souls. Apparently someone recognized we could never save these souls."

"We should check the surrounding houses," I suggested. "We know the revenants aren't afraid to kill neighbors. The guards might've served as a sustainable meal, but we need to be sure. The revenants by Dunning's house were killed. We need numbers. I can't be sure who we killed. We need to know who was in that house, because if Dunning wasn't with the revenants we killed he's still out there ... and a danger."

Cormack blew out a weary sigh. "This is beyond anything we've had to face before. We need to get ahead of this, but I don't know where to start."

This situation was quickly growing out of control and there was no end in sight. If the revenants continued to multiply, we would be overrun quickly. We couldn't allow that to happen.

We were already running out of time.

Twenty-One

I was exhausted by the time we returned to Grimlock Manor. I didn't mount an argument when Braden directed me toward the kitchen. I thought we would be alone, but most of the family was there mixing sundaes. We joined in without saying a word.

"I take it things were bad," Redmond said as Braden dished up a huge serving of ice cream and handed it to me.

"They were bad," Braden agreed. "The revenants ate their souls."

"What?" Horrified, Aisling pulled away from Griffin. They looked to have made up, because they were both in pajamas and giving each other flirty looks. The crackling atmosphere between them died in an instant.

I nodded dully. "I saw what happened to the guards when I touched one of them. The souls didn't have time to flee. They were gone in an instant ... and it was ugly."

"Well, crap." Aisling rubbed her cheek. "Do you think they would've done the same to us?"

Griffin straightened his shoulders at the question. Obviously he hadn't yet worked his way around to that possibility. "You're not leaving the house," he announced.

She slid him a sidelong look. "We've already talked about this. You

agreed it was unfair to keep me locked away from the action. You said
... ."

He shook his head to cut her off. "I know what I said, but I've
changed my mind. You're on house arrest again."

"Oh, that's big talk," Braden challenged. "We both know you won't
be able to back it up. You can't keep her locked away from this. It's not
fair and it's going to blow up in your face."

"It is," Aisling agreed.

"I don't care." Griffin looked determined. "Dealing with the idea of
you dying is enough to cripple me. The thought of losing your soul
forever ... no." He fervently shook his head. "I won't risk that for
anything."

"You don't have a choice." Aisling was matter-of-fact. "I can't turn
away from this. You know that. If the revenants get a foothold, it won't
only be me in danger. It will be Lily. We have to stop them now or risk
losing everything."

"Oh, good grief." Griffin rubbed his forehead. "You just said that
because you know I can't argue with you."

"Oh, if only that were true." She flashed him a smile. "It'll be okay.
I took one down with a real estate sign. It'll be much easier with a
sword."

Griffin didn't look convinced. "I want you to have backup at all
times. No going at this alone."

"Deal."

I sighed in relief when it appeared a potential fight had been
headed off. When I turned to Braden, though, I found him watching
me with somber eyes. I knew what he was thinking.

"I can't make that promise," I offered. "I will do my absolute best
to have backup, but I can't promise not to go after them if I see an
opening. You have to realize that."

"I do." He forced a smile that didn't make it all the way to his eyes.
"We'll figure it out."

That's as close as we were going to get to compromise. "We will.
But now I want to eat my weight in ice cream and then get some sleep.
I'm officially exhausted."

He winked. "Your wish is my command."

. . .

WHEN I WOKE IN HIS bed the next morning he was already conscious and watching me. His expression was contemplative.

"Oh, don't be a pain," I complained, groaning as I stretched my arms over my head. "I don't want to start the day with a fight."

"I have no intention of picking a fight." He was sincere. "I was just ... thinking."

I wasn't sure I wanted to know what he was thinking about, but I asked the obvious question. "About what?"

"You." A small smile played at the corners of his mouth. "You're kind of pretty ... and I'm kind of fond of you."

"Kind of?"

"Just a little bit." He held his index finger and thumb about an inch apart. "It's not out of control or anything."

I didn't believe that. He felt the same way about me as I did about him. I knew, because he often couldn't control the rush of emotions that overtook him at the oddest of times, and I felt the same things he did because we were connected on an emotional level.

"I'm kind of fond of you, too."

"I know." The words were delivered with equal parts charm and ego. "I'm the sort of guy you can't help but be fond of."

"You're ... something." I stretched again, taking a moment to feel each muscle. Surprisingly, I wasn't sore. I didn't feel as much as a twinge. "We need to talk to your father and come up with a plan for fighting the revenants. We should be able to take them. I mean ... Aisling, Paris and I were outnumbered. It wasn't easy, but it wasn't nearly as hard as it could've been. We weren't at risk of dying."

"I've been thinking about that," he acknowledged, his fingers linking with mine under the covers. "Reaper guards aren't trained for heavy combat. We have special teams trained for things like that, don't get me wrong, but the guards weren't helpless. They should've at least put up a fight."

I thought about what I'd seen in the vision. "I don't think they were expecting what happened. They didn't see the danger until it was directly on top of them."

"That's the same thing that happened to the guards outside the hospital wing."

I shifted to stare at his face. "What are you thinking?"

"I don't know." His jaw was stubbled with a night's worth of growth and he looked criminally handsome. Seriously, nobody had the right to look that good so early in the morning. It made my heart roll in pleasure ... and my brain start chiding my hormones for picking now to become active. "Have we considered that they can somehow camouflage themselves?"

It was an interesting notion. "We saw the revenants right after they rose ... or whatever it is they did. I have no idea where they were hiding. We searched that house, and there's no way they managed to hide from us in each location. That means they were somehow hiding in another way ... perhaps even underground.

"When we saw the revenants, they looked exactly like Ray Smith did the night we took him down," I continued. "They weren't hiding anything and they came straight for us."

"Well, that would seem to indicate they can't change their appearances ... except we know they can. They looked like normal humans when they appeared on our side of the gate. They only changed after."

"For Ray, it was after he died. For the others, they didn't die as far as we know. Perhaps it's possible one of them was injured in a fight, but there's no way all five of them went down."

"I didn't really think of that, but you're right. Maybe it wasn't about Ray's death at all. Maybe there was some sort of trigger built into each man."

"But why? Why were they taken in the first place? How did the revenants manage it? Why did they take only the one group of men?"

Something occurred to me. "Maybe it wasn't only one group of men. Maybe it was multiple groups of men at different locations. I mean ... think about it." I was starting to get excited as a specific idea built in my head. "What happened to the cadets here wasn't common knowledge. What if each location had a similar incident around the same time and they opted to keep it to themselves?"

"That sounds like a pretty large conspiracy."

"It doesn't have to be. Reapers are naturally secretive. What if each location kept it quiet?"

"But we don't know that it happened at different gates. That's all supposition at this point."

"Do you think there's a way we can find out?"

"Only one that I can think of." He cast me a sidelong look. "We'll need Dad to call in a few favors."

"Will he do that?"

"Absolutely."

"So ... what are we waiting for?" I moved to climb out the bed, but he stopped me with a wicked gleam in his eye.

"Breakfast is still an hour away," he pointed out. "We have a little time to burn."

I knew how he planned to burn it. "Seriously? We're dealing with life and death here."

"An hour won't change that."

I sighed. "Okay, but if we get yelled at by your father for being late I'm totally going to blame you."

"I can live with that."

MOST OF THE FAMILY WAS GROUPED around the dining room table when we finally made our way downstairs. We were only three minutes late, but since Cormack prided himself on timeliness I wasn't surprised by the glare on his face when we headed toward our usual seats.

"I'm so glad you could join us," he drawled. "I hope this potential apocalypse didn't cut into your play time."

"We're good," Braden replied dryly. He was used to his father's attitude and clearly didn't care if he was upset. "What's for breakfast?"

"It's a normal breakfast," Aisling announced, morose. She looked as if someone had kicked her dog for no good reason. "It's just simple stuff ... eggs and corned beef hash. There's not even any biscuits and gravy."

I found her reaction humorous, bordering on ridiculous. Braden, however, was equally upset. "No way." He shook his head and glared at his father. "Why don't we have a waffle bar? Or pancake bar?"

"Or omelet bar?" Aisling whined. "You know I could eat from the omelet bar seven days a week. That's my favorite."

"I hate to agree with my wife, especially over something so frivolous," Griffin interjected.

"But you will," Cormack muttered.

"An omelet bar would've been good this morning," he argued. "I mean ... we'll all be fighting monsters and stuff to save the world. We could use the protein."

"And you can have protein in regular eggs." Cormack was firm. "Given how some of you behaved yesterday, punishment is still in effect. Since I expected two of you — and you know who you are, Griffin and Braden — to exert some control over this situation, you're being punished as well."

"What about the rest of us?" Redmond complained. "I don't have a girlfriend. Cillian's girlfriend always behaves herself. As for Jerry ... he's annoying but never puts himself in danger. Why are we being punished along with the bad ones?"

"You laughed and encouraged the bad behavior."

"We always do that. We've never been in trouble for it before."

"Well, times change." Cormack sipped his juice. I could practically see the glee wafting through his mind. He was enjoying himself, which only proved his children picked up the majority of their behavioral cues from him. It really was a distressing display.

"Well, this blows," Redmond complained as the kitchen staff started delivering platters to the table.

Everything looked and smelled delicious, and I immediately dug into the corned beef hash. "My grandfather used to make this when I was a kid," I offered, grinning as I reached for the egg platter. "We didn't have much money so we had to make do. We could make a meal out of corned beef hash and eggs — sometimes three times a day — for only a couple of dollars."

Instead of being charmed by the story, Aisling shot me a withering look. "I hate it when you say stuff like that. It makes the rest of us look entitled."

"You *are* entitled," Griffin shot back, his plate heaped with food. "There's nothing wrong with a normal breakfast every now and again. It makes you appreciate the special breakfasts even more."

Her eyes were dangerous lavender slits. "I'm done talking to you this morning if you're going to say things like that."

"Okay." He patted her knee under the table and glanced around the table. "Speaking of people who enable Aisling on the breakfast front, where is Jerry?"

"He's already at work," Aidan volunteered. "He has a big wedding coming up — it's for a prominent family and means a lot of money for our honeymoon fund — and he refuses to work from here. Dad arranged for two men to watch him, but Jerry doesn't know that. He thinks he's safe simply because he watched ninja movies when he was a kid."

Cormack smirked. "He is safe. The odds of these creatures even knowing about Jerry are slim. The guards are simply a precaution. He'll be fine.

"It's the rest of us who have to be careful," Cormack continued. "With that in mind, I don't want anybody alone. Everyone is working in teams. If you even think about arguing with me, you're in trouble." His eyes were on Aisling when he delivered the last line.

"I'm fine working with a partner," Aisling offered. She'd finally started adding food to her plate. She waited long enough to see if her father was playing a cruel joke on her and then gave in. Apparently her hunger was greater than her mouth ... which was saying something. "I want to pick my partner, though. I don't want to work with Braden."

Braden sneered at her. "Right back at you."

"You're not working with Braden," Cormack confirmed.

"That's good. I don't want to work with Cillian either."

"Hey!" Cillian shot her a look. They were close in a way the other Grimlock siblings couldn't claim. It was a quiet closeness. When either of them needed some downtime, they went to each other. It was an interesting relationship. "I can't believe you just said that to me. I'm supposed to be your favorite."

"I'm her favorite," Redmond countered.

"No, I'm her favorite," Aidan snapped. "We shared a womb together. It doesn't get closer than that."

Griffin cleared his throat. "I'm her favorite. I believe I've already stated that multiple times. And, if I have a vote, I would prefer she be paired with Cillian. He'll be researching in the library all day and that's a perfectly reasonable job for Aisling."

"Under normal circumstances, I'd agree," Cormack replied. "I don't want her at headquarters. I think it's unlikely that the revenants would return there, but you never know. Besides, I have a meeting with Renley this morning and it might get loud. I don't want her there in case it also gets ugly."

"Okay. Then where is she going?"

"Well, I've given it a great deal of thought and come up with a plan. Aisling is going to Belle Isle with Izzy and Cillian. There's a library there and they can all conduct research between normal gate duties."

Griffin balked. "I don't think the gate is safe."

"It's as safe as anything right now."

He didn't look convinced. "No. I don't want her on that island."

Perhaps it was because Griffin was setting his foot down. Perhaps it was because her father sounded so sure of himself and she owed him a morning free of strife. I couldn't be entirely sure. Aisling's motivations were often murky, including now. That's why I was instantly suspicious when she started talking.

"I'll go to the island and do research," she said, pinning Griffin with a death glare. "I want to do my part to help. Don't bother arguing, Griffin. It's already decided. I'm going to the island."

He stared at her for what felt like forever and then nodded before reaching for his coffee. "Good enough."

I was expecting more of a fight. Apparently, so was Aisling.

"Wait a second ... ." Suspicion lit her face. "What just happened here? You guys planned that, didn't you?"

"I have no idea what you're talking about." Griffin averted his gaze and focused on his father-in-law. "What are you talking to Renley about?"

"Secrets," Cormack replied, grim. "There are far too many of them regarding what happened at the gate. I want to know exactly what happened sixty years ago and why it was covered up."

That was a relief. I thought we were going to have to push him into questioning his boss. "You also might want to ask if there's any reason to believe similar incidents happened at other gates," I volunteered. "It's just an idea, but I'm starting to wonder."

Cormack's eyebrows drew together. "You're starting to wonder what?"

"If the revenants had this planned, why focus on Detroit? Doesn't it make more sense to set things in motion at each gate?"

He shifted in his chair and I could hear the gears of his mind working behind his eyes. "I didn't consider that, but you're absolutely right. Enacting something like this in one location is folly. It has a better chance of working if multiple locations are under attack at the same time."

"Would Renley tell you if that were the case?" Griffin queried. "I mean ... will he be open with you?"

"He'd better be. My family is at risk. I don't care how he wants to handle things. From here on out, they'll be done to my liking."

"Kind of like how you tricked me into doing research today," Aisling groused. "Everything is coming up roses for you right now."

"Suck it up." It was clear Cormack had no sympathy for her plight. "You're going to be in the safest location we can arrange, and you volunteered for it."

"Only because you tricked me by using my own husband against me."

"You'll be smarter next time." Cormack's grin was charming as he slid his gaze to me. "It's going to be a long day for you, but that's your penance for allowing her to manipulate you. I have a feeling you'll learn quickly from here on out."

I had a feeling he was right.

Twenty-Two

Cillian sent Aisling and me ahead. He promised to join us as soon as he collected a few books — something he had to carry out at reaper headquarters — which meant I would be traveling with Aisling.

Alone.

"I like your sister, but I think I've had my fill of bonding with her for the week," I explained to Braden as we said our goodbyes in the driveway.

He chuckled as he stroked my hair. "She's a lot of work," he agreed. "But she's not always terrible. She's actually fairly good in a crisis."

I studied him for a beat. His relationship with his sister was always a curiosity. They'd been at odds for a long time. Cormack once told me it was because they were the most alike, although he added that Braden, who was unnaturally attached to his mother, struggled the most after his mother died. Aisling did, too, in a way. As the lone girl, she'd lost the only other female in the house and it was difficult.

Maxine filled in a lot of the story for me. She was involved in the final battle, at least on the periphery. She helped the soul of Lily Grimlock return to fight for her children. She had the inside scoop, so to speak.

I didn't know much. I knew that Aisling was taken by the thing that wore her mother's face, that plans were in place for that thing to steal Aisling's body (it was the only way for it to become whole again) and that the Grimlock males arrived as a group to fight. Aisling was pretty much in control of her destiny at that point, thanks to the return of her real mother, and she took off after the evil version. Braden followed.

I wasn't aware of the specifics of the battle. No one wanted to go into that much detail, and I couldn't blame them. At some point, Braden was in danger. One of the balconies in the abandoned theater they were fighting in gave way and he was at risk of falling to his death. Aisling put herself in danger to save him. She held on even as the Lily creature begged to be saved over her son. Aisling ignored her pleas, and with the help of her father and brothers managed to save Braden.

Intellectually, I knew Aisling wasn't really the person I thought of her as. When we'd first met, she was pregnant and due to give birth any day. After, she struggled in the wake of new motherhood. Not everyone embraces it with happiness and light. She needed help. Luckily she came from a family that liked to help.

Now she was throwing herself back into work and I didn't know what to make of it. I'd seen her fight the previous day — and she was scrappy — but I couldn't help feeling I would be spending all day entertaining her rather than getting any work done.

"I wish she was going with you guys."

Braden's eyes twinkled. "My father would never allow that. He's taking Lily with him. I would love to be a fly on the wall in Renley's office when my father strolls in and starts yelling with Lily strapped to his chest. She'll smile. It will be something to behold."

He was far too thrilled with the image. "Too bad your father won't take Aisling with him to headquarters."

"He says it's because he doesn't think she'll be safe there, but that's not true. The majority of the reapers are loyal to him, even over Renley if there's an issue. If he honestly believed there was going to be trouble he wouldn't take Lily. He doesn't want Aisling there because she's liable to stir up trouble."

I could see that. "So instead, I get stuck with her."

Braden snickered. "I can tell you're thrilled about it. The thing is, you might be glad you have her. I know it doesn't seem like it now, but it's true. She's a righteous pain in the behind, but she also thinks outside the box, and in this particular case she's motivated to help. That's good for all of us."

He was so earnest I could do nothing but shake my head. "I never thought I would see the day you'd take up for your sister."

"I know. It's baffling."

I laughed before giving him a hug. "Don't worry about Aisling. I'll take care of her."

"I know you will. Even though you might not be able to see how or why just yet, I believe Aisling might help you, too. She's smarter than she seems ... and she wants to keep Lily safe. She'll work harder than you think."

I knew I was acting out of line simply because he was so determined to stick up for Aisling. When it came to big things, the Grimlock siblings were loyal to a fault. When little things popped up, they enjoyed messing with one another. The fact that Braden showed no inclination to mess with his sister told me he was convinced this was a big deal. It would be wise, I rationalized, for me to do the same.

"I'll do my best for both of us," I promised.

He wrapped his arms around me and kissed my forehead before moving his lips to mine. "You always do."

AISLING WAS QUIETER THAN I'D EVER seen her when we arrived at the small dock. Belle Isle was still closed to visitors — something that was being described as an environmental precaution by the local news to keep looky-loos away — so there was only one way to get to the gate. That was via water.

"This is a nifty little boat," Aisling announced, perking up for the first time as she climbed into the back of the vessel. "I'll drive."

The declaration caught me off guard. "What if I want to drive?"

"Then you can drive tomorrow." She was firm. "I haven't been on a boat in ... well, years. My mother liked boating. She would take us out on Lake St. Clair when we were kids. No one really wanted to get on a boat after she was gone."

The story should've touched me. but I was instantly suspicious. "Are you just saying that because you want to drive?"

She nodded without hesitation. "Yes. My mother did like boats, though. My father wasn't as much a fan. We didn't go out as much after she died. I took lessons when I was a kid."

"You took lessons?" I didn't want to be stuck on this side of the river forever, so I climbed into the front of the boat and got comfortable. If Aisling turned out to be a bad captain I would probably regret giving in. I had to suck it up because it was too early for an argument. "I didn't know they gave motorboat lessons."

"This is a huge boating area." Aisling started the engine with little difficulty and got comfortable as she steered away from the dock and into the river. "Boating is a big deal because of the weather. We get only five months a year when we can enjoy the lakes, so people treat it like the pastime of kings. Even though my father wasn't a big fan, he wanted to make sure knew our way around boats.

"We had classes a lot when we were kids," she continued. "Sailboats ... speed boats ... smaller boats with outboard engines like this. We learned how to operate them all. My father was convinced we were a calamity waiting to happen, so we also had to take survival classes. We learned to strip out of our clothes while treading water so we could survive an extended period in the water."

I watched her for signs she was kidding. "My grandfather saw to it that I took boating lessons, too. New Orleans is surrounded by water. We would head out at night a lot because he liked to collect things for spells. He turned me into his boat captain at a young age so he could focus on the plants and critters he needed."

If Aisling was bored by the story, she didn't show it. "I bet you had fun with your grandfather. I mean ... I know you would've given anything to have your parents back, but your grandfather sounds fun. My grandparents are more boring than a mole in an armpit. You'll find out. They'll be visiting in a few weeks. They're both jerks."

It took everything I had not to laugh at her morose expression. "You don't like your grandparents?"

"They're awful. They used to call us hellions and tell my father he should make us behave."

"And you don't think your father should've made you behave?"

"No. We turned out absolutely fine."

She said it with so much conviction it was impossible to argue with her. I decided to change the subject instead. "Why are your grandparents coming? Braden mentioned they were visiting — he's just as thrilled as you, by the way — and he let it slip that they're almost never around. Why are they visiting now?"

Aisling's lips curved down. "They want to torture us."

"Why really?"

"My grandparents moved out of Michigan when I was young. I can't even remember how old I was. I used to joke with my father that they moved because they didn't want to get stuck babysitting us. He didn't disagree.

"They came to visit after my mother died," she continued, taking on a far-off expression. "They thought my father would fall apart and not be able to care for us. That was true to an extent — he was absolutely wrecked — but he didn't completely collapse.

"We were teenagers. I think Redmond was in his twenties. Our grandparents swooped in and tried to take advantage of the situation. They even suggested taking Aidan and me to live with them.

"That's when my father put his foot down and told them to back off." Aisling smiled at the memory. "He said he would raise us as he saw fit and wouldn't allow us to be separated. I remember thinking at the time that we would be okay. It still hurt to lose Mom, but we were going to be okay because Dad would make sure of it."

I nodded in understanding. "Even though your father overindulges you — all of you — he's a phenomenal man. He did an amazing job."

"He did," Aisling confirmed, smiling. "My grandparents were angered by his attitude and took off. They split their time between Aspen and Florida these days. I was convinced we might never see them again. They barely call once a month to check in with Dad and they always have attitude when they do. They don't like his stories about us."

"And yet they're coming," I noted. "Something must've changed. Maybe they've had a change of heart."

"They said they wanted to meet Lily. She's their first great-grandchild."

The expression on Aisling's face told me she wasn't thrilled at the prospect. "Maybe they're telling the truth," I suggested, the early morning sun making me shield my eyes. "They're getting older now. They're feeling their mortality. Perhaps they realize they made a mistake."

"I think you're giving them far too much credit." Aisling went back to sulking. "I just know they're going to be rude. To them, marrying a cop is pretty much the worst thing I could've done."

"They dislike cops?"

"They dislike anyone who doesn't make seven figures a year."

"Ah. I understand." Actually, that wasn't entirely true. I didn't understand in the least. I'd met all sorts of people over the years – rich people, poor people, happy people, sad people – and I could only imagine how these people thought. Cormack was rich and his children spoiled rotten, but they were all surprisingly down to earth. The privilege aspect was bound to come in somewhere. "Just tell them that you're happy with Griffin and if they don't like it to stuff it."

I remained focused on the approaching shore. I was almost positive I saw movement in an area where nothing ever happened. Maybe fishermen. I happened to love a good morning spent with a rod and reel in hand. If there was a local group that was about to join together for a quiet morning, I wanted to know ... mostly because there was a likelihood I would join. The one thing my grandfather and I liked to do together even as I grew older and discovered my own interests – as well as boys, of course – was fish. We never argued when fishing.

Frogging and reed cultivating was another story.

"Oh, I'll tell them to stuff it. I ... ." The boat grazed something below the waves, the metal walls screeching as Aisling frowned. She slowed the engine and glanced around, confused.

We were dead center in the channel. I'd been over this area several times. There was nothing out here that should've scraped against the bottom of the boat.

So ... what was that?

"Do you think a boat sank or something?" I asked, turning away from the shoreline and focusing on the water. It wasn't exactly the cleanest body of water I'd ever seen, but it wasn't full of garbage either. Still, the water was murky. I couldn't see beyond the first few inches.

"There aren't usually a lot of boats out here," Aisling replied absently. "Most people with boats take them to Lake St. Clair to avoid the current." She looked over her shoulder. There was something about her expression that bothered me.

"What's wrong?" I wasn't worried, but I couldn't shake the feeling that something was about to happen. We were in a fresh-water channel of the river. Thankfully there were no creatures in the water big enough to attack — sharks were a real fear of mine — so I couldn't figure out why she'd gone so rigid.

"I don't know." Aisling rummaged around the bottom of the boat until she came up with a paddle. They were there in case of emergency, like the engine overheating or the boat springing a leak. I'd paid them zero attention the few times I'd been in the boat the past few days.

"What are you going to do with that?"

"See what's under here." Aisling lowered the paddle into the water, frowning as she leaned over the gunwale. She looked as if she was concentrating, and I almost wanted to laugh at her expression because it was so grave. She was so serious that she almost looked like a different person.

When she didn't immediately find anything, I was ready to call it a morning and complete our short voyage to the island. "There's nothing down there. Maybe whatever it was came from a boat way out that way." I gestured vaguely toward Canada. "It might've brushed against us in the current. It was probably nothing."

Aisling didn't look convinced. "Probably," she murmured, moving the paddle around again. Suddenly, she gasped, both hands grabbing the paddle.

"What?" I gripped the side of the boat and peered over. I couldn't see anything. Still, I felt something ... and it wasn't good. "What do you think it is?"

"Something is pulling," Aisling gritted as she gripped the paddle and gave it a vicious tug. "There's something down there."

"Let it have the paddle," I ordered. "We don't need it."

"No way. I'm not giving whatever is down there a weapon."

"Let it go," I repeated. "Crank up the engine and get us out of here."

"No, I ... ." She pulled so hard the paddle jerked several inches out of the water and soared in her direction. For a moment I thought she was going to win the tug of war.

That feeling of exhilaration lasted only a split-second.

That's when I saw a black hand wrapped around the paddle bar. It was mutated ... and rubbery. I knew exactly what that meant.

"Did you see that?" Aisling's eyes were as big as Frisbees.

I nodded, dumbfounded. "The revenants are in the water." I glanced back toward the shore to study the movement I was convinced I'd seen moments before. The shore was still, but my suspicions were out of control. "We have to get to Belle Isle right now. We can't screw around."

Aisling continued to tug on the paddle.

"Now isn't the time for your 'win-at-all-costs' attitude," I hissed, grabbing the paddle so I could pull it from her. "Screw the paddle and get us to the island. We need to prepare for them to invade. It might already be too late."

Aisling held my gaze for a moment and then acquiesced, releasing the paddle. "Okay, but that's the last ground I'm ceding to them. This means war."

I could do nothing but shake my head. "Over a boat paddle?"

"Over everything. They can't have this world. I won't let them."

On that we could agree.

Twenty-Three

Aisling had no fear when it came to navigating to the island. She aimed right for the shore rather than the dock, which was a stroke of genius because we wouldn't have to worry about being dragged into the water from below the rickety wooden contraption. We rammed the shore hard enough that I pitched forward, scraping against the rocks that littered the shoreline.

"Son of a ... !" I glared at Aisling, who didn't look bothered in the least about how I landed.

"Get up," she ordered as she joined me on the beach. Her eyes were on the water as she scanned for movement. "We're too exposed out here. We have to get inside."

I glared at her as I dusted myself off, frowning at the small tear in the knee of my jeans. "You're a menace," I muttered. "I mean ... seriously a menace."

"I got us here safely, didn't I?"

That was a matter of opinion. "You didn't have to ram us in so hard."

"Oh, suck it up." She scuffed her shoe against the ground and then shook her head. "The revenants could be coming from any direction. They'd be stupid to follow us. Given the way they attacked yesterday, I assumed they were stupid. What they pulled off today shows actual planning. We need to get inside."

I nodded in agreement. I was still annoyed, but she was right. "Oliver will be at the aquarium. He might know what to do. Even if he doesn't, at least we'll have more backup."

"Then let's go."

WE RAN, BECAUSE IT SEEMED the thing to do, and were out of breath when we reached the aquarium. The island was shut off to guests, so the workers who toiled in front of the aquarium were gone for the day. Those who fed the aquarium creatures stopped in, but at night. At least that's what I was told. That meant, conceivably, the only people on the island were Oliver, Brett, Claire, Collin, Aisling and me. That wasn't enough bodies to wage a war.

My hands were steady as I swiped my keycard in the reader. We waited until we were inside, the doors separating us from the outside world, to glance over our shoulders. There was nothing out there and yet it felt as if death was closing in.

"Come on." I hurried away from the door and headed for the hallway that led to the gate room. I wasn't particularly thrilled at the idea of returning to where all of this began, but I didn't see that we had much choice.

Oliver was at his computer, a spreadsheet open on the desk next to him, but he was engaged in a conversation with Brett. I pulled up short. I couldn't ever remember Brett just stopping by for a visit.

"Is something wrong?" I blurted out the question without thinking.

"They should be asking us that," Aisling noted. "Just FYI, guys, there's definitely something wrong."

Oliver furrowed his brow, confused. "I wasn't sure you were coming to work today. I got a cryptic message from Cormack. He said something about members of his team stopping by, but he didn't mention you specifically."

Oh, well, I was part of his team. That was a nice sentiment. It wasn't, however, something I could focus on now. "What are you guys working on?"

"We're not working on anything," Brett replied. "Oliver simply mentioned he was feeling lonely working here alone the past few days so I thought I would surprise him with a mid-morning snack." He crossed the room to hug me. He was the demonstrative sort, unlike Oliver. I returned the embrace even though I was agitated. "What's going on with you?" he asked as he pulled away, taking a moment to push my wild hair from my face. "You're flushed."

"If Braden is here with you, I wasn't kidding when I said I would tie it in a knot," Oliver commented. "I don't care how much you like him. He's a pervert."

"He's totally a pervert," Aisling agreed. "But he's not the reason she's so disheveled."

"Yes, *you're* the reason I look like this," I groused, rolling my eyes. "You drive like a maniac and I'm going to make you pay for it later."

Aisling didn't look worried in the least. "I'm looking forward to the effort, but we have other things to worry about now."

"Something happened on our way over," I explained to Brett and Oliver. "We hit something in the water. It turned out to be a revenant."

Oliver very deliberately got to his feet. His expression was unreadable, but there was fire in his eyes. "What do you mean? Why would the revenants be in the water?"

"I think the obvious answer is that they're coming here."

"But ... why?" Brett was clearly bewildered as he glanced between faces. "I don't understand what any of this means."

He wasn't the only one. "We've discovered a few things," I volunteered. "The biggest of which is that revenants are basically bastardized cousins of vampires." I told them the story as quickly as I could, leaving nothing out. When I finished, the doubt reflected on their features was obvious.

"And Claire told you this?" Oliver challenged. "How certain is she that it's true?"

"She seemed pretty certain. She said some minor details might've changed over the years, but the heart of the story was the same. Revenants and vampires both sprung from demons."

"That's true of vampires," Brett noted. "I've read our history books and they all confirm that. The revenant thing, though ... I just don't understand. If they were such a great threat, why wouldn't that story be included in our lore?"

I'd been giving that a lot of thought. "All the paranormals worked together," I volunteered. "That rarely happens. They recognized a threat and worked together to eradicate it. I think they hid the truth for several reasons.

"The first is that each group couldn't very well continue to hate other groups if it became common knowledge that all of them worked together at one point and nobody but the enemy died," I continued. "Old grudges run deep. Each group wanted to continue to hate. Groups might start doubting how smart that was if a truce was not only brokered but achieved for an extended period.

"The second is that I think they were trying to make it so others, those too stupid to see the folly of their actions, didn't try to cross over to see the revenants. If that happened, the revenants might've had the ability to use those individuals as a means to cross back. It's just an idea, but it makes sense."

Brett stroked his jaw. "It does make sense," he agreed. "The problem is that they've put us in a real bind. We don't even know how to fight these things, and now you're telling me that they're descending on the island. How are we supposed to stop that?"

"Fire works well," I replied. "They burn quickly enough."

"You can stab them, too," Aisling offered, pulling a dagger from her pocket and grinning maniacally. "Do you guys have weapons here?"

"We have an arsenal in the closet at the end of the hallway," Oliver replied. "It wouldn't hurt to arm ourselves. Brett and I can also fight with our bare hands. We're strong, but it's possible the revenants are equally as strong."

I immediately started shaking my head. "I don't think so. We took out four yesterday without breaking a sweat. But if I had to guess, most of them were new. I guess it's possible they grow stronger with time. I really should've asked Claire about that."

"She needs to be warned." Oliver's tone was grave. "She and Collin need to be made aware of what's coming so they can arm themselves."

"And stay out of the water," Aisling added. "It's not safe for them to go for a relaxing dip right now. We're not sure where the revenants will make land, but they're probably already here."

"And it won't take them long to zero in on this building," Oliver noted. "The original men were well aware of the location of the gate. They'll probably head directly here."

"So we need to be ready," I insisted. "We need to arm ourselves and keep the revenants out. The one thing we have going for us is that the door is narrow. We can pick them off as they enter easily enough."

"We'll still need backup," Brett added. "You need to call the Grimlocks and tell them what's going on. It's going to take some time for them to get out here."

I hunted in my pocket for my phone. "I'll call now. You guys handle Claire and Collin. Then we'll batten down the hatches and prepare to defend the gate."

"There's one other thing we need to be concerned about," Oliver countered. "Paris. She was due to take a separate boat. She should be arriving any second."

My heart skipped a beat. I'd completely forgotten about her. I wasn't sure what to do, but there was no way I could leave her out there unprotected. "I have to get her."

"*We* have to get her," Aisling corrected. "We promised my father we wouldn't go anywhere alone."

Annoyance reared up to grab me by the throat. "Since when do you listen to what your father has to say?"

"He occasionally makes sense. This is one of those times." She was unnaturally calm. "You can't go alone. You'll need eyes in the back of your head. It will be safer for us to go together."

I didn't like that idea one little bit. "You have a baby. I'll be fine on my own."

"I'm going with you. You can't stop me."

That wasn't technically true. I could stop her with magic. I wasn't exactly keen on the idea, however. "Aisling ... ."

"She's right." Oliver firmly shook his head. "You can't go alone and we can't go with you because of the sun."

"Then we should head out." Aisling gripped her dagger tightly. "She'll be under attack the moment she hits the dock."

"Let's go then." I still wasn't thrilled with the idea of Aisling accompanying me, but we were out of time. "You must do everything I say while we're out there. I'm dead serious."

"It'll be fine." She sounded sure of herself. "We've faced worse. Trust me."

BRETT AND OLIVER WATCHED US from the security room. The camera footage was grainy, but it was good enough for them to warn us via radio if they saw movement.

"You're clear," Oliver offered as we hit the sidewalk on the water side of the building. "I don't see anything."

That was both a relief and a reason for agitation. "Where are they? We know they're out here. I would rather know and fight than constantly look over my shoulder."

"We're better off leaving the fighting for when we're all together," he responded. "Just collect Paris and get back. There will be plenty of blood to spill when you manage that."

I increased my speed. We were jogging by the time we hit the end of the dock ... and that's when the true scope of what we were dealing with became obvious.

"Oh, my ... ." Aisling's mouth was agape.

I was right there with her. "Paris!" I screamed. She looked lack-adaisical as she docked, as if she didn't have a care in the world. She was out of the water, which was a relief, but she didn't seem to sense the danger. Her eyes were quizzical when they turned in our direction. "Run to us!"

Her forehead wrinkled in confusion. "And good morning to you."

The revenants were appearing in the water. It was almost as if they'd been walking along the bottom of the river rather than swim-ming, which made sense. Slowly, methodically, they trudged forward. Once they hit the beach they would be able to cut Paris off. We couldn't let that happen.

"Move your ass now!" Aisling screeched, gesturing toward the water.

Paris finally slid her eyes in that direction and the look on her face would've been comical under different circumstances.

"Run," I ordered. "Right now!"

Paris didn't have to be prodded. Once she understood what we were facing, the sheer horror of it, she raced away from the water as fast as she could manage. She made it to us with time to spare, and I pointed her back toward the aquarium. "We're putting a team together in the gate room. If they attack, it will be easier for us to take them out there."

Paris gasped as she ran. "I don't understand what's happening."

"None of us understand," Aisling shot back. "We don't have enough information to truly understand. It's fight or die."

That was a grim reality for all of us now. We had no other options.

OLIVER AND BRETT MET US AT the aquarium door. They looked relieved when we streamed through. Brett corralled me at the souvenir counter and gave me another hug.

"Are you okay?"

I nodded. "We're fine. They're coming."

"Then we must get back to the gate room." Oliver was calm in the face of certain destruction. "Cormack called while you were retrieving Paris. They're on their way. It will be at least thirty minutes before they can get here. Your paramour was bellowing to talk to you in the background. When Cormack asked about you and I explained where you were, numerous vile threats were issued."

I could only imagine. "I'll handle Braden when he gets here. We have to worry about survival now. We should probably go to the security room so we can watch them through the security cameras. Once they get close enough, we'll return to the gate."

"I've patched the security feeds into the gate room computers," Oliver countered. "We can watch from down there. I don't think it's wise to be anywhere else at this point."

I didn't have an argument to the contrary, so I simply nodded. "What about Claire and Collin?"

"Claire is in the botanical gardens. She says she's ready should they approach. I doubt she'll be a target. Collin is at the casino. He was checking the kitchen equipment when the call came in. He wanted to come, but I told him to stay. He'd only be a distraction if we worried about him."

I was already weary when we descended the stairs to the gate room. "All we have to do is hold them off for thirty minutes. Then we'll have help."

"I saw about twenty of them," Brett offered. "We checked every feed while we were waiting for you to return to the aquarium. I think the five of us can take twenty of them."

"I agree," Oliver said. "The doors are heavy, the opening narrow. Only one — two at most — will be able to enter at the same time. We will make a large dent in them before any manage to muscle through the door."

The fact that they were so upbeat made me feel better. "We're going to be okay," I confirmed. "We're strong ... and Aisling is a total badass when she wants to be."

Aisling grinned. Despite the circumstances, she was clearly enjoying herself. "You've got that right."

My spirits were bolstered until the moment we opened the door to the gate room. I heard the whispering right away. It was so strong it almost took my knees out from under me.

I reacted on instinct. Paris was behind me, so I turned and shoved her out of the room. Brett was at the rear of the formation, so he caught her, his eyes going wide with an unasked question I couldn't possibly answer. When I turned back to the front of the line, Oliver was already at his computer. I could see his furrowed brow from fifteen feet away as he registered the data flying through his equipment.

Aisling was too close to the gate. In fact, she was almost standing on the first step of the gate platform.

"Aisling, get away from there!" I bellowed the warning so loudly her shoulders jerked in surprise.

Puzzlement wafted over her features as she shifted her eyes to me. She was confused. She couldn't hear the whispering.

"The gate," I snapped. "The gate is about to malfunction. You could be sucked to the other side."

Realizing the danger inherent in her position, Oliver started racing toward Aisling. I had the same idea, but Brett had grabbed me from behind, pulling me from the room. There was a glint of light as the gate kicked into overdrive. That was the last thing I saw as Brett dragged me away.

The noise was overwhelming again, but it didn't knock me out. I had to press my hands over my ears to stay upright, though, and I closed my eyes as blinding heat flashed three times on the other side of the door.

It was over as quickly as it began.

I slapped Brett's hands to get him to release me and raced through the doors, desperate to find Aisling and my godfather. My heart gave a terrific heave when I realized the room was empty.

Twenty-Four

T he revenants never came to the gate room. We waited, even as every horrible possibility crowded my mind, but they never entered the building.

Brett, who looked as shaky as I felt, held it together as he watched the camera feeds. Once the gate stopped flashing, the revenants turned on their heels and returned to the water. Were they hiding there? Were they biding their time? Were they returning to their previous haunts? I had no idea. All I knew was that I'd lost Oliver and Aisling ... and I was positive my heart might break.

"Is everybody okay?" Cormack and his Grimlock army arrived exactly when we expected them. They clutched swords in their hands, wild looks in their eyes.

My heart lodged in my throat when I tried to answer. What could I tell them?

Braden pushed past his brothers and made his way to me. His arms were strong, his emotions warm, and yet I felt so cold all over I didn't know how to react.

"Are you all right?" He tipped my head back and stared into my eyes. "I was so worried we wouldn't get here in time."

"I'm fine." Somehow I found my voice. It sounded normal, which felt miraculous given the circumstances. "They didn't even come down here. I was certain they would, but ... they didn't."

"Where did they go?" Cormack asked, glancing around. "I mean ... I would've jumped to the same conclusion. If they weren't heading for the gate, what were they doing?"

I didn't have an answer.

"Where is Aisling?" Redmond demanded. He was either the first to notice that his sister was missing or the first to give voice to his worry. "I bet she was gung-ho to fight those things. Is she feeling sorry for herself in the bathroom? That sounds just like her."

He moved in that direction, as if he was going to stroll into the ladies' room to mess with his sister. Paris stopped him.

"She's not here." Paris's voice was strong. I had to give her credit for holding it together. All I wanted to do was fall apart.

"What do you mean?" Cormack's eyes flashed with annoyance. "I gave her a specific order. She was to stick with Izzy the entire day. Are you telling me she shirked her duties and left you here to fight those things on your own?"

I immediately started shaking my head. I couldn't stand the disappointment in his voice. "She didn't abandon me." I worried I would suddenly burst into tears. I knew if that happened I would likely never stop crying. "She would never leave me during a fight."

"She wouldn't," Paris agreed. She was obviously steeling herself for the big reveal. It should've been my job, but I couldn't force myself to say the words. Once I did, they would be real.

"I have some bad news," Paris announced, sucking in a breath. "I'm sorry to be the one to tell you this, but something happened while we were preparing for battle."

In slow, concise terms, Paris laid out everything that happened. She didn't embellish. She was matter-of-]fact and straightforward. And when she finished, the Grimlocks were in tatters.

"You take that back!" Redmond's face was red with exertion as he took a purposeful step forward and jabbed a finger in Paris's direction. "You're playing a game or something."

"Why would I do that?" Paris held her hands palms out. "I'm not the sort who plays games when it comes to love and loss."

"Loss?" Cormack stirred. He looked like a man who had aged ten years in two minutes. "We haven't lost her. I ... she's not gone."

"She's not," Brett agreed, speaking for the first time. "She's most certainly not lost. She's with Oliver. He'll take care of her."

"But you're saying she's on the other side of the gate," Braden countered. "You're saying she ... crossed over."

"That's the assumption," Paris agreed. She refused to fall victim to emotions, instead holding herself together in a manner I envied. "There's no other option for what happened to them. They were here one second and gone the next. That's not necessarily a death sentence. We know from recent experience that the men who disappeared sixty years ago managed to return ... and they were alive when they did."

Cillian, always the calm Grimlock, completely lost his cool. "They came back sixty years after the fact! They came back as monsters! If you think we're going to allow that to happen to our sister ... you're crazy. We're getting her back right now." He moved toward the gate, and I was certain he was going to throw himself through the shimmering wall of magic. Cormack caught him before he could.

"We have to think about this," he growled as he wrestled his son. "We can't run off half-cocked. That won't help your sister."

"We can't leave her." Cillian struggled against his father's grip as his voice broke. It was enough to crack my heart. "She's probably on the other side of the gate waiting for us. She expects us to come for her. We can't just leave her."

"Do you think that I'm going to leave her?" Cormack was beside himself. Aisling mentioned a broken man when she told me the story of her mother's death on the boat ride over. She said her father stumbled in the immediate aftermath, but then pulled it together because he had to. His children needed him. That's what I was seeing now. Cormack looked as if he was about to fall down, but he was strong enough to keep his children upright. "We're going to find her. I promise you that. We have to come up with a plan first."

I rubbed my forehead as I struggled with my emotions. I couldn't help feeling this was my fault. I should've kept her out of the room. I should've been the first through the door. I should've ... done anything other than what I'd done. Aisling would still be here if I'd thought faster, reacted quicker. Now the family I'd started thinking of as my own was about to lose the most important piece.

"I have a plan," Aidan interjected, his eyes fierce. "I'm going through that gate and I'm getting her. If you think you can stop me ... . You raised us to take care of her, to protect her. You can't stop us from doing that now."

Cormack was clearly at a loss. "We'll all go through that gate to get her if it's necessary. We need to think first. We need to figure this out before we act. We have to ... call Griffin." He choked over the last bit, and the ache that had begun to dull in the pit of my stomach ripped into a fresh wound. "He doesn't know. We have to tell him."

"No!" Braden immediately started shaking his head. "We have to get her back. Then we'll tell him after the fact. He'll fall apart if he knows what happened."

"I can't help that," Cormack shot back. "Aisling is his wife. He has a right to know. I ... the baby is at the office daycare center. We can't leave her there long. I needed to run out and I just left her there. It wasn't safe to bring her to the island and ... I just left her."

"He's right," I offered when I thought I could say the words without bursting into tears. "Griffin needs to be informed. While we're waiting for him to arrive, we'll discuss plans to get Aisling back. We have to work together. That means talking things through before reacting for a change."

Aidan's glare was dark when it landed on me. "You don't get to decide what we do to get back our sister."

Braden moved in front of me and met his brother's accusatory gaze. Nothing had been said, but I knew they blamed me. I could feel it ... and I understood the reaction. It was my fault. All of this was my fault.

"Let's take this one step at a time," Braden growled. "Call Griffin. After that ... well ... we'll figure things out. Aisling isn't gone. We won't let her be gone."

If love was powerful enough to bring the youngest Grimlock sibling back, she would already be here. Unfortunately, it wasn't.

GRIFFIN WAS FULL OF FURY WHEN he stormed into the gate room. Cillian met him on the main floor and filled him in. Cillian was the calmest Grimlock, so the others assumed he would have the most soothing effect on Griffin.

They were wrong.

"Where is she?" He practically spit the words he was so worked up. "I'm not playing around. I want my wife now."

Cormack moved away from the computer Brett was operating. They'd been reviewing the data from the most recent gate malfunction, comparing it to the previous instance. His face, usually a master class on aging gracefully, looked craggy and caved in. The loss of his youngest child would likely kill him, I realized. Oh, he wouldn't kill himself, but he couldn't deal with the loss of one of his children. Life would simply run him over if we didn't get Aisling back.

"We don't know where she is," Cormack replied. His voice sounded stronger than he obviously felt. He had realized he had to hold it together for his son-in-law's benefit. Aisling would want it that way. She wouldn't want Griffin to feel as if the world was against him. She would want her siblings and father to rally to hold him up.

That's what they all intended to do.

"How can you not know?" Griffin gestured toward the gate. "Is she in there? Is that where she is?" He moved to start up the stairs, but Cillian and Redmond cut off his approach.

"We're assuming she's in there," Cormack replied, drawing Griffin's attention back to him as the detective gripped his hands into fists at his sides. "We're trying to work out how to get her."

"How? You just walk across and find her. It seems pretty obvious."

"There is a question whether one can survive crossing the gate," Brett explained. "She might already be gone. If so, who does it benefit for anyone else to sacrifice himself in a vain search to find her?"

Griffin's glare was sharp enough to cut glass. "She is not dead! Stop saying that!"

"She's not dead," Cormack reassured him, shooting Brett a quelling look. "We won't allow that sort of negative thinking. We just don't know what to do. If we cross over, there's every chance we'll never be able to return. I'm willing to do that to find Aisling. However, the rest of you ... ." He left the sentence hanging.

"No, I'll go over." Griffin was firm. "You stay here and I'll cross over. If we can't come back, then ... at least we'll be together."

Cormack's eyes glistened as he shuffled closer to Griffin and rested his hand on the discombobulated man's shoulder. "Is that what you really want?"

"Are you asking if I want to be with your daughter? Um ... yes. She's my wife. I love her. I'll cross ten worlds to find her if I have to."

"That's not what I meant." Cormack paused, choosing his words carefully. "If you go over, you could find Aisling and be together for all eternity. I know you would be okay with that. Have you considered what you would be leaving behind?"

It was only then that realization dawned on Griffin's handsome face. "Lily," he muttered under his breath.

Cormack nodded. "Lily. It's not just you and Aisling any longer. You have a child. You need to take care of her."

Griffin looked legitimately torn. "But ... she's my wife."

"I know. But she's my daughter. It makes sense for me to cross over. I've lived a full life. If we can cross back, I'll bring her with me. If we can't ... then you all should know that we're over there together. We'll be with your mother. We'll be waiting when you all ... ." His voice cracked before he could finish.

"No." Redmond immediately started shaking his head. "We need you on this side in case you can shake information out of Renley. You're the only one who will be able to pull that off. I'll go. You told me when she was born that she was my responsibility. I'll go over and be with her."

"No. I won't allow that." Cormack was firm. "The rest of you have lives that still need living here. I'll go."

Griffin looked numb as he dropped his head in his hands and sank to the floor. He was torn between the two most important things in the world to him. He didn't know the right thing to do. Nobody did.

I finally found my voice. "It should be me," I volunteered, causing every head in the room to snap in my direction. I barreled forward before I lost my nerve. "I saw the vision of what happened to the others," I reminded them. "That was for a reason. Maybe the gate was trying to tell me something. I think ... I think ... I think I'll be able to get them both back."

Braden was already shaking his head. "No way. You're not going over."

"I have to agree," Brett offered. "Oliver would not be happy if you sacrificed yourself for him. In fact, he would be downright apoplectic."

Braden was fervent as he grabbed my wrist. "You definitely need to stay here."

"I think that's probably a good idea," Griffin agreed, lifting his head and meeting my gaze. There, for the first time since I'd met him, lurked something dark and hateful. "You've done enough. I don't want you to go after my wife. It has to be someone who loves her."

My heart threatened to implode at his words. I did love her. It wasn't in the same way he ... or her brothers ... or her father did, but I loved her. Every contrary inch fascinated me even as I wanted to strangle her. She'd almost become a sister to me. I couldn't explain that to him. He didn't want to hear it.

"You can't blame this on her," Braden challenged, stepping in to shield me from Griffin's anger. "She didn't cause this."

"Didn't she?" Griffin's voice was hard. "She knew the gate was dangerous and yet she decided to put my wife in this room. She did that even though there was no way to predict what would happen when the revenants arrived. Obviously they were drawn to the island because they knew the gate was going to malfunction."

Cillian lifted his head. "I hadn't really thought about that, but it makes sense. The gate called to them. Then something else happened and they were cut adrift so they didn't continue with whatever mission they had planned. We need to figure out why they came to the island."

Everyone ignored him.

"Izzy recognized the noise," Griffin continued. "Cillian told me. She knew there was trouble. What did she do? She pushed Paris out of the way and let Aisling walk headlong into danger. She's responsible for all of this.

"Don't bother arguing with me, Braden," he continued with a hiss. "It's true. Izzy chose to protect Paris. She probably wanted Aisling gone. We don't know that she hasn't been controlling what happened at this gate since she was a child."

"Aisling told me the story." He got angrier with each word. "Izzy heard noises from the gate, whispering, and something passed over. It was probably one of these things. Her parents ended up dead and she survived. How do we know that she's not the cause of all of this?"

It never occurred to me that the thing that came through the gate the night my parents died was a revenant. In hindsight, that was ridiculously stupid. I may not have called to the creature but it made sense. All of it made sense.

"You don't want to go there." Braden's fury was on full display. "I know you're upset — we're all upset — but you can't blame Izzy. She's not the one who ... this isn't her fault. I can't sit back and watch you attack her."

"You don't have to sit back and watch anything, Braden," Griffin replied dully. "You're probably happy your sister is gone anyway. This is what you've always wanted. You hated her and now she's gone. I bet you and Izzy had this planned."

"Griffin, that will be enough of that," Cormack warned. "Izzy is not to blame for this. We'll figure this out. You need to have faith."

"I think I'm all out of faith." His shoulders were heavy as he moved toward the door. "I want to see Lily. Where is she?"

"At reaper headquarters, in daycare. She's safe."

"I want her." Griffin was so forlorn I thought I might fall over as the weight of his angst hit me smack in the face. He was a normal human, so he wasn't good at shuttering. Every emotion was on display ... he would fall apart before the evening was over. "I want my daughter. I want her right now."

"We'll get her," Cormack promised. "Son, this isn't over. We're going to figure things out. I ... we'll come up with a plan."

"I want my daughter now. I want my baby."

With that, he walked out of the room without even looking over this shoulder. He didn't look at the gate. He'd made his decision. He was going to protect his daughter because it was the right thing to do, but the loss of his wife would leave Griffin Taylor a broken man. There would be no coming back for him.

A quick look at the remaining Grimlocks told me there would be no coming back for any of them.

Twenty-Five

B raden didn't leave with the others. He was steadfast in his refusal, even though I could've used a bit of breathing room. He understood we had data to explore and secluded himself in a corner.

There he sat and stared at the gate.

It wasn't much of a stretch to figure out what he was thinking. He was worried about his sister, wondering if she was already gone. He was regretting every nasty thing he'd ever said to her, thinking back on all the horrible things she'd said to him.

He was picturing the moment on the crumbling balcony. I could see the memory in the forefront of his brain.

"Oh, that's not true." The half-wraith Lily Grimlock turned smug as the sound of frantic footsteps became obvious. "I think someone would be happier if I stayed. Isn't that right, Braden?"

Angst rolled over Aisling's furious face. "You should go back downstairs, Braden," she said quietly. "I've got this."

Braden's tone was hard to decipher. "What exactly have you got?"

"She plans to kill me, Braden," Lily hissed, adding a bit of panic to her voice to manipulate him. "She wants to hurt me. Don't let her hurt me."

"I see."

Aisling risked a glance at Braden. "She's not our mother. You know that. Deep down, you understand. You saw our mother downstairs."

"That was a trick," the creature spat. "Whatever you saw, it wasn't your mother. I'm your mother. You know that."

Braden remained silent, so Lily talked to fill the gaps.

"Think about all the time we've spent together since I returned, Braden," she wheedled. "I listened to all your stories, commiserated with you about how your father always favors Aisling. Do you want to know why I did that? Because you were always my favorite."

Aisling's expression was fierce. "You know that's not true, Braden. Dad loves all of us. Sure, he spoils me because I'm the only girl, but you can't possibly believe that he doesn't love you. That's just ... ridiculous.

"He's spent the better part of the last few months worrying about you above everyone else," she continued. "He knows how much Mom's death gutted you. He doesn't want it to happen again ... but there's no choice. This is not our mother."

"I am your mother!" Desperation rolled off the thing claiming to be their mother. She knew this was her last shot. "You need to let me go, Braden. I promise I won't hurt the family. Aisling simply doesn't understand what I was trying to do. She's hated me from the second I returned, resented me. I'm not a threat. You know that."

"That did it." Aisling raised the letter opener clutched in her hand and stepped toward the Lily monster. "I won't let you hurt my brother. We're finished here."

Lily retreated. The only place to escape was the ramshackle balcony. It was small, and she managed only four steps before she backed into a wall. Aisling gave chase, ready to plunge the letter opener through her heart, but Braden grabbed her arm.

"No."

"Braden, we have to do this." Tears filled Aisling's eyes. "I know you think she's our mother, but she's not."

"Don't let her murder me, Braden." Lily turned shrill and there was a momentary glint of mayhem flitting through her eyes. "I'm your mother. I love you. She's trying to separate us. If she kills me, she'll win."

"She's not going to kill you." Braden's voice was hollow as he forced the letter opener from Aisling's hand. "I'm going to do it."

Shock washed over the room as Braden grabbed the letter opener and raised it.

"Braden!" Lily screamed his name at the same moment a ripping sound caused Aisling to jerk her head to the left.

The rotting floor finally gave way and the balcony tipped forward. The desolate chairs left from better days flew forward and broke through the weakened balusters, causing the balcony to jerk as it buckled.

Braden pitched forward and Aisling scrambled behind to catch him. Things happened fast, and she missed with her first grab, skin touching skin before he slid further away. Somehow she managed to grab his hand with her second attempt, and even though his body went over the edge she held tight, planting her feet against the balusters and praying that they wouldn't give and take them both over the edge.

"I've got you!" Aisling gasped as she fought Braden's weight. He wasn't large, but he was well-muscled, which made him heavy. "Don't let go."

"Aisling, look out!" Braden yelled out the same moment Lily grabbed her other arm in an attempt to stop herself from sliding over the edge.

Aisling bellowed out her frustration as she struggled to hold steady.

"Son of a ... !" She gritted her teeth as she fought to keep her grip on Braden. "Somebody help me!" she screamed, knowing there was no way she had the upper body strength to pull Braden to safety. That was doubly true now that her mother's added weight worked against her.

"Let me go, Aisling," Braden instructed, his voice cracking. "If you don't, we'll both go."

"I'm not doing that." Aisling looked determined as she met his gaze. "We're both getting out of here. I'm getting married the day after tomorrow. You're going to be there with me."

"I might survive the fall," Braden offered, choking on the words. "If you hold on we'll both be hurt ... or worse. There's still a chance I'll make it."

"Listen to your brother," Lily snapped. "Let him go. If you do, you'll have the strength to pull me up."

Hatred washed over Aisling's features. "I am not saving you." She jerked her arm, grim satisfaction rolling across her face as Lily's fingers slid down her *wrist. The desperate creature dug its nails in. "A parent is never supposed to outlive her child. That's a lesson you simply haven't learned."*

Aisling yanked her arm away from Lily again. This time, the soulless creature couldn't maintain its grip. Its eyebrows flew up its forehead as its fingers slid down Aisling's hand. For one long moment — it seemed an eternity — it was as if the monster floated there, accusatory eyes blasting Aisling with a lifetime of hate and disgust. Then it plummeted, rapidly falling out of sight. Aisling didn't watch the fall. She was already focused on Braden ... and there was no need to look.

Her hand was bloody from Lily's fingernails, but that didn't stop Aisling from wrapping both of her hands around Braden's wrist. "We're going to make it."

"Aisling, you have to let me go."

"No! Somebody help me!" Aisling screamed.

"Aisling!" Griffin's voice echoed throughout the darkness behind them. He sounded close. The shocked look on his face when he poked his head over the threshold of the rapidly faltering balcony wouldn't be forgotten. "Baby." He dropped to his stomach and crawled until he wrapped his arms around her waist. "Hold on."

"We need to get Braden up," she growled. "I don't have the strength to pull him."

"You won't be doing it alone," Cormack announced, appearing near Griffin. "Redmond, I want you to hold Cillian's legs and lower him on the other side of Aisling. Aidan, I'll hold you. I want you to each take an arm. Aisling can't hold on much longer. Then we'll all pull at the same time. Everybody got it? Good. Go."

Cillian and Aidan were lighter than Cormack and Redmond, so it made sense they would be the ones to crawl forward. Aidan made it down to Aisling first, and grabbed Braden's left wrist to ease the tension on his sister's arms.

"I've got him."

"I've got him, too," Cillian called from the other side.

"Let go, Aisling," Cormack instructed. "You don't have to hold on any longer."

Aisling ignored him. "Just pull."

Cormack heaved a sigh. "Fine. Be stubborn." He ordered everyone to pull at once. For a second it didn't appear the effort would work. Braden remained where he was. Then, as if by magic, everyone grunted together and dragged Braden from the precipice to safety.

The naked emotion on both of their faces when they were reunited with the rest of the family made my heart hurt.

I wanted to go to him, but what could I say? His sister was gone because of me. I should've pulled Aisling, rather than Paris, back. I could've saved them both. Instead, I reacted on instinct ... and now Aisling was gone. The odds of her returning weren't good. And even if she did return she wouldn't be the same. She would be one of the creatures hunting us as we tried to figure out how to end them.

What would it be like? Would it be another sixty years? Would Griffin even be alive? I had my doubts. And what about Oliver? He couldn't be turned into a revenant. What was his fate?

I risked a glance at Brett and found him focused on the computer. He wasn't as familiar with the gate as Oliver, but he'd been around for a long time. He understood the gate, recognized the data scrolling across the screen. He wasn't giving up.

"Stop doing that," he chided, never moving his eyes to my face. "We'll get them back."

He sounded certain. "How can you believe that? You know everything we know. How are we supposed to get them back?"

"I don't know, but we will." He patted the open chair next to his. "Sit. You haven't eaten since breakfast. I'm afraid you're going to fall down."

I sank into the chair and slid low. "This is my fault."

"Nonsense. We don't know why this happened. Aisling isn't dead. And she isn't alone. Oliver will protect her."

"Against how many revenants? We're assuming it's the revenants who will intercept them on the other side of the gate. Oliver can't hold off an army of them."

"No, but he's smarter than he looks." Brett offered me a lopsided grin and weak wink. "They'll be okay. We need to figure out why Oliver was taken this time. I think that's key to solving this."

I'd wallowed so long he was clearly ten steps ahead of me. "I don't understand," I said. "Why do you think that's important?"

"He wasn't taken the first time. He was just as close as the rest of them, yet he was left behind. Why was he taken this time? Nothing has changed. He's still a vampire. He can't be recruited to their cause."

"Maybe it was an accident."

"I don't think any of this has been an accident. We need to figure out what's different this time."

That was easier said than done. Still, chasing something that might turn out to be a disappointment was better than doing nothing. "What do you want me to do?"

PARIS LEFT WHEN THE GRIMLOCKS departed. They saw her to the other side of the bridge. They'd managed to drive across, calling in a few favors along the way. The bridge was closed down again, but it was safer to drive than boat at this point. She'd texted that she was home safe, promised she would be back the following day, and then reiterated what she'd said before: It wasn't my fault.

And yet it was.

"I just can't figure it out." Brett stretched his arms over his head. We'd been at it for hours and he hadn't moved a muscle. I'd been pacing for the better part of the afternoon.

"Maybe there's nothing to figure out," I suggested, rolling my neck. "Maybe we can't figure it out because we don't have enough of the puzzle pieces to put the picture together."

"So ... what do you suggest?"

I had a few ideas. Nothing I could say out loud, though. Instead, my eyes drifted to the gate.

As if reading my mind, Brett started shaking his head. "Don't even think about it," he warned, his voice barely a whisper. He had the common sense not to explode in front of Braden, which I was thankful for, but the warning was obvious. "I won't let you walk through that gate. If you try, I'll tell your boyfriend. Do you want to completely kill him?"

That was the last thing I wanted. Still, I couldn't shake the idea. I was starting to believe that crossing the threshold wasn't a death sentence. I had no idea if my magic would work over there, but I was willing to give it a try to get Aisling and Oliver back.

While I was thinking of an argument to bring Brett around to my way of thinking, Braden left his perch and moved to my computer. "I need to call home and I would prefer doing it via video chat," he said dully. "Can I use your computer?"

I nodded as I watched him sit. He was listless and broken-hearted, scenes spent with his sister rolling through his head at a fantastic rate. Some of the memories were funny, others mean. All of them now tragic.

"Go ahead," I supplied.

Brett and I went back to staring at the computer screen. We obviously couldn't continue our conversation with Braden so close. I was thankful for the reprieve and started building arguments in my head as Braden called home.

Redmond answered the call. "Anything?"

"No," Braden replied. "They're still looking, but they can't find anything. They don't want me to know that, but it's obvious. What's going on there?"

Redmond was grim. "Nothing good. Griffin tried to take the baby and leave."

"To go where?"

"Home. He's angry at all of us and wants to shut us out. I don't want to say that he's trying to punish us, but that's what it feels like."

"He's not punishing us," Braden countered. "He's ... grieving. He wants to go after Aisling more than anything, but knows he can't leave Lily. I mean ... she wouldn't even have a memory of him if he crossed over and couldn't come back."

"I know that. He's just ... out of it. Dad stopped him from leaving by reminding him that the revenants were still out there and he couldn't protect Lily without help. Griffin yelled, called him a few names, and then locked himself in the nursery with the baby. He won't allow any of us to see her."

"Maybe that's for the best," Braden suggested. "He needs time to get his emotions under control. It's not as if he's going to hurt Lily. After a few hours with her he might come to his senses."

Redmond's expression reflected doubt. "I don't think that's going to happen. I'm not a psychologist or anything, but I think he's angry ... and not just at Izzy. I think he's mad at Dad ... and us ... and even Lily."

I kept my lips zipped.

"Why would he be angry at Lily?" Braden challenged. "She's a baby. She obviously didn't cause this."

"No, but she's the reason he can't go after Aisling. That's what he really wants to do. He'll always question whether he could've done something if he doesn't go, and yet he knows he can't. Aisling would never forgive him if he left Lily. I'm afraid he's going to break."

"He won't." Braden was matter-of-fact. "He's strong. That's the only way he could take on Aisling and match her fire. He's upset. We're all upset."

Redmond agreed. "Dad is just as much a mess as Griffin, although he's trying to hide it. You should know that if we don't come up with anything by morning he's resolved to go through the gate himself. He's going to go after Aisling."

"I know. He would do it for any of us."

"He would. I'm just afraid that it's already too late for Aisling, and then we'd be giving up Dad. I don't know how we get through this." Redmond's voice cracked. "It's too much. I know that Mom dying felt like it was too much, but we had each other. We're splintering now. I just ... I don't know that I can take this. I keep hoping I'll wake up from a bad dream."

"We can only take it a step at a time," Braden said. "I just wanted you to know that I won't be home tonight. I'm staying here with Izzy."

"Are you sure that's wise? Don't you want to spend some time with Dad?"

"I still think we'll find a way out of this so he won't have to cross over. I want to see Dad. I can't leave, though. If I do, Izzy will cross over and sacrifice herself to get Aisling and Oliver back. I have to watch her."

My mouth dropped open as dumbfounded disbelief washed over me. "How ... ?" I didn't finish the sentence.

Braden replied. "You're not going across. We'll figure out another way."

"See." Brett extended a finger in Braden's direction. "He's smarter than he looks. We're going to find a way. In fact ... ." He broke off when the alert on the third computer started beeping.

I was on my feet and in front of the computer before anyone else could react.

"What is it?" Braden asked, his hands resting on the desk as he prepared himself for battle. "Is it the revenants?"

I furrowed my brow as I tried to work out what I was seeing on the security feeds. "I don't think so ... unless they suddenly learned to drive. There's a van on the bridge. I'm not sure how the driver managed that with traffic blocked at the far end."

"A van? What kind of van?"

"I'm not sure." I squinted to make out the writing on the side of the van, my heart clenching when I read it. "It says 'Get Baked' and there's a giant peach cupcake on the side of it."

"Ugh." Braden briefly shut his eyes before recovering. "Jerry."

"He's coming for Aisling," I surmised. "He's going to try to go through the gate."

"We need to intercept him." Braden sighed as he stood, his eyes flicking back to Redmond. "Tell Aidan we have his fiancé and we'll keep him safe. I'll send Jerry back as soon as I can."

"I'll send Dad and Aidan to you," Redmond corrected. "Nobody but them will be able to talk Jerry down. You know that."

"I do, but I don't think they'll be enough."

"Just keep him from doing something stupid," Redmond instructed.

Twenty-Six

isling had brought Jerry with her to the aquarium on more than one occasion when trying to talk me into a frivolous lunch. He was familiar with the set-up and already messing with the card reader on the front door when we found him.

"Oh, good, you're here." His expression was hard to read, but I sensed trouble. "I need to get to the gate."

"Why are you going to the gate?" I asked. I already knew the answer, but I wanted to hear him say it.

"I'm going after Aisling."

I had to hand it to him. He wasn't good at subtlety, and finesse was out of the question. He put it out there and didn't care who argued with him.

"Jerry … ." I licked my lips. I wasn't sure what I was supposed to say to him.

"You can't stop me, Izzy." His lower lip quivered and almost undid me. "I'm going after my best friend. No one — and I mean no one — can stop me."

I opened my mouth to argue but no sound would come out. I was completely at a loss.

"Come on, Jerry." Braden slid around me and put his hand on

Jerry's shoulder, prodding him inside the building. "We'll get you some-thing to drink and have a talk."

"You can talk all you want. I'm still going through that gate to get Aisling."

"We'll talk," Braden repeated. "There are a few things you need to know before you head over. The other side of the gate is ... different ... from anything you've ever seen."

"Wait ... you're not going to argue with me?" Jerry was instantly suspicious.

"I'm not going to argue with you. I want to make sure you're prepared. You'll die within five seconds if you're not."

I didn't miss the way Jerry's face paled or how hard he swallowed at the words. Braden was using psychological warfare on him and Jerry was oblivious. That didn't mean he was going to simply forget about his best friend. Instead, he squared his shoulders. "Anything you can tell me will be good."

"Great." Braden feigned excitement. "Come downstairs. I have a lot to tell you."

I UNDERSTOOD BRADEN WAS stalling. He was keeping Jerry busy with horror stories of what lived beyond the gate until Aidan and Cormack could get to the island. By pretending to go along with Jerry's wild idea, he was keeping him safe.

"Then, when you get to the cliff, you have to make sure that the revenants hiding in the trees don't get you," Braden said, somber. "You need to make yourself as small as possible, as quiet as possible, and keep away from the sheer cliff edge. If you fall over that cliff, there's no coming back and there's not much room to maneuver in that area. Have you got it?"

Jerry was so white you could almost see through him. He nodded. "Got it."

I wanted to sigh ... and then throttle him. The Grimlocks were loyal to a fault. They attracted people who displayed the same type of fervent loyalty. Jerry wasn't a Grimlock by blood, but he'd been adopted into the family long before he became engaged to Aidan, and he was a Grimlock in his heart. No matter how frightened, he was determined to go after Aisling.

I had to admire him for his dedication ... even if I was certain he would be killed within five seconds on the other side.

I was never so relieved as when I heard footsteps at the door and turned to find Cormack and Aidan standing there. They both looked exhausted, beaten down by life. They also looked exasperated ... and broken-hearted.

"What are you doing here?" Jerry was on his feet. "You called them!" He swung on me with a viciousness that would've been surprising under different circumstances.

"I called them, Jerry," Braden countered. "In fact, I was in the middle of a video call with Redmond when we realized you were here. We knew what you had planned. I told Redmond to send Aidan and Dad before we even saw you."

Jerry narrowed his eyes to slits. "And I thought you were really trying to help me by explaining what to expect on the other side. I knew I shouldn't have trusted you."

Braden held up his hands. "I'm sorry. Aisling would never forgive me if I let you cross to the other side."

"Aisling won't be around to be angry if you don't let me go," Jerry barked.

"I can't let you go." Braden was firm. "We're going to get her back. I promise you that. I just ... you're going to be needed here when it finally happens. Who do you think she's going to want to see more than anyone?"

"Griffin," Jerry replied without hesitation. "And then Lily ... and then her father, because he's going to spoil her ... and then me. I'm not an idiot. I know I'm not at the top of her list any longer. That doesn't mean I'm not going to get her."

Cormack cleared his throat, drawing Jerry's eyes to him. "You'll always be at the top of her list." He looked pained as he took a step toward the obviously crumbling man. "Aisling loves you, Jerry. She's always loved you. When she brought you home from kindergarten that first time — I swear — she loved you that very first day. She's always loved you and that's never going to change."

"That's why I have to find her," Jerry sniffled. "She needs me. I can't live without her."

Cormack was adamant. "Tomorrow morning, I'm going through the gate to get her. It's already settled."

Even though I was aware of his plan, I couldn't tolerate the idea. Cormack was needed here. His family would fall apart without him. He couldn't be the one to go through the gate. We had to figure out another way ... just as soon as we got Jerry home.

"Then I'll go with you." Jerry refused to back down. "It will be better if there are two of us."

"I don't know that I believe that, Jerry," Cormack hedged. "We can't guarantee that we'll be able to cross back over. There's a chance I won't come back. There's a chance Aisling won't either. I'll find her and make sure the revenants can't keep her ... and then we'll go to our final destinations if we have to."

Jerry immediately started shaking his head. "No. I want her back here."

Aidan stirred. "We all want her back here, Jerry." His voice was ragged and I could tell he'd been crying for the better part of the night. "We'd all cross the gate threshold to get to her and make sure she's okay. But she wouldn't want that."

Jerry was incensed. "Are you kidding? There's nothing Bug wouldn't like more than knowing we were all willing to die to get her. She likes being the center of our universe. She'll be fine if we all go over.

"And, while I don't believe staying on the other side will be necessary, I can live with it if it is," he continued. "I just can't lose her. She needs me ... and I need her."

"And I need you," Aidan pointed out. "I need my sister, but I need you, too, Jerry. We're trying to come up with the best possible outcome and this is what we've landed at.

"Lily cannot cross over," he continued. "Griffin has to stay with Lily. Maya has to stay with Griffin because that's her brother and he needs her. Cillian can't make it without Maya. It's a house of cards that could fall at any second. We're doing the best we can. I'm sorry it's not good enough for you."

Jerry murdered Aidan with the darkest look in his repertoire. "Nothing is good enough for me until we get Aisling back."

Instead of exerting the infinite patience I'd gotten used to with Aidan, the man absolutely exploded. "We're doing the best we can, Jerry! I've known her longer than any of you, loved her longer. We're connected in ways you can't understand.

"We don't know what to do," he bellowed, his voice cracking. "We don't know if it's already too late. We don't know if we can bring her back. We don't know if we're sacrificing our father for nothing or there's a chance he can find her. All we know is that you're making things harder for all of us."

I didn't realize tears were coursing down my cheeks until I tried to breathe and discovered my nose was stuffed. I let loose a soft gasp, fighting the urge to sink to the ground and bury my head as Braden slid an arm around my waist. He was as wrecked as any of us, but he was determined to hold it together.

"I can't just leave her." Jerry refused to back down, even in the face of Aidan's misery. "She needs me."

"She needs all of us," another voice offered from the doorway.

I was stunned when I turned and found Griffin there. His hair was a mess, his eyes red and puffy. I was certain he might fall over at any moment because of the grief enrobing him like a suit of armor. He remained standing, though, and headed straight for Jerry.

"What are you doing here?" Cormack asked, confused. "Where is Lily?"

"She's with Cillian and Maya." Griffin didn't meet his father-in-law's concerned gaze. "I heard the commotion in the hallway after Redmond got off the call with Braden. I heard what was going on and I knew I had to come. Aisling would ... she would ... ." The tears were back clogging his voice.

"Aisling would want you to take care of him," Cormack finished knowingly. "She'd want all of us to take care of him. The thing is, son, she'd want us to take care of you, too. I need you to let me help you. I want to spend some time with Lily back at the house. I ... just need to see her."

Griffin nodded as he collected himself. "I'm sorry about that. I just needed a few hours."

"I know." Cormack squeezed his shoulder. "I'm sorry all of this happened. You'll never know how sorry I am. I shouldn't have sent her here. I thought I was so clever keeping her out of trouble that I sent her into the abyss instead of protecting her. I just ... I'm so sorry."

Griffin's gaze turned keen. "It's not your fault. I agreed to the plan. She was going to do what she was going to do. It made sense at the time."

"I'm going to get her," Cormack promised. "I'm going to bring her back ... to you ... and to Lily ... and to Jerry ... and Aidan. I'm going to bring her back for myself."

"I know you are." The two men held each other's gaze for a long time before Griffin turned back to Jerry. "You have to stay with me. Aisling would want that. I promised her I would always take care of you if something happened. She promised you would always take care of me. We're going to need each other ... and Lily definitely needs her favorite uncle."

Jerry, although obviously touched by the "favorite uncle" bit, didn't look convinced. "I can't just leave her."

"We're not leaving her," Griffin reiterated. "We're preparing for tomorrow, when we're going to get her back. I need you with me for that."

For a moment I thought Jerry would continue putting up a fight. Instead, he nodded in defeat and threw his arms around Griffin's neck.

There, in the middle of the room where his wife had disappeared, Griffin comforted her best friend. His heart was broken, his strength waning, yet he did the one thing his wife would've wanted more than anything. He stood as a pillar for her family, and no matter where she was, she had reason to be proud.

AFTER CORMAC, AIDAN, GRIFFIN AND JERRY LEFT, Brett went back to studying the data and I returned to my pacing. We didn't have much time before Cormack would slip through the gate. I wanted to come up with a plan that would guarantee his safety.

I paced by the duffel bag on the desk at least twenty times before I noticed it. When I did, I slowed my pace. Without thinking, I opened it and peered inside. "Where did this come from?" I asked.

Jerry brought it," Braden replied. He was watching Brett work, which was probably annoying to the vampire, but Braden had been invigorated by witnessing his fractured family join together and he was now determined to help. "I don't know what's in there."

It was a hodgepodge of assorted items I couldn't quite wrap my head around. "I wonder what he planned to do with this stuff," I mused, pulling each item out in turn. There was a flashlight, a huge knife, a frying pan — perhaps for all the cooking they would have to do on the other side — and a rope. There was also a survival magazine that looked as if it had been purchased recently, extra clothes and a bag of cupcakes.

"At least he was prepared." I pulled out the cupcakes and stared at them. "There are sharks on them."

"Jerry probably made them special for Aisling," Braden volunteered. "He's an excellent baker ... and Aisling is an excellent eater."

"Yeah." Absently, I drew out the rope and stared at it. Then, slowly, an idea formed and I glanced toward the gate.

"What are you thinking?" Brett asked. It was obvious he'd been watching me and picked up on the change in my mood.

"I don't know." I played with the end of the rope. "I'm thinking that maybe Jerry had a good idea."

"About crossing to the other side and giving Aisling cupcakes?" Braden challenged. "Yeah, I think that's the best idea he's ever had. He still would've died."

"Not that part." I waved off the comment. "Jerry definitely should not cross over. I don't think your father should either."

Braden's eyes went dark as he looked at me. "You're not going over. Before you even suggest it, know that I will fight you on that. It's not going to happen."

"I hate to point out the obvious, but you're not the boss of me."

"You're not going!" Braden stomped his foot. "I won't allow it."

"Smooth," Brett intoned. "That's exactly how to get her to agree to what you want. Talk down to her like you're the boss and she has no say. Women love that."

Braden shot him a withering look. "You can't tell me that you think it's a good idea for her to go."

"I don't," Brett conceded. "But neither one of us can truly stop her if she makes up her mind. We have to talk to her rationally if we expect her to change her mind."

"Do you think talking about me as if I'm not here is talking to me rationally?" I barked. "Speaking of things I don't like, that's right up there."

"I apologize for the grievous error," Brett deadpanned. "If you run toward that gate, though, I will stop you. I know I said that I won't be able to stop you in the long haul — and I mostly agree that's true — but I will stop you tonight. You're not going over."

Oh, but I was. "I have to. Cormack can't be the one. He doesn't know what to expect on the other side. I do. I've already seen it ... because the gate wanted me to see it."

Braden growled. "You keep acting as if that vision was shown to you on purpose. What if it wasn't? What if it was just something that happened?"

"None of this just simply happened." I pressed my tongue against the back of my teeth and rolled my neck back and forth until it cracked. "All of this has been by design. The gate — or rather someone on the other side of the gate — knew something bad was about to happen. They tried to show me, but I didn't understand."

"Didn't understand what?" Braden was beyond frustrated. "What makes you think you can cross over and come back?"

"I have a plan." I held up the rope by way of proof. "I'm going to the other side, but I'm going to remain anchored to you. It will be a way of keeping a foot in both worlds."

"But ... that rope is only about fifteen feet long. That won't allow you to get very far."

"It will if I magically extend it," I replied, unruffled. "The rope will work."

Braden looked pained. "And how can you be sure you'll be allowed back?"

"I'm a Bruja. I wear the mask of the dead when using my magic. I can pass as one of them. It was always supposed to be me."

Braden continued to shake his head, but I could already see the resignation settling in the depths of his lavender eyes. He knew he couldn't stop me. There was legitimate fear there ... and a small kernel of hope. I decided to stoke the hope.

"We need to figure this out," I ordered, moving back toward Brett. "We need to come up with a definitive plan ... and we need to do it in the next two hours, because that's when I'm going in."

"What? No!" Braden's eyebrows flew up his forehead. "We need to think about this overnight."

"No." I knew what had to be done now and was unwilling to wait longer. "The more time we take, the more danger Aisling is in. I'm going over in two hours. I plan to be back well before your father arrives to go through the gate on his own trip. That's the best thing for all of us."

"It might not be the best thing for you," Braden persisted.

"It will be absolutely fine." I felt that to my very marrow. "I promise everything will work out. You need to trust me. Do you think you can do that?"

"I've already trusted you with my heart. I really need you not to break it."

"I feel the same way. This will work. We just have to iron out the details."

Twenty-Seven

We couldn't plan for every contingency. It was impossible. We tried to work out as many as we could. By four in the morning, I was ready.

"You should get some sleep first," Braden insisted. He almost sounded desperate.

"No. Your father will be here soon. I need to be on the other side when that happens so he can't cross." I was insistent ... and committed to my plan. As much as it hurt me to leave him — his unease was strong enough to bowl me over — I had to try. I would never forgive myself if I didn't.

"You don't know that my father won't follow you anyway," Braden pointed. "Even when I tell him what you've done, he might come after you."

I'd considered that. "You're in charge of making sure that doesn't happen." I slid my eyes to Brett as he approached with the rope. "Tie it around my waist. I'll magically lengthen it as I go. I'll send magic through the rope if I need you to start pulling."

"We've already been over this." Brett was calm, but I saw the storm behind his eyes. "I'm not sure I should let you do this, but I do think it's our best shot, so ... don't even think of staying over there."

"I have no intention of staying." I meant it. "I will be back." I held Braden's eyes when I said the last bit.

He jerked me to him, his arms banding around me as he buried his face in my hair. "Don't leave me. Please. I just ... don't do it."

I felt caught. "I'm not leaving you. I'm retrieving your sister and Oliver, and then coming back." I held him tight because he needed it. "I will be back. I swear it."

In truth, that was a vow I couldn't make. I had no way of knowing what I would find on the other side. In my heart, though, I felt I could pull this off. If I didn't make the attempt we would eventually be torn apart by different circumstances. He didn't realize that now, couldn't wrap his head around it, but I understood what we were truly facing ... and it wasn't good.

"I'm coming back," I whispered as I rubbed my cheek against his. "Before you know it, we'll be sitting around an omelet bar listening to your sister's tall tales about what she saw over there."

He didn't let go. I could feel tears on my face and recognized they were coming from him. Finally, he pulled back enough to stare into my eyes. The despair I found in his was almost enough to bring me to my knees.

"I love you," his voice cracked. "I ... love ... you so much."

I was struck silent. Then I was angry and smacked his arm. "I can't believe you just said that!"

His wounded eyes opened wider. "I said it because I felt it."

"This isn't the moment for that. We're not trapped in a movie. That should be said when we're alone, in the middle of a romantic moment. I just ... you're unbelievable."

Now, instead of morose sadness, I felt anger vibrating through him. That was preferable to the fear. "I can say 'I love you' when I want to say it. I mean it, too. I love you and you're coming back."

I managed to crack a smile. "I *am* coming back. I'm not saying it back until we're together again ... and alone."

Brett leaned closer to Braden. "Basically that was an 'I love you, too' whether you realize it or not."

Braden nodded, his eyes going fierce. "If you're going to do this, now is the time. We'll be here, waiting, and ready to pull. Tell my sister when you see her that I'm going to beat the crap out of her for causing all this fuss."

This time the smile I managed was genuine. "You can tell her that yourself when we get back."

Braden grabbed my chin and gave me a fierce kiss. I was nearly gasping when we parted.

"I really do love you," he murmured.

Brett grabbed my arm and directed me toward the gate, perhaps fearful our goodbye would last forever if we weren't forced to separate. "Don't dilly-dally," he ordered. "Find them and get out. Even if you think you can find answers about the revenants, this is a search-and-rescue mission, nothing more."

I nodded as I gripped Braden's hand a moment longer and then moved toward the steps. "Keep your hands on the rope even if you get bored," I insisted. "I don't want you guys playing solitaire or something when you're supposed to be pulling ... and don't start pulling until I signal you. That could be bad."

"We've got it." Brett gave me an impulsive hug when we reached the top of the platform. "Bring Oliver back."

"I'm bringing them both back."

I SHOULD'VE BEEN NERVOUS approaching the gate. I was about to cross into the land of the dead. While nerves were present, they weren't the overriding emotion coursing through me. No, that was love. Love for Braden ... his sister ... Oliver ... this life. I wanted it all back the way it should be and nothing was going to stop me from getting it.

I extended my fingers when I reached the shimmering surface, furrowing my brow as I slid them through the barrier. I expected pain, maybe a jolt of electricity. Instead, all I felt was a vague itch.

"I'll see you soon." I glanced over my shoulder one more time, met Braden's glassy gaze, and then pushed forward.

Passing through the barrier was like walking through a lightning bolt. It didn't hurt, but it was bright. It took almost three seconds before I reached the other side, and when I emerged from the blinding light I found myself on the same cliff I'd seen in my vision. Nothing had changed, which made sense because this wasn't a room that needed redecorating.

The first thing I noticed was the pallor of the atmosphere. Our world was painted in vibrant colors, a sun high in the sky. There were no sun or clouds here, and yet it was as if I'd been trapped in an overcast day, all gloom and depressing grays.

There was nothing else to focus on in the area, so I ignored the cliff and looked toward the woods. In the vision, the movement came from that direction. There was no place else to go but over the cliff, so that's the direction I headed.

It didn't take long to reach the tree line. I tested the rope with each extension I made. It held strong, the magic I doused it with glowing bright. That was the only hint of color in this world and I was grateful for it. The sparkling rope reminded me that I had a tie to the other, no matter how tenuous.

I poked my head into the trees to look around. I wasn't sure what I was expecting — more trees, maybe some excited morel hunters — but instead I found myself looking at the interior of a brightly-lit cave. I was so surprised I jerked my head out and glanced around, convinced I was imagining things. When everything appeared normal at the tree line, I poked my head in again.

Yup. It was a cave. Roots poked through the roof, which was higher than I felt it should've been, and rocks jutted from the walls. As far as caves went, it was fairly posh. Er, well, at least it had elevated ceilings.

"You're late."

I jolted at the voice, jerking my head to the left, to a large room where a rectangular table sat. There, sitting at the head of it, was the dirtiest man I'd ever seen. His hair was long, a *Duck Dynasty* beard full of what looked to be twigs and leaves on full display. His eyes were a clear blue that reminded me of a summer day spent at the seaside. And his face ... well, his face was completely normal, other than the huge and creepy smile spread across it.

"Are you talking to me?" I asked finally.

He nodded. "Please come and sit down. We don't have much time before you go back."

This was the strangest conversation I'd ever taken part in and it had barely started. "Why do you have a cave in what's supposed to be woods?" I asked, taking the final step and completely entering the dark space. "I saw people moving through here in my vision ... and I'm fairly certain they weren't in a cave."

"There are many different realities," he replied. "Some beings travel to and from their homes. I take my home with me wherever I go. You're right in ascertaining that things aren't normally like this. I've ... taken over ... for a bit. Things will revert to normal shortly."

"Uh-huh." I was leery as I moved toward the table. I had several questions. I went for the one I cared about most first. "Where are Aisling and Oliver? Do you have them?"

"I do."

I waited for him to expound. When he didn't, I pushed harder. "Can I have them?"

"All in due time." He patted the seat next to him. "We need to have a talk, Isabella Sage. Once that is complete, I will give you those who you came for and send you on your way."

He looked crazy, but sounded so reasonable. It was a weird total package.

"I want to see them," I countered. "If you allow me to see them I'll sit and talk to you."

"I would rather not see the reaper right now." He made a face. "She's got a mouth on her and the vile threats that she issues remind me of a mage I once knew. She's giving me a headache because she won't stop talking. I swear you'll get her before you leave. I definitely don't want to keep her."

I pursed my lips, considering. Finally, I slipped into one of the chairs ... although not the one he indicated. "Who are you?" It wasn't the most auspicious of greetings, but I wasn't in the mood to be polite. "Are you an angel?"

He chuckled. "No. I am not an angel. I'm also not here to discuss theology. If you have questions about life and death, I cannot answer them. That's not my place."

"You still haven't answered my questions," I pointed out. "You know who I am — I prefer Izzy to Isabella, by the way — but I don't know your name."

"I am Cernunnos."

I recognized the moniker. "You're a god."

"I am."

"You're the god of life and the underworld."

"I am ... among other things."

I frowned. "You're supposed to have a horn."

"Not all horns are visible. Also, I wouldn't mention the horn to your reaper friend. She's already offended by the beard. She says if I try to make her eat frog legs she'll castrate me. She is quite worked up. Your vampire friend is trying to calm her."

Well, that was good news. Both Oliver and Aisling were alive. If I had to guess, they were somewhere close. That meant I could retrieve them ... as soon as I was done talking to a god.

Wow. That's something I'd never thought I would think.

"The revenants are a problem," he announced, drawing my attention back to him. "They have managed to punch a hole between worlds. They spent years trying to take over this world. They failed, so they made a hole into another plane. They are ... tedious."

"Are you saying the revenants don't live in this world?" That was interesting ... and confusing.

"The revenants live between worlds. They created their own world. They travel to this one occasionally, but only because they've figured out they cannot cross to the other planes without a gate. They need to use the one here. We've managed to destroy great swaths of their army over the eons, but now they have a plan to reproduce."

That made sense. Well ... kind of. "They plan to invade our world and multiply. They've already started."

"They have." He nodded. "You must stop them before they get a true foothold. You will get your opportunity in the next few hours. They will move on your gate with the express purpose of bringing more of their kind through. You must not let that happen."

"Okay. Give me my friends and we'll go back and prepare for battle. We'll stop them."

He chuckled. "You're impatient to see your friends. You will be reunited shortly. I promise no harm has come to them. I wasn't aiming for them when I reached to the other side. I was aiming for you ... and missed."

My heart sank. "You're saying you accidentally took them."

"It was a mistake. I can walk on your plane — and have many times — but I'm needed here because the revenants are starting their big push. I cannot let them take over this world. It serves a very important purpose."

"It's the waiting room," I mused aloud. "The souls cross over and then are met by guides who take them onward."

"You're very smart."

"That's common sense."

"Don't sell yourself short." Cernunnos steepled his fingers on his stomach as he leaned back in his chair. "It is not my job to alleviate the woes of men. I'm supposed to stay out of things.

"I'm supposed to let the various races fight their own battles. This one is too important to risk failure, though, so I'm giving you a warning. You must stop the revenants on your side. Even then, they will continue to push. This is only the first battle. The war is yet to come."

He was grave and somehow — although I wasn't sure how — I knew he spoke the truth. "We can fight them. We're aware of the threat now. But how did the revenants get the reapers in the first place? If you're supposed to be watching the gate ... ?"

"I don't watch the gate. In fact, I spend very little time at the gate. The process is streamlined. I haven't been needed here for a very long time. Besides, there are many gates. Spending my time guarding one – the only one we seem to have a problem with, mind you – sounds like a terrific waste of time."

He was blunt, I had to give him that. "So ... you're saying the revenants somehow took over the gate long enough to grab the reapers and then hold them for sixty years. I don't get it."

He let loose a heavy sigh. "That's not what I'm saying at all. There was a malfunction with the gate sixty years ago. Word spread quickly that we had visitors. We dispatched personnel to intercept them, send them back.

"Believe it or not, we don't want to keep people when it's not their time," he continued. "The business of life and death is a balancing act, and they were taken before they should've been. The revenants somehow got wind of the reapers first. There is bureaucracy in everything. While we were discussing how to handle the situation, they took the reapers back to their plane."

I was still confused about this alternate plane of existence business. "How did they create their own plane?"

"They pooled all the energy they had into it, sacrificed a great many of their kind, and even then the world they created is small. They can't expand as they wish. It's a dark and depressing world ... but it is free of us. That's all they care about.

"They took the reapers sixty years ago and there was no way for us to get them back," he continued. "I don't like admitting defeat, but we figured they were a lost cause. We did not realize what they were planning to do.

"It isn't easy for them to cross back into this world. They lose numbers whenever they make the attempt. They tried for decades to cross over again. The only time they managed it was a few days ago ... when they sent revenants disguised as reapers through. It was an imprecise drop.

"We managed to intercept eight of them," he explained. "One was mortally wounded as he fell through the gate. Five crossed to the other side intact. We were hopeful you would realize something was wrong and destroy them, but things didn't work out that way. Instead they began breeding."

Things were finally starting to make sense. "They're coming back to the gate because the revenants are going to try to cross again."

"Yes. We will be fighting the revenants on this side. We need you to fight them on the other."

"Okay." That sounded easy enough ... in theory. "What happens after that?"

"As I said, killing all the revenants won't be possible today. We can only hope to hurt them. They will retreat and regroup. That will give us time to work up a battle plan. We need that time now that we know what they have planned. They will stay secluded on their plane only so long."

I nodded in understanding, my mind busy. "So we kill the revenants on our side and you kill as many as you can here. That gives us some breathing room."

"For a time," he agreed. "They will continue to try."

I was determined as I rose to my feet. "If what you're saying is true, I need to get moving. I would appreciate you giving me my friends ... and next time you want to chat, don't cause the gate to malfunction and steal people I love. You have everyone thinking they're dead."

"The gate doesn't kill people. This is not the afterlife. It is a stop on the way to forever. There is nothing to fear."

"Yeah, well, I'm starting to believe that the reapers don't understand the mythology they're peddling."

"That is very true. Now is not the time for that discussion, though. If everything works out, I can answer some of your other questions at a later date."

"Okay, well ... ." Something occurred to me and I switched course. "Just for my own edification, was it a revenant that came through the gate and killed my parents?"

He nodded. "It was."

"What happened to that revenant?"

"We don't know. It disappeared."

"How do you know it's not out there right now creating other revenants?"

"We don't. We can only deal with one problem at a time, and this is our current problem. I ... ." He broke off, furrowing his brow when a man — equally as dirty — appeared in the archway at the far side of the room. "What is it?"

"The reaper is demanding an ice cream bar," the man replied. "She will not shut up."

Instead of reacting out of anger, Cernunnos shook his head. "She really is something." He stood and gestured toward the man. "Bring her and the vampire out. They're leaving ... and not a moment too soon."

My heart leapt at the news that I was about to be reunited with Aisling. Still, I had a few more questions. "Will I see you again?"

"Most assuredly. This isn't our final meeting. I will be in contact when I can manage … and you don't have to worry about me pulling you through the gate. I've learned my lesson."

That was a relief. "How do I let you know that we've won?" Honestly, losing wasn't an option, so I didn't let doubt creep into my mind.

"I'll know." He made a face at the sound of scuffling at the door, and when I turned I found a furious Aisling being pushed through the door.

"I don't see why you're being such jerks," she complained, her hair wild. "It was a simple request. Ice cream always makes me feel better." She pulled up short when she saw me. "What are you doing here?"

"I came to get you." It was the simplest answer. I met Oliver's steady gaze over her shoulder. He looked much calmer than she did. "Both of you. We're about to head back. The revenants are going to attack the gate and we need to stop them. Although … why were they heading toward the gate yesterday in the first place?"

"They intended to carry out their plan," Cernunnos said. "I intervened, caused the gate to malfunction early, which interfered with what they wanted to do. I accidentally grabbed your friends instead of you." He held out his hands and shrugged. "Nobody is perfect. Not even a god."

He was hard to dislike, but I wasn't certain I couldn't manage it if given a bit of room to breathe. "Well, don't do it again." I held out my hand to Aisling. "Come on. Your family is wrecked and your father intends to cross the gate to find you. We need to get back before he does something stupid."

"My family." She shook her head as she moved toward me. "I bet Dad will give me an ice cream bar." She looked happy at the prospect, although she darted a dirty look toward Cernunnos.

"Your father will give you the world he'll be so happy to see you. Your husband and Jerry are so upset they'll smother you when they finally get their hands on you."

Aisling's smile dimmed at the information. "Then let's go. I want to get out of here. This guy is the worst host ever." She jerked her thumb in Cernunnos's direction. "I mean … who doesn't have ice cream?"

It was such a surreal conversation, I wanted to laugh. Before I could, the dirty god called out to me.

"Before you go, tell Paris Princeton that Bob sends his regards."

I was understandably confused. "Who is Bob?"

"I am. She'll understand. Also, inform her that the mage will likely have to get involved before all is said and done. She's not done fighting quite yet."

Everything he said sounded like gibberish. "Am I supposed to know what that means?"

"No, but she will. She will understand. I will be in touch with her and the mage, too. Make sure she warns the mage. I don't want to be set on fire when I come calling."

I wanted to question him further, but didn't have time. "We have to go. We need to prepare for a fight."

"You definitely do." His eyes momentarily traveled to Aisling. "I won't miss you in the least."

Aisling simply rolled her eyes. "Right back at you."

Twenty-Eight

I thought the hardest part of our return would be crossing through the gate with Aisling and Oliver. I was determined to keep a firm hold on each in case there was a problem. Other than the itchiness returning, however, it was a smooth trip.

We emerged into absolute chaos in the gate room.

"How could you let this happen, Braden?" Cormack was beside himself as he glared at his son. "The plan was for me to go through."

"Izzy thought she was better equipped to deal with it." Braden, still holding the rope, was morose. "She's got a mind of her own. I couldn't stop her."

"So she tied a rope around herself and just waltzed over?" Redmond was flabbergasted. "Well, that sounds like an awesome plan. Oh, wait ... ."

Griffin was with them, looking as though he hadn't slept a wink. Everybody started talking at once, blaming each other, and no one looked in our direction. Finally, I cleared my throat to get their attention. When that didn't work, Aisling stepped next to me and screeched.

"Doesn't anyone want to make a big fuss over the fact that I'm back?"

Seven heads snapped in our direction in unison. Griffin shoved past Redmond and Cillian as he raced to his wife.

"Baby!" He burst into tears the second he had her in his arms, his shoulders shaking as he held onto her for dear life. "I thought I'd lost you."

She patted his back as her brothers descended on them. "I'm fine. There's no ice cream on the other side, though. Prepare yourselves for that."

The Grimlocks turned themselves in a mass of hugs as they surrounded the couple. There wasn't a dry eye in the house. Well, other than Oliver and Brett, who reunited in much less dramatic fashion. Braden broke from his family and came to me, his eyes wide.

"You did it."

"Obviously you had doubts I would be able to pull it off," I said dryly. "I told you it would all work out."

"Yeah, but ... ." He didn't finish. Ultimately, it didn't matter. Instead, he drew me to him and kissed my cheek as he held tight. "I always have faith in you," he whispered. "I was just afraid."

"I know." I held on for as long as I dared and then pulled back, my eyes drifting to Aisling and her family. She stood in the center of fawning brothers, a relieved father and a husband who refused to stop touching her. She grinned so wide it almost swallowed her entire face. It was a beautiful moment. Sadly, I was going to have to wreck it. "We have a problem," I announced. "I'm sorry to cut the reunion short, but the revenants are on the way. We have to take them out. All of them."

Cormack shifted his eyes to me. "How do you know they're coming?"

I gave him an abbreviated version of my conversation with Cernunnos. When I finished, the Grimlocks were already springing into action.

"Where are the weapons you keep here?" Redmond asked Oliver.

"I'll show you." Oliver moved toward the hallway, his eyes holding mine for a moment. "Thanks for coming to get me, by the way. I had everything under control, though. He was going to release us at any moment."

"He *was* going to release you," I agreed. "He was sick of Aisling's mouth."

Aisling beamed. "I have a way with people."

Griffin planted a smacking kiss against her cheek. "You're magical all around, baby ... and I want you to go back to Grimlock Manor right now, before the revenants get here. I'll stay and help your father and brothers."

Aisling's eyes widened and lit with fire. "Excuse me? I am most certainly not going home. I'm part of this."

"I just spent almost twenty-four hours thinking you were dead ... or trapped on the other side ... maybe forever." Griffin didn't back down in the face of her fury, which was fairly impressive given what he'd gone through. "I wanted to go after you. I would have, but your family stopped me. Do you want to know why?"

"Because of Lily," Aisling answered without hesitation. "If you'd come after me and we couldn't get back, Lily would've been left alone."

"Not alone," he corrected. "She would've had your father and brothers. My sister certainly would've been there for her. But she wouldn't have had any parents. That didn't stop me from wanting to come after you. The only thing that stopped me was that it would've hurt you if I'd left Lily ... even if it was to go after you."

"I would've kicked your ass," Aisling agreed.

"Losing you would've broken me," he pressed. "It did break me. I'm not risking you again. I want you at home with our daughter."

Instead of exploding as I expected, Aisling was calm. "You didn't break. You might've thought you did, but you didn't. You did what you had to do, what was necessary for our daughter. I know you've been through it. I can see that." She pressed her hand to his cheek, a lifetime of love and compassion wrapped in the gesture. "I was always coming back, though. I know you can't see that because you're so worked up, but I was never going to leave you. You're stuck with me forever."

He cupped the hand she held against his face. "That was beautiful. But you're still going back to Grimlock Manor."

"No, I'm not."

They stood toe-to-toe, all the mushiness of the earlier moments forgotten. They were ready to throw down ... until Cormack put himself in the line of fire.

"She needs to stay, Griffin," he supplied, meeting his son-in-law's death glare without flinching. "We can't risk her being separated from us right now. I know you want her safe, but she'll be safer with us."

"We don't have time to argue about this," I added. "They'll be here soon. We have to be ready ... and we can't let any of them escape."

"We won't," Cormack replied simply. "We're all back together and we're strong. We can win this."

I hoped he was right. The alternative was too difficult to think about.

WE WERE LOCKED AND LOADED five minutes later and we had a plan.

"They're coming for the gate," Cormack noted. "We need to keep them out of this room. I think we need to space ourselves between the aquarium door and here. I'll take the boys to the main floor. Oliver, I want you and Brett to be the last line of defense in the gate room. If something gets past us, start ripping off heads ... or whatever it is you do."

Oliver nodded absently, seemingly unbothered by the order. I, however, was agitated by the distribution of the workload. "And what about me?"

Cormack's expression never faltered. "I think it would be best for you and Aisling to take up positions in the security room. You can shut the door, call out locations while watching the cameras, and they'll be none the wiser that you're even here."

Oh, that wasn't going to happen. "No way. You want to take me off the playing field? I'm your best player."

Redmond cleared his throat and I shot him a look, practically daring him to argue with me.

It was Aisling who smoothly stepped in to handle things. "She is your best player, Dad," she pointed out. "She crossed to the other side to get Oliver and me. I've seen her work her magic other times. You can't bench her just because she's a girl and she saved me when you wanted to be the hero."

Cormack's mouth dropped open. "I'm not benching her because ... because ... ."

"You're jealous?" Aisling arched an eyebrow. "I get it. You wanted to be the one to get me. You wanted to bring me back and fix everything for Griffin. You were afraid and wondering if you would die in the attempt. You were willing to die because you love me. You also wanted the glory."

Cormack made a face that would've been funny under different circumstances. "I hardly think I wanted glory. I wanted my child back."

"Well, I'm back and you can't hide me away. I'm helping. I'm part of this whether you like it or not."

He blew out a long-suffering sigh. "Fine. But if you get hurt we're all going to lock you in your bedroom for the next month. And you won't be allowed to leave the house. I'm warning you now."

Her smile was designed to melt the heart of her father ... and it worked. "I'm fine with that. Do you think we can have an ice cream bar tonight?"

He nodded without hesitation.

"And an omelet bar tomorrow?"

Another nod.

"And how about a seafood extravaganza tomorrow night? I want crab legs ... and lobster ... and scallops."

Cormack didn't even pretend to put up a fight. "Kid, you're going to get whatever you want for the foreseeable future. We got a glimpse of what life would be like without you and none of us liked it."

"I was fine with it," Braden lied, raising his hand and earning a stern glare from his father. "I'm just saying ... ."

He was all talk. He loved his sister as much as the others. There were times I thought he might even love her more because they'd bonded in the wake of their mother's most recent death.

"We're all going to spoil you," Cormack continued. "We're all going to help with the baby ... and give you whatever you want. We're not even going to pretend to do anything but what you want."

"Awesome." Aisling rubbed her hands together. "I also want a beignet bar for Izzy. She deserves it for coming after me. She didn't know it was going to be as easy as it was. She could've died trying, and I appreciate that ... even if I still think she should've kicked that dirty god in his special place for keeping me from my family for so long."

I pursed my lips to keep from laughing. "You can have your bars first. I'll survive until it's my turn. Until then ... ." I trailed off. Talk of Cernunnos made me remember the last part of the conversation we'd shared. Paris. He knew Paris. I needed to talk to her about that ... and then I realized what time it was ... and the one little detail we'd overlooked. "Son of a ... !"

I raced from the gate room and up the stairs. I was already through the aquarium before the others caught up. I made it to the door and threw it open before anyone could stop me and was outside in a flash.

It was already too late.

There, in the center of the small outdoor park, five revenants stood in a half circle. Paris was on the ground in front of them. She was alive, breathing and whole, but it was obvious she was in a vulnerable position. I should've thought about her safety instead of getting distracted by Grimlock hijinks. That was another mistake on my ledger.

"Hello, girl." One of the revenants spoke. It was the first time I'd heard any of them attempt to communicate. His voice was raspy, but I recognized Doug Dunning's voice. That meant the other four revenants standing with him in the park must be the men he'd crossed over with. The remaining revenants — and there had to be ten or twelve as far as I could see — were the family members they'd turned.

"Hello, Doug," I replied, hoping I sounded calm. "It's a beautiful day, huh?"

He was haughty. "We're here for the gate. You can either cede us this location or die. Those are your options."

"Wow," Aisling said from behind me. "That escalated quickly."

I was thinking the same thing. "We're not ceding the gate. You can forget that. We're also not going to die. If that's what you're expecting ... well ... you're about to learn an important lesson."

One of the revenants lashed out with his foot and kicked Paris in the side, causing her to yelp ... and my fury to overflow.

"You want to stop that," I warned. I was deadly serious. "I'm not in

AMANDA M. LEE

the mood to play games. We're not giving you the gate room no matter what you do. By the way, that horrible thing you did to the lily garden is going to be avenged, even though I have no idea why you would dare go after a bunch of flowers."

"It was a warning," Doug responded. "You didn't heed it. As for my earlier declaration, I stand by it. Flee or die."

Ugh. I hated heavy-handed threats and there was no way I was bowing to this one. "We've been informed of your plan. We can't allow you to win, so ... we're going to have to kill you."

"Oh, that was so polite," Aisling shook her head. "You really should just send a flaming arrow into his balls or something."

"Aisling, I love you, but it's time to shut up," Cormack warned. I felt him move in beside me. He was a picture of gravitas as he glanced between faces. "I'm sorry for what happened to you. I really am. You did nothing wrong and through no fault of your own your lives and families were stripped away. I can only imagine how difficult that was for you."

Even though his eyes no longer looked human, there was something familiar in the gaze when Doug rolled them. "We're better than we were. We're ... enlightened. We work for a common goal now."

"You want to take over. I get it. The thing is, we won't let you. We can't. So, while I feel sorry for what happened to you, I won't let you threaten my family. We're going to end this here."

"And how are you going to do that?"

Doug was so full of himself I reacted without thinking. Fire erupted from my fingertips and I could feel the Bruja mask slip into place. My magic was tied to my emotions, and I fancied myself an unstoppable killing machine when I focused my energy.

That's exactly what I did.

The first fire ball I unleashed smacked directly into Doug's chest. He was obviously confused by the phenomenon because he just stood there ... and then exploded into a fiery ball of ash.

"Holy smokes!" Aisling was beyond excited when she saw the results of the magical blow. "That was awesome!"

Things happened quickly after that. Without their leader, the revenants broke apart. Confusion reigned as they scattered, but they didn't stop their attack. Instead, they doubled their efforts. I reacted as quickly as I could, hopping a bench and positioning myself next to Paris. She was already scrambling from the ground when I arrived.

"That was impressive," she noted. "Can you do that with the rest?"

I was fairly certain I could. Because it seemed the best move, I shot out my hands and sent fire toward two of the closest revenants, causing both to ignite. Just like that, we were down to two of the original creatures.

The Grimlocks and Griffin were going after the other revenants. They were newer and appeared weaker. I was hopeful that meant they would go down fast. Even though their brethren were dying around them, the other members of the group didn't stop their assault. Instead, they pushed harder ... and fell on a sea of swinging swords.

"You can't stop us," one of the two remaining revenants in the center of the park hissed. I recognized his voice, too. "We're inevitable. You can't fight this. We've been planning for so long ... even if we fall here, our numbers are enough to stagger you. We will not go gently into the night and leave you the world you stole from us."

"You were once a member of this world, Manuel," I reminded him. "You had a family."

"I still have a family."

"Do you?" I inclined my chin to the area beyond the park, to where the Grimlocks were steadily hacking through the remaining revenants. There were only a few left now, which was a relief. Obviously the older the revenant, the stronger it was. The newer ones fell with little fight. I filed that information away for later ... because there would be a later. This was only the first round with the revenants. I'd been warned of that and I believed it. "Your family is dying. They would've been fine if you hadn't turned them."

Manuel growled as his eyes jumped from body to body.

"Do you love in that form?" I was genuinely curious. "Do you remember what you were? Long for what you lost?"

"I am better now," he snapped.

I didn't believe him. There was horror in his voice. "I wish I could help you." I meant that with every fiber of my being. "I wish I could fix what's been done. But I can't let you escape. This has to end here."

Manuel's eyes flashed red. "This is merely the beginning."

"Then we'll fight the other battles to come." I lifted my hands again, fire exploding from my palms. I directed the first blast at the second revenant and sent Manuel a pitying look before I did the same to him.

They didn't even try to run. They had to realize that the end was upon them, and yet they didn't try to flee. They took it, their bodies turning to ash within seconds as the fire roared and then diminished.

All that was left was smoke ... and the boasts of the Grimlocks, of course.

With a heavy heart — we'd won the battle but lost too many souls to count in the process — I glanced up to make sure the Grimlocks had everything else in hand. Apparently they'd already dispatched the lesser revenants and were now reenacting the brief battles with one another so they could puff out their chests and clap each other on the back.

Instead of joining them, I sank onto one of the benches. Paris sat with me without saying a word.

"You're okay, right?" I asked finally. "They didn't infect you, did they?"

"No, but they'd planned to once they'd taken you guys out. They didn't have me more than a few minutes."

"That's good." I meant it. "I'm sorry I forgot you were coming ... again. I'm still getting used to this 'being the boss' thing. I'll do better."

"It's fine." Paris waved off the apology. "I see Aisling and Oliver are back. How did that happen?"

It was a surreal conversation. We were acting as though we hadn't destroyed a small monster army only moments before. It seemed somehow right given the moment, though.

"I crossed over to get them."

"Really?" Her eyebrows hopped. "I guess that went better than expected. They weren't dead or anything, huh?"

"No. They were hanging with a guy. I think you know him. He had a message for you."

"Someone I know?" Paris didn't look convinced. "What's the message?"

"He said to tell you 'Bob says hi' and 'the mage will have to join in the fight before it's all said and done.'" I focused on her. "Does that make any sense?"

Paris was taken aback. "Bob?" Her voice was weak. "I told you about him. I didn't think you would actually get to meet him. I guess I should've seen that coming. It makes sense when I think about it."

"He didn't want me to call him Bob," I explained. "I had to call him by his given name ... and he absolutely hates Aisling's mouth. He couldn't give her back fast enough."

"He's always been weird. He's a good guy, though. He knows what he's doing."

"I'll have to take your word for it. For now, at least." We lapsed into silence for a moment. I really meant to let it go, but I couldn't quite force myself to do it. "Do you want to tell me about the mage?"

"Not really."

"Eventually?"

"Maybe. I need to think."

That seemed fair. "Okay. We can talk about it later."

"That sounds good."

"I'm dying to hear about your interactions with Bob. I'll bet those stories are fascinating."

"They have their moments."

Twenty-Nine

I was weary to the bone when we returned to Grimlock Manor. To give myself time to decompress, I took a long shower in Braden's suite. When I exited, I realized I didn't have anything to wear. I'd forgotten to grab a few items from my apartment before fleeing the island. Braden had obviously thought ahead, though, and hit up his sister for comfortable jogging pants and a T-shirt, which were on the bed when I emerged from the bathroom.

I was grateful for his consideration and took the time to run a comb through my hair. I didn't bother drying it. I was starving, and vanity could wait. I wanted dinner and then bed. Everything else was inconsequential.

When I hit the main floor, I followed the sound of murmuring voices to the parlor. Only a portion of the family was there, but I knew the rest would soon arrive. They could smell prime rib from a mile away.

Aisling and Griffin were on the couch, their arms wrapped around each other. Griffin's back was to the settee cushions and Aisling was curled into him. They looked to be asleep, Lily in her carrier on the floor directly next to them. Oddly enough, the baby was staring at them ... and smiling.

I moved closer to her, hunkering down as several sets of eyes drifted toward me, and rested my hand on top of the baby's head. She couldn't shutter. She wasn't yet strong enough. The few times I'd seen stray thoughts from her they'd been simple. A bottle. Her grandfather's face. Her mother.

Now when I took a peek, all I saw was her parents. They were content, so she was content. It was ... fascinating.

"What do you see?" Cormack asked quietly as he moved closer. "Can you see inside her head?"

I nodded. "She's happy."

"Of course she's happy. I'm her grandfather."

I smirked. "She thinks of you often. But right now she's picking up on Aisling's and Griffin's emotions. She's definitely empathetic. How powerful she'll be is up in the air. I think it's going to be a long time until we know for sure."

"Wait ... are you saying she's happy because her parents are happy?"

"That's exactly what I'm saying. She senses their emotions and it makes her feel safe."

Cormack glanced between me and the baby and then sighed. "I think that's nice."

"It is."

"I'm also terrified at the prospect. Aisling and Griffin are lovey-dovey now. That will change when Aisling decides to get back into the swing of things full time. I mean ... what's going to happen the first time Aisling and Angelina go after each other in front of the baby?"

I already knew the answer to that. "Aisling gets such a charge out of torturing Angelina, the baby will pick up on that and feel the same emotions. She'll be fine."

"You're saying Lily will get a charge out of being evil because Aisling enjoys messing with people."

"That's a rather succinct way of putting it, but you're not wrong."

"Ugh. I just know she's going to turn the rest of my hair gray."

I laughed as I stood. "Maybe, but you'll be okay with it." I moved to the drink cart and accepted the martini Braden had mixed for me. He leaned close and gave me a kiss. He seemed much more relaxed.

"We should probably talk about the things the god told you,"

AMANDA M. LEE

Cormack noted as he settled in his usual chair. He looked to have a bourbon on the rocks in hand. Obviously everyone was in the mood to relax.

"He said we had to take out the revenants. We did that."

"Yes, but he said more would be coming. I think we need to come up with a plan to deal with them."

I'd been thinking the same thing, but had no idea where to start. "Sure. You go first."

He didn't chide me for the snark, instead offering a weary grin. "I didn't mean right this second. I was talking about the next few days. For tonight, I figured we would just hang out as a family and get some sleep."

"I definitely think that's a good idea," Braden agreed, snagging me around the waist and tugging me toward the other settee. "I don't want to think about anything more taxing than Aisling's ice cream bar."

"I went all out," Cormack conceded. "Prime rib, chili fries, crab legs, an ice cream bar with a side of cupcakes. I ordered absolutely everything."

"Oh, good," Braden deadpanned. "That should solve that whole 'Aisling is spoiled' thing. Way to go." He flashed his father an enthusiastic thumbs-up. "She's going to be unbearable to deal with from here on out."

"At least we'll have her to deal with." Cormack's voice cracked and he quickly sipped his drink to cover.

Instead of giving him a hard time, Braden simply nodded. "There is that. I guess spoiling her for another week or so won't be the end of the world."

Cormack's eyes turned to his sleeping daughter and her lightly-snoring husband. "It might be longer than that."

Braden snickered. "I have a feeling we'll all be spoiling her ... even me. I wasn't sure I would ever see her again. I didn't like the feeling."

"I knew I would see her again," Cormack volunteered. "I just didn't know about the rest of you." His eyes were glassy. "I didn't get a chance to thank you, Izzy. What you did ... ."

"Was the only thing to do," I finished, discomfort washing over me. "It always had to be me because ... it's my job."

"Crossing the gate isn't your job. Monitoring the gate is your job. You risked your life for my child."

"No, I risked my life for our future. I'm talking everybody's future here. We all needed her back ... and I needed answers. I needed to see, to know. More than one thing propelled me through the gate, and I don't regret it."

"It was a risk." Cormack refused to back down. "You might not have come back. That would've hurt our family ... even if you don't yet realize that."

"I knew it would be hard for all of you, but I also knew that I had to try. Losing you would've crushed your family more than losing me."

Braden stirred. "I would rather not qualify my feelings for either of you. Trading one for the other ... either of you for Aisling ... it's an impossible choice. It's done. We all survived. Can we please not dwell on it?"

I patted his arm. "Sorry, but I blame your father."

"I blame him, too." Braden snuggled closer to me, his face disappearing into my hair. "Let's talk about something else. Believe it or not, I preferred talking about how spoiled Aisling is."

Cormack chuckled. "We don't have to talk about any of that. Your sister is home. She's right over there. In twenty minutes I'll wake her and watch her overload on ridiculous amounts of food and sugar. Two hours from now, Griffin will chase her upstairs.

"They'll make a big show of flirting," he continued. "They'll gladly hand over baby duty to me – and I'll gladly take it because I wasn't sure I would ever see Lily again either – and then they'll disappear into her bedroom.

"Once on the other side of that door, any façade they're hiding behind will crumble. They'll give in to the emotions they've been running from for the better part of the day. They'll cry ... and hold each other ... and pass out from sheer exhaustion."

I watched him for a moment, expecting him to continue. When he didn't, I had to laugh. "Is that personal insight or what you want to happen so you don't have to imagine the other way they might celebrate?"

He cracked a smile. "Personal insight. They held it together all day.

They'll hold it together for dinner. Then they'll fall apart behind closed doors. It's okay. They've earned it."

"And you?" I was genuinely curious. "What have you earned?"

"I ... ."

He didn't get a chance to finish because there was a flurry of movement by the door. Jerry stumbled into view. It looked as if he'd been crying for the better part of two days. Aidan trailed behind him, looking sheepish as Jerry raced toward the settee.

"One little problem," Aidan said. "I forgot to call Jerry right after Aisling walked through the gate ... and then I was distracted by a fight for our lives ... and then there was the gross cleanup. He just found out thirty minutes ago that she's fine."

"Oh, no." I leaned forward, ready to offer Jerry solace, but he didn't as much as look in my direction.

Instead of waking Aisling, instead of picking up the baby and cuddling her, he shoved Aisling until she was practically on top of Griffin and then he rolled in behind her, wrapping his arms around her from behind.

I expected her to wake and start complaining. I thought for sure Griffin would make a fuss about his wife being crushed between him and her best friend. Instead, they continued to sleep as Jerry pressed his face to her back.

"That's kind of sweet," Braden said finally. "Do you think we can leave them out here so dinner is quiet?"

Cormack shook his head. "Your sister needs her food."

"You need my sister to have her food," Braden corrected.

"Either way, she's getting her prime rib ... and chili fries."

Aisling stirred. "And ice cream bar." Her voice was thick. "Did you get the other thing I asked for?"

"The beignets?" Cormack nodded. "They're not really for you. I thought we would surprise Izzy with them after dinner. She earned them, after all."

"Okay." Aisling's eyes were still squeezed shut. "Just give us ten more minutes."

"No problem, kid."

I didn't realize there was a lump in my throat until Cormack turned to me.

"I had to get your beignets on the fly," he explained. "I hope you like them."

I seriously thought I might start bawling. "You didn't have to get them," I argued. "This is Aisling's night."

"No, this is a family night," he corrected. "You're our family ... and today you're our hero. You get whatever you want, too."

"Yay!" Braden clapped his hands, causing me to jolt. "What? That means I get whatever I want because we're together. I want some pie."

Cormack sighed. "Sometimes I wish I didn't have children," he lamented.

I didn't believe him for a second. "I think you might miss them."

"That's the sad thing. I know I would."

It was quiet after that. For once, Grimlock Manor wasn't burbling with noise. Love was another story.

We still had an enemy to contend with, but for one night at least, we could rest. With that in mind, I slid my eyes to Braden and leaned in close to whisper. "I love you, too."

Emotion stormed his eyes and I thought he might start crying, but he held it together. "We're not alone and you said it."

"I felt it. That's all that matters."

"Yeah." He rested his forehead against mine. "Just remember who said it first."

Ah, yes, there was that Grimlock competitive streak. That was still going to take some getting used to. Thankfully, we had plenty of time.

Made in United States
North Haven, CT
10 June 2022